MR. COWBOY

MEN OF STONE RIDGE

HEATHERLY BELL

For Tyler and Felicia, who loves horses, and each other.
Though I should probably dedicate this to Phoebe, your rescue
horse.

PROLOGUE

*G*reat news! We've finally selected a bachelor for Mr. Cowboy, our reality dating show! As y'all know, we lost Wade Cruz last year to one of our local women (who always get first dibs, you understand.) However, I never dreamed Sean Henderson would finally step up and agree to be our first ~~victim~~ Mr. Cowboy. He's a confirmed bachelor, that one, but I know exactly why. And also, that it's my job to fix this mess. Two birds with one stone, you see.

More than a decade ago, I thought I was doing the right thing for someone I loved dearly. No one could blame me. With hindsight being twenty-twenty, I do now see I've been instrumental in Sean's bachelorhood. But his days are numbered, yes, they are. By the time we're done here, Sean will be happily in love and engaged. We'll have more women in Stone Ridge and bring one back who got away. But that's another story.

Folks, this rancher played right into my hands. All because he has his own obsession with saving every wild horse in the west. Like a magician with a slight of hand, while he was over there looking at one thing, I've single-

1

handedly engineered his happily ever after. This is true or my name isn't Beulah Mae Hayes.

You are welcome, Sean Henderson!

Please don't be too stupid to see who is right in front of you.

~ BEULAH HAYES, President of SORROW (Society of Reasonable, Respectable, Orderly Women) and keeper of the *Men of Stone Ridge* bible, tenth edition. ~

CHAPTER 1

What were they thinking?

A *new reality show is coming to streaming next year and is in fact in pre-production as we go to publication. Get ready for Mr. Cowboy, a dating show in which a small-town cattle rancher will pick his bride from among a gaggle of beautiful and young contestants. The only unique part of this particular show is that it will be held entirely in Stone Ridge, Texas, home of the cow. Yes, you read that right. Their claim to fame? Cows.*

Word is the dates will all be held locally, the ladies housed in the newly remodeled home of local multi-millionaire and owner of the largest horse ranch in Texas: Mr. John J. Truehart.

So, no traveling to all four corners of the earth to swanky dinners wearing beautiful ball gowns. This little lady had better arrive wearing her spurs and chaps. In the span of a couple of weeks, the cowboy will date his heart out. Women will arrive from all over the United States to spar for the heart of this handsome and wealthy cattle rancher.

I've seen early photos of said bachelor and can report he's not hurting in the tall, dark, and handsome category. Thirty-seven-

year-old Sean Henderson has never been married and is reportedly ready, willing, and able to settle down. Suffice it to say if a wedding proposal doesn't result at the conclusion of this show, we have little hope left for humanity.

Though there isn't much 'Hollywood' from this sweet offering, we might possibly see some Nashville-style performances from the bachelor's own sister-in-law, CMA award winning singer Winona James (now Mrs. Winona Henderson), and from Jackson Carver, a local rancher and musician who started his career in Stone Ridge.

~ The Hollywood Blogger

SEAN HENDERSON TIPPED his hat and summoned all the genuine interest he could when he had a cow in labor and other matters on his mind.

"Hey, y'all, I'm ah…Mr. Cowboy. I'm thirty-seven and it's time to settle down. I'm lookin' for the right woman. She should…um, she…wait. Let's…let's start over."

Elton, the head camera man, threw up his hands in disgust. "This is take ten in case anyone is paying attention. And next time, look into camera *one*."

"Oh, shitfire. I thought you said camera three."

"Okay, that's exactly the kind of language we can't have on the airwaves."

The director and emcee approached, a young sprightly woman of about twelve. Okay, he was exaggerating. She had to be at least eighteen given what they'd told him about their union rules, but she sure didn't look it.

"Cursing? Even on a streaming network?" He narrowed his eyes because he'd seen some rather questionable stuff on said networks and didn't think a simple curse word would kill anyone. "Sorry, darlin' but I'm a cowboy."

Lori fanned herself. "Don't try that aw shucks crap on me."

Sean chuckled. He liked to have his fun with Lori, who reminded him of a Pitbull someone had slapped some lipstick on. Short, cute, and misleading sweet when she wanted to be, she'd fooled everyone. She'd rolled into Stone Ridge kicking ass and taking names. She complained daily about paying her dues by being stuck directing reality shows when everyone knew she was the next coming of Martin Scorcese.

"What are you doin' now?" The feminine voice came from behind him in the faux studio set-up they had fashioned in the new barn. "Don't you dare ruin this."

He turned to see his second biggest pain in the ass, Winona, his older brother Riggs' wife. She had her baby girl, Mary, in her arms which gave her an unfair edge. She knew how much Sean loved that little girl.

"Hey, sweet Mary," he said, ignoring Winona. "Your Uncle Sean is over here tryin' to find himself a wife, but these studio lights are too bleepin' hot and I don't know which camera to look into. Also, did I mention I got a cow in labor?"

"Riggs is takin' care of all that and you blasted well know it."

"That cow is one of my favorites. I'm worried," he lied.

Winona bustled up to Elton. "Which one is camera one?"

He pointed and she went to stand behind it, holding Mary. "Look over here, Uncle Sean."

Little Mary, barely three months old, kicked her chubby legs and squealed in delight.

"Finally, some help," Elton said.

"Here we go again," said Sean.

"Just be yourself and you'll be fine." Lori rolled her hand in a circular motion. "Keep the camera rolling. We'll get this reel down if it kills me."

"What are you looking for in a future wife?" Winona prompted.

"Well, someone nice. Sweet." He tugged at the tie they'd made him wear around the collar of a shirt he'd wear again the day they put him a coffin.

"*Sweet*?" Lori barked. "Define sweet. We need a little more depth. Go deep, cowboy. What makes a woman sweet in your opinion?"

"Um…well, I take that back. Not *sweet*."

Lori threw her hands up. "Why me, God?"

"Would it kill you to make somethin' up?" Winona said. "How about a script?"

"Sure, yeah. Whatever."

Sean wanted children, which meant he should have a wife because being a traditional man, he didn't put the cart before the horse. Even if he'd put the cart before the horse plenty of times so to speak. Yes, sir. But no babies had come out of all that putting the cart before the horse repeatedly and with much gusto. Unlike Riggs, who'd knocked Winona up, Nashville royalty, and then got her to marry him and *stay* in Stone Ridge.

Keeping a woman here was a challenge in a place less a town than a huge man cave.

"It's not that complicated," Lori said, her nose flaring. "And a script is the very antithesis of what we're doing here. What part of reality do you not understand?"

"Reality." Winona snorted. "Yeah, right."

"Fine, fine. I know what you want." Sean cleared his throat and looked into the right camera this time. "I've got this. Look, I'm thirty-seven years old and I've waited a long time for the right woman. The perfect woman, for me, won't be afraid to get a little dirty. But by dirty, of course, I'm not talkin' about sex."

"Cut!"

"Oh, shit."

Winona covered her mouth with one hand and burst into laughter.

"That does it!" Sean pulled his tie off and next off came the ridiculous shirt. "Here we go. See, I don't wear shi-stuff like this. Where's my dagum flannel?"

Elton threw him the shirt he'd worn when he got up this morning.

Sean shrugged it on and began buttoning. Maybe now he could actually *be* himself.

"I'm not showy. I don't wear ties, but I'll wear one on my wedding day if my wife insists. And the next time I wear one will be when they lay me down in my coffin, six feet under. If a woman can handle that, plus living on a cattle ranch in the middle of nowhere, super. I'm your man."

"I hope you were rolling," Lori said to Elton. "We can use the footage of his abs if nothing else."

"He still hasn't said what *he's* lookin' for in a woman," Winona protested.

"Right," Sean said. "How about y'all tell me about some of these women, and I'll reverse engineer this whole thing?"

"You mean tell you what kind of women we have, and you can make those your requirements?" Lori asked.

"That's utterly ridiculous," Winona said.

"Now, now. Let's not be hasty," Lori said, looking through several print-outs. "We have been here a while. Okay, there's a teacher."

"Great. I want someone educated, and good with children."

"Bingo!" Lori said. "Why didn't I think of this. We have a neonatal nurse who put herself through school by stripping."

Sean smiled, remembering why he signed up for this deal. He would be dating. A lot. And hot damn it had been a while since he spent quality time with a beautiful woman. It didn't seem fair that he'd be saddled with about ten of them at once. All vying for his attention and affection in this contest which he couldn't possibly lose.

But hey, he was taking one for the team. Heh. Heh.

"I want a compassionate woman, well versed in First Aid."

"Last month, Sean nearly put a nail through his finger," Winona explained. "Mendin' fences."

"True story. Doesn't usually happen but I was in a hurry."

"Next, we have a financial planner from New York City."

Sean considered this. "I'd like a wife with money?"

"Try again." Lori tapped her foot. "Goes right back to education."

"Yes, my wife should be intelligent and able to do accounting."

"Too specific," Winona said. "Eliminates many of the women if you're looking for an *accountant*."

"Okay, let's take a break," Lori said. "They don't call me Ms. Scorcese for nothing. I'll just bet I can splice something together here and create our first commercial reel."

"That's what I like to hear, Marti, Jr.," Sean said. "I'll be in the pens if anyone needs me."

Lori wrinkled her nose. "The pens? Where's that again?"

"Where the cows give birth." Winona made a face.

Winona wasn't exactly rancher's wife material, either, but she'd acclimated, giving Sean a smidge of hope for the woman from New York City. He wanted to be fair and give every woman he met a chance. They were coming from all over the country. He'd seen photos and boy howdy, he was going to have a *great* time. Of course, there were a few conditions to this contest. He'd read over them carefully when he'd agreed to this deal and signed the contract.

No kissing any of the women until the final ceremony.

Definitely no sex.

No playing favorites too early on. Give every woman a chance.

Agree to allow the producers to choose one woman who, in their opinion, would be the best match.

Propose with a ring offered by one of the top jewelers in Dallas.

Yes, propose, even if he had no intention of following through with a wedding.

The last rule was a tough one, because Sean never did anything half-assessed. When he proposed, he'd wanted it to be the real thing. He hoped he could connect with the woman they chose, even if he believed that the odds of falling for someone in a couple of weeks were long.

Still, when Winona and Beulah Hayes had approached him for the seventh time, he'd had a rough and tumble kind of day. The kind which made him wonder what he was doing with his life. When they laid him down six feet under, who would care other than Riggs and Colton? How had he made a difference anyone would remember when he was long gone?

And that's when he'd asked: *what's in this for me?*

Beulah, as usual, feigned a stroke when asked why anyone would want more than love out of this deal. Forever love. Companionship. The right woman. Yeah, been there done that, and Beulah knew better than most. Sean wanted a dagum *guarantee* that even if he didn't find a lifelong partner, quite likely in his opinion, he'd get something out of this.

Sean wasn't interested in a public life and being in front of the camera felt like an invasion of privacy. But he had his pet causes, like the plight of wild horses of the southwest. With Riggs help, they'd written in that the producers would issue a large donation check to the foundation Sean wanted to start here in Stone Ridge.

The Mr. Cowboy contest was the brainchild of Beulah Hayes, founding member of the ladies of SORROW, and Winona, who still had contacts in the entertainment industry. The reason for the contest? For a town well known for having far more men than women, this seemed like a good opportunity to bring more women in for all their single bachelors.

Beulah hoped at least some of the women would stick around and check out all the other cowboys. In fact, said cowboys were already paying careful attention and would be watching a dating show for possibly the first time in their lives. They loved the idea they would be the first to know of his fiancée, way before the show actually aired.

Sean did not like the idea of "selecting" a woman and having to eliminate anyone. He figured these women would become his friends even if he didn't feel a "love" connection. Unrequited love was no picnic and he'd certainly been on the other end of that situation.

More so than most, he understood the pain of being left behind and hated to inflict that on anyone.

Quite frankly, while it might be childish, he hoped a *certain* woman would be watching the show when it aired in a few months.

Hopefully she'd regret the choice she made years ago when she left town and broke his foolish heart.

CHAPTER 2

Hollywood, California

"Go on in, Ms. Wheeler. He's expecting you."

"Thanks." Bonnie stood and walked inside the offices of Marvin Cain, her talent agent of over a decade.

"Bonnie!" Marvin stood and came around his desk to hug her.

She nearly jumped back in surprise at the sudden rush of affection. "I thought you'd still be upset with me."

"Not at all. You were right about Oopsie Underwear."

"So, you agree they're basically adult diapers?"

"Well, I wouldn't go *that* far." He waved a hand dismissively. "It's lingerie with a little extra padding. You started your entire career as the 'it' girl for Topanga Lingerie."

"I was *nineteen*, and it was my first and only modeling job." And, apparently, nearly twenty years later, she'd never live it down.

"Look, it only makes sense to ask you all these years later. You're still a beautiful woman and this was your chance to be

11

the face of their new middle-age line. Full circle. Look, you can't always afford to be so picky."

"I'm hardly qualified to be the spokesperson for women who are ready for adult diapers."

"You're right, you're right." He waved at her to have a seat. "I have something much, *much* better for you."

By now, Bonnie didn't get as excited as she had in the old days. Once, she'd almost nabbed the part in a Marvel Studios picture but in the end, they'd chosen someone smaller. Someone who wouldn't make their average height leading man look *short* because God forbid.

She could die her hair blonde, jet black, brown, pink, or stay with her natural red, but she could not get any *shorter*. Her only serious professional success remained the Irish mafia show she'd starred in at the start of her career over a decade ago. She'd been so good in it, Marvin said, that she'd been typecast. Again. Tired and jaded, once a week she considered quitting show business and moving back home.

She'd already missed so much from life that many took for granted. Marriage and children for instance. After too many failed relationships, she'd finally found someone she could count on in Eric Cavell. Both struggling actors, they'd met a year ago at an audition for Chicago Fire. She got the part of a firefighter's girlfriend, he *didn't* get the part of a man buried under rubble.

Many cocktails and war stories later, they spent most of their free time together. Her condo was the place he laid his head to rest most nights since he lived with roommates the way Bonnie had when she'd first moved to Hollywood. He was younger so she cooked for him and lent him both emotional and mental support. She'd long ago given up on falling in love again, and tired of being alone, Bonnie had become pretty fond of Eric this past year. He was so easy to like. So easy to get along with. Like a Golden Retriever, always so happy. Plus, she always had a date for an industry cocktail party or awards show.

"Tell me about the role." Her foot began to jiggle with the typical raw nervous energy of living in the city.

"Well, first, keep an open mind. It's a reality show." Marvin leaned back in his chair and steepled his fingers together, which she noticed he often did when he wanted to appear pensive.

Informed enough about the seedy underside of the business, she realized many so-called reality shows hired a plant for conflict and controversy. Often, they were actual actors in the screen actors' guild picking up a little extra work on the side.

"I'm not doing a *reality* show."

"This one is right up your alley. They're looking for beautiful and accomplished women and they specifically wanted women your age. Plus, you'll be the only actress."

"I'm the plant. What do they want me to do? Cause trouble among the women? Be the house bitch? I won't do it. You know how I feel about pitting women against each other."

"No, no. Well, you are the plant, but there's a specific reason."

"What's the reason?" Bonnie had begun to smell a rat. "Are they worried that they're not giving so-called 'older women' enough of a chance? Do they have some organization after them? What's the end game here?"

"Bonnie, Bonnie, Bonnie." Marvin slid a piece of paper toward her. "Jaded much? This is the salary you'll make for a few weeks' worth of your time."

Bonnie gaped at the figure, nearly the amount she'd made, years ago, on her last season of *Kavanaugh's Way*. The Irish mafia show which had been her first break and starring role. It might have turned her into a bankable movie star but when a strike delayed all future productions for months the series ended after three seasons. Many actors returned to work as waiters and never went back. She was one of the lucky ones to have found work after the series ended.

The show had recently been picked up by a major streaming network, but no one seemed to be watching. Including her.

So, why were they offering her so much money? "Did you explain I don't do nudity?"

"Of course. This is a family show. Well, it's streaming, but we all know streaming is the future and the future is now."

"This is lot of money. I don't see the catch."

"No catch. They desperately want you and I think you should consider this opportunity before you immediately say no."

"Hm." Bonnie quirked a brow. "*Why* do you think I'll say no?"

"It's complicated." Now, Marvin pushed something else toward her. It appeared to be an eight by ten glossy. "*This* is the bachelor."

A face from her past stared back. Now several years older, his face was thinner, the jaw more cut and defined. The eyes hadn't changed, of course, still the same amber hue serving a stark contrast to the shock of dark hair. There were tiny little crinkles at the sides of his eyes. Laugh lines of a life well lived and well loved.

Sean.

She didn't even realize she was staring blankly until Martin cleared his throat.

"M-mr. Cowboy?" Bonnie's hand shook, joining her still jiggling foot, and she handed the photo back. "That's the name of the show?"

"The show is the brainchild of Winona James, Nashville superstar. She's retired and living in Stone Ridge and would like to bring more women into town. Since it's your hometown I'm sure you're aware there's a—"

"I know."

They had a shortage of women and had since the dawn of time if you wanted to listen to town folklore. Her Aunt Beulah was currently the President or the ladies of SORROW (society of reasonable, respectable, organized women) and her own mother, Maybelle, still a member. When she'd been widowed after Bonnie's father died in a rodeo accident, they'd struggled. Even if the men of Stone Ridge did their best to take care of them, Bonnie eventually left town for a better future for her and her mother. A future she thought only Hollywood could offer. How wrong she'd been.

So, Sean Henderson was looking for a wife, because God only knew if there were enough women in Stone Ridge, he'd be married with plenty of kids. It was what he'd always wanted. A wife, kids, the ranch. The simple life.

"While the money is attractive, I can't do it. That's my hometown, as you know."

"Are there any problems with going back?"

"Yes, because I don't have a time machine. There's no going back for me."

"Surely there are some people you'd love to reconnect with. How long has it been since you visited your mother? It's only a few *weeks*, Bonnie. Like a paid vacation." His eyes narrowed. "You know him, don't you? Is that the problem?"

"Of course, I *know* him. There's about 1,000 people in the entire town. We went to school together."

There was more, far more, but she wouldn't allow the producers to know just how much more. She'd finally learned to protect herself in this business and wasn't interested in going home so Sean could stomp on her heart. It had taken years to get over him.

"That's perfect! I wonder if the producers know about this. I could ask for more money."

"They *know*. This must be why they're offering this kind of money. It's not difficult to track me down. I kept my real name."

"That's the angle for them, then. A blast from the past. Drama and conflict. I strongly urge you to consider this offer. Times are tough. Productions have been halted for one reason or another. Wildfires. Union strikes and pandemics."

"What about the pilot we talked about? The frazzled mother of three who's trying to save her family's floral business?"

The script was witty with sharp dialogue and Bonnie had been inspired for the first time in a long while.

"They went with more of the 'girl next door' look."

Translation: someone younger.

"Are you sure you won't even consider Mr. Cowboy? Just as a short gig while you wait for another part to come along. Who knows? You might get into some westerns this way."

"No. I can't do Mr. Cowboy. I'll just wait for another opportunity."

She assumed Sean understood exactly what he'd gotten himself into. By her count, he'd been engaged twice and remained unmarried. There had to be a reason for that. And if in more than ten years he still hadn't found the right woman, he wouldn't likely do it in two short weeks under that kind of intense pressure. Then again, these shows were created to indulge good looking men. And while Sean had grown up in their lopsided town, now several women would fight for his attention. He'd probably be in hog-heaven. One thing for sure: she didn't have to *watch*.

. . .

THE BRIGHT POOL of California sunshine made Bonnie blink. Maybe a drive to the beach to contemplate life was in order. She readjusted her shades and headed for the parking lot. As she pulled out, a car rushed into her space so quickly it almost clipped her. The driver then flipped her the birdy for not getting out of his way fast enough.

Not for the first time, she wondered if she *should* move to Vancouver. She and some of her actor friends had discussed the idea. The number of Hallmark and other streaming service productions filmed in Canada increased yearly. One of her friends had moved there a few years ago and found steady work. She adored the small quaint town she'd settled in and had invited Bonnie to visit many times. Eric regularly compared himself to the Hallmark Hunks on Instagram. Maybe she'd bring the idea up to him again tonight.

The fact she'd seen Sean's photo and suddenly wanted to put even more distance between herself and Texas was mere coincidence. She had to find work, and if that meant following the locations, so be it.

Tonight, she'd invite Eric over and make his favorite dinner: her creamed corn, mashed potatoes, and chicken fried steak. Then she'd suggest it was time to make the move to Canada and just suck up the cold weather. If she, a Texan, could brave the subzero temperatures surely Eric could. If he came along, they could share rent and expenses.

He felt like her child most days, even if he was only seven years younger. Much of the time he behaved far younger than thirty and was one of the most insecure actors she'd ever met. She felt incredibly protective over him at times, like a Mama Hen. When he got turned down for a part, she'd assure him the casting directors had no idea what they were doing. When he got a bad review, she comforted him and told him she understood what this felt like. It would pass. He couldn't be everyone's special snowflake, but it would be okay because he was hers.

She whipped out her cell in the produce aisle and texted Eric:

Come over for dinner at six-thirty. I'll make your favorite, chicken fried steak.

Eric replied:

I'll be late. Have an audition.

Interesting. Eric hadn't told her about any audition today. He was always so neurotic about them and forced her to recite lines with him for days before. Most of the time, truth be told, she was his support system and not the other way around. She'd become his cheerleader whenever he felt uncertain.

She texted him to break a leg, slipped her phone back in her purse, and continued shopping. But when they didn't have Eric's favorite wine, she drove to Pasadena and the specialty store. His favorite meal, favorite wine. She aimed to please even when it wasn't reciprocated. Long ago, she'd gotten over being special and held in high regard by any man. The men in Hollywood needed a keeper half the time. Now, she was content with friendships which always skirted around love. Never too deep, never too emotional. This made it easier to focus on her career for years and this had always been her goal, so it worked.

On the way to the store, she flashed on a memory of Sean's favorite IPA beer and wondered if he still enjoyed it. As teenagers, they used to sit on the banks of Lupine Lake, drink beer, kiss…and…other stuff she'd best not think about now.

Passing the peanut butter aisle, temptation gripped her. She went ahead and reached for a jar of her favorite brand of peanut butter. Face it, after seeing Sean's photo, she needed a fix. Besides she'd been good for six months and was the thinnest she'd ever been.

From her grocery cart child safety seat, an adorable little girl, so cute she looked like a doll, offered Bonnie a toothless smile. Her heart and womb tugged simultaneously. Somewhere along the line she'd forgotten to pencil in a baby. Oh, well, she wouldn't have had time for one anyway. Too late now, as she'd made it a practice to ignore the proverbial ticking biological clock.

The baby's frazzled mother, or babysitter, bent to pick up the pacifier she'd dropped again. "If you do this one more time, just one more time, I'm *not* picking it up again."

Down went the pacifier and the baby smiled with utter delight. It was a game, quite obviously, one she didn't even realize she was playing.

"Here you go." Bonnie bent to pick up the pacifier and hand it to the mother.

She would not be outwitted by a one-year-old.

"Thank you. Some days I just can't take another minute of her *attitude*." The woman brushed it off and stuck it in her purse. "My boyfriend and I think she has early oppositional defiant disorder."

"Oh?"

"Never too soon for early intervention." She threw in a jar of organic vegan baby food and passed Bonnie.

A few minutes later, the checkout clerk announced a ridiculous price for Bonnie's purchases, but she was too embarrassed to put anything back. Besides, she was fairly certain Jennifer Lawrence waited in line two customers behind.

This is what she should expect for shopping in a specialty store. Her hand shook slightly, and Bonnie offered her credit card. She promised herself to pay it off in full when the bill came. Her income was sporadic, and she had to plan accordingly. At least she lived in one of the only rent-control areas of the city and her rent hadn't been raised in years.

A road crew had blocked off the section of the parking lot where she'd parked, so Bonnie had to go around. As she passed the local Thai restaurant, a sun ray glinted and nearly blinded her with its gleam. She blinked and found herself staring inside the glass paned window right at Eric.

He sat extremely close to a gorgeous brunette Bonnie recognized immediately. She was the principal player on a popular network sitcom now in its sixth season.

This must be his audition. It wasn't unheard of, she supposed, though unusual. Maybe she'd taken a hand in choosing her co-star. She was certainly a big enough name to do it.

It would be just like Eric not to jinx the opportunity to be on a hit sitcom by even *mentioning* it to Bonnie. On top of all his other neuroses, Eric was extremely superstitious. For his auditions, he wore purple socks and green boxers. *Seriously.* She'd tried to understand superstitions, quite common in Hollywood, but being a Texan and a Protestant, she didn't.

Then something odd happened. Eric…yes, he…he started to *kiss* the woman. What was her name? Um, Vicki? Vicki Something. Think, think, think. Bonnie *should* know this. She read the trades even if she couldn't stomach watching shows with a laugh track and hadn't viewed a full episode. Kissing the woman's neck, Eric lifted her hand to his lips and kissed it. They were now in a full-blown lip lock.

Was this in the script?

"Oh look, it's J.J. from that show, what's it called?" This was from a teenager at Bonnie's elbow.

"A Family of my Own," Bonnie said.

Vici Milan. That was her name.

"Yeah, that's right. Ma'am, can I help you with those bags?"

Ma'am.

In Stone Ridge, every married woman, irrespective of age, was referred to as ma'am out of respect. But Bonnie had just been dissed because in Hollywood ma'am meant "old lady." She held on tightly to her bags, fully capable, as the osteo arthritis had not yet set in. Oh, fine. He was a good kid to offer, and frankly to a teenager, she probably seemed ancient. He was simply being kind, enough of an anomaly in the bustling metropolis to have shocked her into silence.

"No, thank you."

Did she *look* old? Because Bonnie didn't *feel* old. But from the offers to be the face of Oopsie Underwear, to auditions for the parts of middle-aged mothers, she got the message. She was done in this town.

And Eric was still kissing that woman.

Carrying her bags inside the restaurant, she tried to get past the hostess, but the young lady was dead serious about her job.

She blocked Bonnie. "Ma'am, do you have a reservation?"

"No, but I see my party has already been seated."

She nudged her chin toward the table where Eric and Vici now sat, making-out. There was just no other word to describe it as they grappled for each other and seemed to be surgically attached at the lips.

"Oh," the hostess said. "Right this way to Ms. Milan's table."

Phone cameras were not so discreetly filming Eric's "audition" to be the lover of the year. This was also a trick of the trade. Be seen with someone more famous and watch the publicity machine do its thing. She'd been guilty of this in the past, and everyone had at one point or another. But she and Eric were supposed to be a *couple*. They were still together last she heard.

She followed the hostess and plunked her grocery bags down on their table. "I came straight from the store."

This made them both come up for air.

"Sorry, I don't give out autographs when I'm dining," Vici said, giving a wide smile with her bruised lips. "But please call my agency and I'll be happy to send you an autographed photo of the entire cast."

"Oh, how kind of you." Bonnie went hand to heart.

"Bonnie," Eric blubbered. "This is...I want...I..."

"How cute, you're tongue-tied. I think she knows who I am, babe," Vici said. "But how do you two know each other?"

Bonnie smiled through gritted teeth. Eric was a *horrible* actor. How had she not noticed this before? Couldn't he at least *act* like he *hadn't* been caught cheating?

"Is this the audition you told me about, sweetie?" *Cheating. So* predictable.

"No, I..."

"Is this your mother, Eric?" Vici, not the sharpest crayon in the box, smiled widely. "Gosh, you look so *young.* You must have had him when you were ten! You'll have to tell me all your anti-aging secrets."

Oh, good. She did not look old enough to be the mother of a thirty-year-old! Yay.

"Seven. I would have to have had him when I was seven. That's *not* a joke about how young I look, it's a physical impossibility. Eric, tell her I'm not your mother!"

Eric shook his head. "No, no, she's not my mother. She's my...my..."

Bonnie stared, watching the last ten months crumble before her. More wasted time with a man in love with himself, or at the very least, with the idea of fame and fortune.

"Roommate," Eric finished. "She's my roommate."
Roommate.

"Okay, well, I guess we're done here. Eric, I came here to tell you I can't be your roommate anymore. I'll leave your stuff on the sidewalk."

Bonnie turned in a huff, tossed back her hair, and prepared to make a dramatic exit. As she walked by, someone at a table not far from the entrance could be heard asking:

"Isn't that the woman from the Irish mafia show? What's it called?"

"Kavanaugh's Way. It's on Netflix. Yeah, she's kickass on that show, too."

Bonnie nodded and smiled. "Bonnie Wheeler playing Meghan Kavanaugh. And thank you."

She would have loved to leave on that particular note, but unfortunately, she did have go to back.

"I'm *taking* my peanut butter with me." She grabbed the bags from the table and turned to face the rest of the crowd. "And...end scene!"

This time, she received applause, and took a bow.

PULLING up to her old residential street, Bonnie found a spot on the street and carried her bags to her second story condo. No chance anyone would offer to help here, certainly not the grown men who passed her on the sidewalk, on the way to something much more important. No longer a perky young woman, or a hot commodity, she felt invisible at times and missed the polite teenager from earlier. It was fine since she'd been on her own for years. She reached her door and set down the packages.

She noticed an official looking taped notice on the front door:

This property has been seized by the Bank of the West for non-payment.

Obviously, this had to be a mistake. Bonnie faithfully paid

her rent every month. She ripped the paper off and juggled her packages inside. Within minutes, she was on the phone to the kindly landlord to whom she made her payments. Bart Longmire had been an actor in the seventies, and now retired, ran celebrity golf tournaments and helped other aspiring actors whenever he could. When Bart didn't answer, and his voice mail box was full, Bonnie dialed the number listed on the form.

"I'm sorry, ma'am, but the property has been in arrears for months," a representative said between keyboard clacks. "I'm surprised no one contacted you."

"T-that can't be right. I pay the rent every month." She gave him Bart's name and phone number.

More keyboard clacking. "Ah, yes. Looks like this particular landlord received rental payments on several of his properties but did not pay the mortgage with them."

"Sorry? I don't...don't understand. What did he do with the money?"

The representative sighed. "Whatever he wants, apparently."

The room seemed to spin as Bonnie clutched the edge of the countertop and took shallow breaths. "H-how do I get my money back?"

"Ma'am, you're likely *not* going to get your money back. The bank will repossess the property, but..."

"They're not going to pay me back either, are they?"

Silence ensued followed by a few keyboard clacks. Silence. More keyboard clacks. "I'm really sorry, ma'am."

THAT NIGHT, Eric texted that they both needed to "take five." Breaking up via text was an interesting gesture but one she'd come to accept. He'd be staying at "Vic's" because he needed to center his chi before the audition and she'd harshed his mellow. Besides, Vic had an extra bedroom. Right. Sure.

"Extra bedroom my ass," Bonnie said as she dug into her peanut butter with a spoon.

Someone new had arrived to take her place. Someone younger. Someone better connected. She'd been the stupid one, hanging on to Eric because she liked spending time with him, even if he couldn't do a thing for her career but run lines. Even if, truth be told, she wasn't all that invested in him emotionally.

She couldn't even claim to be heartbroken. Having experienced real heart ache firsthand, the kind that made your heart feel like it had been harvested, then skewered over an open flame, Bonnie knew the difference. This was disappointment, pure and simple. Add in a bit of outrage simmering on a low flame. But she couldn't even call up a single tear for the guy.

She was actually more upset about this rental scam.

God, she was so *tired* of everything. Back home in Stone Ridge, women were revered from birth to eighty. They were not disregarded and set out to pasture when they got to middle-age.

She had no current work, and would need to move out, too.

Picking up her cell, she dialed Marvin. She desperately needed to work.

"Hey, if I take the part in this reality show, do I get paid even if I don't even survive the first elimination?"

"I'll look over the contract, but that's usually the way these things go. You'll be paid regardless. But remember, you're there for the drama so it's likely they will want to keep you, regardless of what the bachelor wants."

"And...he knows *I'm* going to be one of the contestants, right?"

"Oh, sure. Yeah. Of course, he does."

Sean was apparently okay with this, which meant she should be fine with it, too.

She needed a job and at least a temporary place to live. But she didn't want him to believe she'd come crawling back to him when he'd broken up with her. She'd have to walk a fine line between acting the part of a woman interested in vying for a cowboy's heart, and someone who was there for a role and a roof over her head.

Bonnie understood that the minute Sean laid eyes on her, he'd get rid of her. But knowing Sean, and how and where he'd been raised, being rude to her would be unthinkable. So, at least she had that going for her.

"Just one other thing." Marvin cleared his throat. "You can't tell him you've been hired to do this gig. Given your history, obviously the producers think it would be far more interesting if he doesn't know."

"You mean create more drama when he eventually finds out. So…he's supposed to think I'm there because I want another *chance* with him?"

Oh hell no. How utterly humiliating! Come crawling back to the man who'd feasted on the spoils of her broken heart?

"Yeah, well, is that such a huge deal?"

"The joke's on them. There won't *be* any drama when he kicks me out after the first day. Alright, Marvin. I'll do it. Send over the contract."

What difference does it make? You're practically dead to him anyway.

After he eliminated her, she could take the time to visit with her mother, see old friends, regroup, and decide where to go from here.

Because she didn't know if she had it in her to be a Hollywood player anymore.

CHAPTER 3

"*A*round of drinks for Mr. Cowboy!" Jackson Carver announced from the stage of the Shady Grind, where he'd just finished performing his last set.

Sean accepted shoulder claps and fist bumps from the crowd at the only bar and grill in town.

In anticipation of the excitement and extra revenue the show would create the few businesses in town had spent months preparing. After buying the bar from the original owner, Jackson had been renovating slowly, taking his time. But news of the production lit a fire under him. Now there were four new state of the art flat screens in each corner of the bar.

"Thanks to you, we're goin' to have ourselves a slew of beautiful single women traipsin' through town for a couple of beautiful and amazing weeks." Levi, the part-time bartender and full-time horse trainer, slid Sean a cold beer.

He'd been drinking free for weeks.

"You are welcome. Happy to do my civic duty." He lifted his bottle in salute.

"Aw, you ole dog!" Lenny, a regular, said. "If only I was ten years younger, I'd give you a run for your money. Back in the day women said I was the cat's meow."

"Back in the day, women said a lot of stuff," Levi said. "The important thing is, we're going to have some young and single women moving to Stone Ridge."

"Well, I can't see them staying here for long if they can't stomach life on a ranch." Jolette Marie Truehart, only daughter of the wealthiest man in town took a seat on the stool next to Sean.

"Right, Jo, go right on ahead and tell us about your tough as nails life on a ranch." Levi crossed his arms.

"Hey, I can muck a stall with the best of them."

"Uh-huh. But do you?" Levi said.

"No, I leave that to you, smartass." She threw a chip at him, and Levi caught in mid-air.

Sean had taken a tour after the complete remodel of one of Mr. Truehart's large homes on his horse ranch. It would accommodate the bachelorettes and entire crew. Let's just say it wouldn't give them a good impression of *his* family ranch. Mr. Truehart's place was far more like staying in a five-star resort than a working cattle ranch.

Sean was happy they'd be comfortable while far from home, but he'd like the women to see what real ranch life was like. His cabin, though built on hilly acres of Henderson land with a great view of the river, was modest, like him. Four upstairs bedrooms, one for each child he had hoped to have someday. An open kitchen complete with island and granite counter tops. A large dining room for family dinners. A wrap around porch. It was his dream house.

He'd sketched the blue prints himself and done much of the actual construction with help from Riggs and the other men of Stone Ridge. Around here, everyone lent a hand. It was one of the best parts of his hometown. He and his brothers hadn't been born here, but they'd had the enormously good fortune to have Calvin and Marge Henderson for foster parents. Sean's biological parents had lost custody of their children, finding their drug of choice far more important than family. But Cal and Marge, childless and in their fifties when they'd taken them on, had instilled a love for tradition, family, and this town. When their biological parents' rights were officially terminated, they'd adopted Sean, Riggs, and their youngest brother, Colton.

Riggs was already a teenager when all three moved in, Sean and Colton school-aged kids. But they'd acclimated well and worked hard. Years later, when Cal and Marge died within a year of each other, they were left the ranch.

A rallying cry came from the crowd as a commercial for Mr. Cowboy flashed across the muted TV screens.

"Turn it up, Levi!" Someone shouted.

Within seconds the volume was up, and Sean got to see for himself why Lori had nicknamed herself the second coming of Scorcese. She'd spliced together parts of his lame answers with film of horses, cattle grazing on acres of land, and used the footage of Sean ripping off his tie and shirt. It was misleading enough to look like he'd pulled it off in passion and not frustration. Using some from each of his answers, she'd spliced something cohesive together, making him sound like a man who knew exactly what he was looking for in a wife. Man, she was *good*.

"Hoo boy." Jolette Marie fanned herself. "Are we going to see some more skin?"

"That's about *all* you're going to see."

"Sean, you want someone educated and good with children?" Jeremy called out from several feet away.

Around ten years younger than Sean, he'd auditioned to be Mr. Cowboy after Wade Cruz, one of their local retired rodeo champs, had turned down the opportunity. He'd been off the market anyway the moment he reconnected with

Daisy Carver. But Jeremy hadn't passed the first interview, sounding too much like a kid who wanted to fool around rather than *settle* down.

"Sure," Sean said.

Those qualities were great in a woman. He already knew what he *didn't* want so he was going in the opposite direction.

"I thought you'd want someone like Bonnie Lee," Jolette Marie said and a hush fell over the bar.

"Bonnie Lee Wheeler is precisely what I *don't* want in a wife." Sean tamped down on the resentment that bringing up her name did to him.

"Um, beautiful, kind, and the daughter of a rodeo champ?" Levi said, voice heavy with sarcasm. "Yeah, what man alive would want *her* in his bed?"

Sean shot him a glare and Levi threw up both palms and went back to wiping the bar.

"Bonnie already proved she won't stay in Stone Ridge. And I'm only leavin' here when they put my body in the ground." He slammed the beer down and waved. "Early mornin'. See y'all when I see ya."

Next month, he would meet all the women for the first time, then after speaking to them each individually, the producers would ask him to eliminate all but four contestants. The next day he and the last four women would drop by Wade's new rodeo training school for their first group date event. Even their new clinic might see some business, and Dr. Judson Grant had ordered in extra supplies and equipment, including an x-ray machine.

"Sean?"

He turned to see Jolette Marie had followed him out and now stood behind him.

"You're not mad, are you?"

"No." He was a little irritated, however. Leave it to Jolette Marie to be the first to bring Bonnie up.

"Because all I meant is that you have to know who you really want as a wife. Not just what you don't want."

"Good point, got it."

"Bonnie had a dream that was different from yours, but otherwise you two were a good match. So, I say find someone like her, who has more of your values in mind."

"I think I'll know my future wife when I meet her, you know? *If* I meet her. I'm keeping my options open."

"Because Bonnie Lee was a good person. Maybe she didn't want to be a wife and mother, but she was the motherly type. So, see beyond what the women tell you. Try to see who they are. Remember the time I fell of a horse and everyone laughed at me? It was Bonnie who took care of me. Cleaned me up, bandaged me, made me laugh, and took me home. She was like the big sister I never had. I miss her, too."

"Yeah, she was good that way." He threw his arm around Jolette Marie. "That's good advice, ya know. Maybe I should take you along as a consultant. Help me weed through the women who don't want to be here for the right reasons."

She quirked a brow.

"You think I haven't heard of these shows? I've done my homework."

He'd watched the "other" more popular dating show and all the clips and drama. Winona and Beulah had insisted this be a "decent" show that children could watch with their parents. So, no "overnight" dates.

More important, this was entertainment. And he understood many, if not all, of the women were simply interested in furthering their own careers. For instance, a lawyer might be interested in a career broadcasting as a "legal analyst." A personal trainer might want her own health show or at the very least an appearance on Dr. Oz. Yeah, he knew the drill. This wasn't so much about finding a future wife but about entertainment and bringing more women to Stone Ridge.

"They will be stayin' on our property, so I can be a fly on the wall if you'd like."

"You would do that for me?"

"The women tend to inform on each other. Who's in it for you, and who is interested in something else. Or someone else. But I can be the final say if you have any doubts."

With that, she finger-waved to him and headed back into the bar.

He should go home as he already felt guilty about all the time he'd spend away from his ranch duties. But considering his new job was dating almost 24/7 in the hot pursuit of a lifetime partner, he had to take this seriously. Jo was right.

What did he want in a woman, besides someone who would stick around?

He hated that Bonnie's best traits immediately came to mind, but that had to be simply because she'd been the longest relationship he'd ever had. His first crush, first kiss, first date, first love, first…everything. From the time he was sixteen years old, he'd been in-love with Bonnie Lee Wheeler. He'd chased after her, hard, until she'd finally agreed to kiss him. One kiss and he'd forever after had a preference for redheads. They'd been on and off again for almost a decade before she finally left for good. Bonnie had plenty of options and suitors in Stone Ridge, but she'd always come back to Sean.

The first time she broke up with him was because, at the immature age of sixteen, she'd wanted to date a boy who owned a car. Sean didn't have his license, even if he'd been driving around the property since he was fourteen. Still, on hearing the news she'd chosen to go out with wily, screwy Joe Bob, Sean promptly put his hand through his bedroom wall. He later spackled the hole himself before his father could get on him.

Two weeks later she was back. "I like you and I don't care that you don't own a car."

That night they'd made out for hours in the bed of his beat-up pick-up truck under the starlit sky.

"I'll get my license," Sean said, tugging her close and pulling the blanket around her.

"Whatever you want. I can be silly sometimes, and I'm sorry. But I really like you."

"I like you, too, baby."

But whether or not he'd said it out loud, he'd been in love almost immediately. Desperately so.

She'd had some catching up to do.

It wasn't surprising that Bonnie's head was easily turned in those early years, given she was the only girl of Maybelle and "Buck" Wheeler, a champion rodeo star. They'd lived on one of the larger properties in Stone Ridge and Bonnie's dad spoiled her rotten, according to Sean's mother, and her best friend, Delores. Neither were Bonnie's greatest fans. It wasn't until the year Bonnie lost her father in a tragic accident that his mother changed her mind.

"That darling girl," she'd clucked as she baked pies and casseroles to take over to their home. "Where on earth will she and her poor mama go now."

There were rumors they'd have to move, and in sheer teenage panic Sean hatched a plan. He'd ask Bonnie to marry him, and until he was old enough to get their own place, he thought maybe his parents would let her live with them. They were both eighteen by then and it seemed like a grand idea to him. Regular sex. The girl he loved. He couldn't see beyond that fantastic picture.

But when he'd suggested the grand plan to his father, he'd simply sat him down in the living room for a serious "talk."

"Son, your heart is in the right place. But the last thing the young lady needs right now is a horny toad teenage boy after her."

Sean fought for his composure since his father had seen right through him as usual. Maybe he did want to do less taking care of Bonnie and more meeting his own needs.

"But—"

Calvin patted Sean's knee. "One day things will be better for her and then you can reconsider."

At her father's funeral, Sean couldn't help thinking Bonnie looked like a cone someone had scooped all the ice cream out of. The first chance he could get her alone, he'd pulled her into his arms.

She fisted his shirt, burying her face in his neck, wetting it with tears.

"Mama says we have to move. But I don't want to leave you."

I don't want to leave you.

For a kid whose own parents had abandoned him, the sentiment hit Sean hard. Those single words changed him from a boy to a man.

"You won't. I won't let it happen."

And if only that had been true.

CHAPTER 4

One month later, on arriving at San Antonio International airport, Bonnie made her way to baggage claim and grabbed her suitcases. If it seemed she'd brought everything she owned with her, this wasn't far from the truth. She'd moved out of Eric's apartment the day after she caught him with Vici. In classic celebrity fashion, but a first time for her, Bonnie broke up with Eric via text:

In case I wasn't clear, we're done.

I took a role on location and I'll be gone for weeks. Don't call me.

Marvin had indicated someone from the show would be at the airport to greet everyone and drive them to Stone Ridge. Among the crowds of families rushing to loved ones and couples embracing at their reunion, Bonnie looked for someone with a sign that either had her name on it or "Mr. Cowboy."

That's when she saw him, standing patiently, holding up a sign that read, "Mr. Cowboy." Older, his hair now completely white, he was still a sight.

Her heart tugged with the familiarity and comfort of home.

"Lenny!" Bonnie ran to him. "I'm so glad yours is the first face I get to see."

"*Bonnie Lee?*" He tipped his cowboy hat, eyes wide. "Well, hell's bells, darlin', I sure didn't expect to see you here! Just as beautiful as ever."

She went into his arms, accepting the hug of a man who'd been a pseudo-father to her for many years.

He sat her back, inspecting her like a proud papa. "Does your mama know you're here?"

"No, I decided to surprise her."

"She's goin' to be happy as a pig in shit." Lenny slapped his knee, then took two of her bags.

Bonnie pulled her other luggage toward the curbside. "Where are you parked?"

"I drove the Hummer the Beulah and the ladies bought the town a few years ago. Just as nice as a limo and roomier, I bet. I put in an ice chest and a twelve pack of beer in the back for y'all. We're drivin' in style."

Just then a blonde zipped up to them. "I'm here for Mr. Cowboy, too!"

Bonnie turned to introduce herself. The young lady couldn't be a day over twenty-five. Did she realize Sean was thirty-seven? She shook her head, remembering Hollywood would do their thing. Didn't matter. She'd be out of here soon enough. If she wound up being the oldest here, big deal. Her age was the least of her problems when it came to Sean.

"Bonnie Wheeler." She reached out with a free hand. "Also a...um, contestant."

"Tabitha Eden." She proceeded to hand Lenny everything she had, which was more than Bonnie did.

And she thought *she'd* overpacked.

"I'll get a cart," Lenny said and excused himself.

"This is so *exciting*!" Tabitha said. "I've always wanted to get married. And did you see his photo? Oh, swoon! A real cowboy, not those guys who model for the book covers."

"Where are you from?"

Tabitha had a lovely southern lilt to her voice that had Bonnie feeling right at home.

"I'm from Atlanta! How about you?"

"I'm a fourth generation Texan, but I've been in Hollywood for the last few years."

"Are you the actress? I heard we'd have an actress in our group!" Tabitha nearly levitated with excitement.

"That's me. I'm originally from Stone Ridge. I…I know Sean." She wasn't certain how much she should tell this young lady about her past.

It was…complicated.

"You know him? Wow. So, I bet you know where all the bodies are buried, yeah?" She chuckled and elbowed Bonnie.

"Yep."

"Have you been in any movies I might know?"

Ah yes, people always wanted to know about the *movies*. Never theater or sitcoms. *Movies* were the big time. She used to feel the same for the first few years, then settled on making a living. Not everyone could be Meryl Streep.

"You may have seen me on an Irish mafia show several years back, Kavanaugh's Way. Most people recognize from there. Three seasons."

"That was you? Oh wow, my brother *loved* that show. A little violent for me, but hey, this is probably going to be *great* for your career!"

Marvin seemed to think so. He thought Bonnie could use the show as a springboard into a secondary career in broadcasting if nothing else. He hadn't even asked Bonnie if she'd be interested in becoming a TV "personality," or famous simply for being famous because the answer was a resounding "no."

"Your Twitter is going to explode!" he'd said triumphantly as if that made her a great actor and an overnight success.

But Bonnie considered Twitter a necessary cesspool. She live-tweeted the Emmys, Golden Globes, and Oscars once a year and otherwise occasionally re-tweeted something which didn't tear anyone else down.

"And what do you do for a living?" Bonnie asked Tabitha as she helped Lenny load the suitcases.

"I'm a NICU nurse," she gushed. "Oh, I *love* me some babies. I can't wait to have my own. Sean is ready to settle down too and have a big family. We sound perfect for each other."

"Is this the place for Mr. Cowboy?" A tall, lean brunette rolling only two suitcases with her joined them. "I didn't see anyone with a sign, so I followed the women."

Bonnie chuckled. "Good plan. I'm Bonnie Wheeler, nice to meet you."

"Angela Stacey, lovely to meet you."

Angela had flawless latte skin and an air of suave sophistication Bonnie had spent years perfecting. She didn't know whether she could even be considered in Angela's league. Time would tell.

In the next few minutes three more women joined them and then Lenny held up his hand. "No more room. Might have to come back if there's any more of y'all."

"I'm sure they can send out a car later if needed," Bonnie said.

"Oh, so you've done this before?" Angela asked.

"Um, no. But I'm an actor and I've been involved in a few productions on sets in New Mexico and Georgia. Believe me, they'll get everyone where they need to be."

"What a relief," Angela said. "I had hoped this wouldn't be

some rinky-dink project just because it's a western version. I applied for the other dating show, but they turned me down. At least I made this call."

"Where's all your luggage?" Tabitha piped up.

"This is it." She pointed out her two bags.

"For two weeks? How do you manage?"

"I travel all the time. You have to know how to pack with some basic pieces of clothing that you can simply accessorize in many different styles."

"Besides, wardrobe is going to fit us for some outfits," Bonnie said.

Approximately six women were packed into the Hummer. Most of them appeared a lot younger than Bonnie. But she was at last coming home where her age wouldn't matter. She was Bonnie Lee Wheeler, daughter of Maybelle, member of the ladies of SORROW. Daughter of the late, great William "Buck" Wheeler. Niece to Beulah Hayes, President of the ladies of SORROW. Even if she hadn't been home for years, she wrote home often and sent money to her mother. She'd be welcome, if not by Sean, by everyone else.

"Woohoo!" Tabitha pulled out a beer from the ice chest and cracked it open. "Let's get this party started."

From beside Bonnie, Angela smirked. "I think she'll be out after the first day."

Bonnie didn't want to say, but she thought so too. Sean had never been into party girls and he claimed to be ready to settle down. Considering he'd been ready since the age of eighteen, she had no doubt.

"Do you have a strategy yet?" Angela said.

"A *strategy*?"

"A strategy to win this thing or at least get into the final four. You're a smart woman. Are you the nurse?"

"No." Bonnie pointed to Tabitha. "She's the nurse."

Angela blinked. "I thought she was the actress."

"Nope, that's me."

Angela waved her hand dismissively. "Long flight from La Guardia. I must be off game."

"The producers probably wanted me for the drama factor, but I've a feeling I'll be gone after the first day."

"Why? You're beautiful and, so far as I can tell, not crazy."

Bonnie laughed. "He won't be interested in me."

"You never know. Maybe you're the one the producers will insist on keeping."

"Insist on *keeping*?"

"Yes," she said patiently. "Every one of these shows needs the drama. And most of them want the option to keep at least one candidate the bachelor can't eliminate until they tell him he can."

"What? Until they *tell* him he can?"

Bonnie swallowed hard. She pulled out her cell and viciously texted Marvin to examine the contract for the *fine print*. She did not want the producers forcing Sean to keep her. He should be able to let her go when he wanted to. She figured that would be immediately, unless he wanted to toy with her. Perhaps he'd like to torture her by making her watch him date all these gorgeous women.

"I've done my research." She patted the laptop case she hadn't let go of once. "Financial planner here. My strategy is to wind up in the top three, then I'll slowly pull back, and let him know I'm not interested in starting a family right away. I'll drop a few hints here and there. That's what's most important to this guy, believe me. Then, I'll be eliminated."

"You *want* to be eliminated?"

"I don't think it's fair to string him along until the end the way some of these women will do. Believe me. But if I at least wind up in the top three, it will be an incredible boost for my new podcast, 'Girl, you should be a millionaire.' Have you heard of it?"

Podcast? Bonnie gulped, feeling decidedly naïve. Her strategy was to leave this show with the least amount of damage to both her heart and mind.

She needed a better strategy.

SEAN HADN'T BEEN this nervous in years. He waited in the Truehart's great room decorated in a classic western theme, if the cowboy was a multi-millionaire. The fireplace was stone hearth and massive, the plush leather couches were big enough to accommodate a crowd.

The hair and make-up crew were playing with his hair, spraying something that made him sneeze. Then someone bent to shine his boots.

"I should do that." He pulled back his foot.

"That's what we're here for," the wardrobe lady said. "Every guy in America would want us to be on a first date with them. You're a lucky man."

"Yeah."

Lucky and nervous. Possibly even a little bit...worried. He didn't scare easily but he hadn't experienced the adrenaline rushing through his blood at this level since he heard a gunshot over a year ago. He'd run outside with his shotgun to find Winona had been shot while attempting to save Riggs from the madman Henderson cousin. He thought he deserved the ranch instead of the foster kids Cal and Marge had adopted. Everything worked out, and Sean nicknamed Winona "Shotgun Annie." But he'd been on edge for weeks afterward.

In a few more minutes, ten women would arrive, one by one, and introduce themselves. The rest of the evening, so-called "cocktail" hour, would involve him spending a little time with each woman. After conferring with Lori, he'd eliminate six of them in the same night. His neck had already broken out in a sweat as he pictured hurting someone's feelings. But Lori was here for moral support and direction, and also Elton and the rest of the small crew.

"You've got this!" Lori now said with a thumbs up.

She'd changed from her standard jeans and T-shirt into a black pantsuit and high heels.

He did a double-take. "Thanks for making me sound intelligent. That reel? First rate."

"No prob. You're the one with the abs." She motioned for him to walk outside. "Ready for this, champ? Now, we're rolling all the time, so no worries if something goes terribly wrong or you trip, spill a drink on a lady, or curse. We can cut all that out in editing."

"You can cut out all my cursing? Shit, why didn't you tell me that before?" He grinned and positioned himself just outside the front door to the Truehart mansion.

"We're rolling!" Lori said. "Look happy!"

"I am happy," he mumbled under his breath.

He would get his foundation started.

Plus, within a few months, I could be married. Maybe even with a little one on the way if I work fast.

And after the longest dry spell in history, he was ready and willing.

Just out of camera shot, he spied a crew member guiding a young lady toward the walkway leading to the front door. She was dressed in tight jeans and a yellow top dipped low to showcase an amazing rack. Gulp.

"Hi, I'm Tabitha Eden. And I'm..." She stared up at him. "Oh, gosh I forgot what I was going to say."

"It's nice to meet you, Tabitha." Warmly, he took both of her hands in his, accepted a hug, and waved her inside the mansion.

Another beautiful woman approached, tall, elegant,

dressed in a dark suit with a tight skirt and matching jacket. She had incredible legs.

"I'm Angela, and I don't believe in wasting time. I'm a financial planner and the only thing lacking in my life is a serious relationship. I want to settle down. Feel free to ask me any questions. I'm an open book."

"Well, thanks. Good to meet you."

The next girl they brought out looked like the proverbial girl next door. Sean couldn't help but smile. Dressed in a short yellow dress with matching cowgirl boots, he thought for the first time: *maybe this could work.*

"Hi, I'm Jessica, and I teach first graders in my home state of Massachusetts. I can work as a teacher anywhere in the country as long as I get my credentials."

"You would like winters in Texas."

"Oh, I bet I would." She smiled shyly.

Nice. Very attractive.

One after another, Sean met beautiful, intelligent, and educated women. A real estate agent who swore she could and would live anywhere in the USA, a dancer, a teacher, a fitness trainer, a lawyer. He thought many of the women could easily relocate to Stone Ridge and keep their careers. It would be up to Sean to get this message across. Stone Ridge was home base and there would be zero negotiating.

"How's it going?" Lori came up to him.

"I'm going to have a hard time, that's for sure. These are some truly incredible women y'all have chosen."

"Well, we do our best. We have one more lady."

Sean turned expectantly but coming up the walkway was none other than *Bonnie Lee Wheeler.*

Thick outrage uncoiled in him and pulsed through raw and untethered. She was from Hollywood so of course she'd think this was a great opportunity to advance her career. Still, this was a cheap trick.

For a moment he couldn't speak.

"Hello, Sean. As you know, I'm Bonnie Lee Wheeler from Los Angeles. Originally from Stone Ridge."

"Is this a joke?"

"They didn't *tell* you about me? I understood you knew I'd be here and were okay with this."

"No, I didn't. And I'm *not*."

"I'm here because I'm also ready to settle down."

He snorted. "Are you?"

"Yes. Probably." She tipped her chin in the way she always had when he'd challenged her. "Why *else* do you think I'm here?"

"I have no idea. Look, I don't have time for this. I'm serious. This..." He waved around to indicate the production. "Isn't a joke to me."

"Me, either."

"We had our chance."

"I'm here anyway and what happened before is ancient history. We've both changed so you can't blame me for trying again. If you want to get rid of me, that's your choice."

Sean stared back at her. He'd be lying to say he didn't online stalk her from time to time when feeling nostalgic. Sean had watched every movie, every series, every commercial she'd appeared in. Now, standing before her, she was more stunning than she'd been at twenty-four, when she'd left him for the last time.

A little older, thinner, her eyes not as earnest and open as he remembered. She eyed *him* with suspicion. Then he remembered the contract allowed the show to choose one woman to stay through each elimination.

This could be the woman. Who better than an actress to stir up drama?

"See you inside."

Bonnie made to walk past him into the house, but he blocked her way. "Hang on."

Sean motioned to Lori to join them and then pointed between him and Bonnie. "Did you know about this?"

"About what?" Lori said.

"This is my ex, Bonnie Wheeler. She's an actress from Los Angeles."

"Oh, get out of town! That's absolute genius."

Sean glared at her until she wilted.

"I mean, it's maybe good TV?"

"Listen, Sean." Bonnie reached for his forearm and squeezed. "I can help you navigate through all this, if you'd like."

He shrugged her off. "Help me? How are you going to help? I've had all the *help* I'll ever need from you."

"Okay, if this scene gets too intense, I'll cut in edits, but keep it going," Lori said, moving to the side, rolling her hand behind the camera. "Good work here."

"This isn't funny. No one told me about her."

"What part of reality did you not understand?" Lori went hands on hips.

"The part where y'all mess with my life and waste my time."

"No one's wasting your time. We want a little entertainment while we watch you fall in love, if that's not too much to ask."

"Maybe it *is* too much to ask."

He didn't want Bonnie here, making him crazy and edgy, wondering what she'd do next. Hadn't she tortured him enough over the years?

This is what I wanted, or at least what I agreed to. The foundation will get a hefty grant. And I'm supposed to have fun with beautiful women. If all this results in a real marriage, great.

If not, it's only a few weeks of my life.

CHAPTER 5

The moment Bonnie stepped through the archway of the great room, she sensed the mood among the women had shifted. Earlier in the day they were chatty and friendly as they discussed Sean and what their chances were with him.

"I heard he likes women who are good with children," Jessica said. "So, at least I have that going for me."

She had a lot more going for her in Bonnie's opinion. Sweet, curvy, and blonde, she was kind. She'd helped with everyone else's luggage as they hauled it into their respective bedrooms and reassured anyone with doubts.

"Of *course* you deserve to be here," Jessica had said.

It would be between Bonnie and Jessica for the title of "house mom."

"Well, I'm a NICU nurse so I can take care of our baby if its ever sick," Tabitha added.

"I can plan and secure our financial future," Angela said smugly, as she held out and inspected her beautifully manicured hand.

"You all have a good chance. I'm rooting for you," Bonnie said.

Like a big sister, Bonnie took on a supportive role. Tomorrow, she'd go surprise her mother, and stay with her, eating peach pie made from locally canned peaches. Sleep for about a week. She'd take long walks, luxuriate in the scent of fresh cut grass and clean air. She would fall asleep at night listening to the soothing sounds of Lupine Lake, behind her Mama's house. The birds twittering as they jumped from tree to tree.

She and Mama would bake cookies, cakes, and casseroles for anyone in need. Bonnie would unwind for the first time in a decade.

Later that day, Bonnie advised the women on clothing and hair style choices for the cocktail party. For herself, she'd decided on a simple pink shift dress and strappy pumps. Obviously, she wanted to look professional for the cameras, but didn't want to mislead Sean. So, she'd split the difference between sexy and sophisticated.

"You look so classy," Tabitha said.

Maybe this won't be so bad if I get to hang out with the women and help them while I'm here. In the process of getting to know them, she'd figure out who might be best for Sean. Then she'd try to help him out. If he'd allow her.

But now, a few of the women were eyeing her with no small amount of curiosity. Others threw downright hostile looks in her direction. Bonnie gave everyone her practiced "audition" smile, nodded, and sashayed up to the bar for a flute of the champagne everyone else already had.

Angela wasted no time in joining her, holding her flute out with one hand and the other planked on her hip. "You could have been honest with me. I shared my strategy with *you*. And I told you I'm not really interested him, but you know what? I could change my mind. He's extremely good-looking. How long did you two date? And how long ago did you break-up?"

Angela, the strategist.

"We didn't end well, and it was a long time ago. The two of us mutually hate each other. I didn't think it was important enough to mention. And I didn't share a strategy with you because I don't have one. Honestly, I don't expect to be here after tonight."

"I see. Okay, okay, got it."

Bonnie could almost see the wheels turning as Angela readjusted and tweaked her strategy. It wasn't much different than what she'd seen the most successful actors in show business do, and maybe if Bonnie had learned to do it too, she'd have been more of a player. Instead, for years she'd focused on craft, not understanding how to play the game. Maybe even not wanting to.

Tabitha wasn't as understanding as she approached, wiggling her neck like a duck. "I mean, you could have *told* me y'all had a thing."

"An unfair advantage above the rest of us in my opinion," Jessica said. "I'm sorry to say, but you shouldn't be here."

"It didn't end well," Angela explained, waving a hand dismissively.

"So...he hates her, or he *love-hates* her?" Tabitha cocked her head.

Lori entered the room, clapping once. "Okay! That's all of you. All ten women vying for the heart of one man. And without any further ado, let's get this party started. Here's Mr. Cowboy!"

Like a school of fish, all women moved forward and gathered together, a few jockeying for better position. Bonnie stayed near the back and safety from the occasional wilting glares in her direction.

"Welcome, ladies," Sean began. "I can't wait to get to

know y'all a little better tonight. I'm looking for my wife and I know she could be in this room tonight."

Well, someone had obviously been through some media training. Bonnie couldn't help but be impressed. The Sean she remembered was all emotions and...abs. Oh, yeah, those abs. She hadn't *forgotten* in case the commercial hadn't showcased them enough.

"Tabitha, would you join me out on the patio?" Sean held out his hand and Tabitha nearly launched herself to him.

"Oh my gawd, oh my gawd."

The two walked hand in hand through the French open sliding doors out to the garden patio. Sean then shut the door and led Tabitha to a bench, where he waited for her to sit first.

"Wow, pick the tits right off the bat," Angela said. "*So* predictable."

"Now, let's not judge too hastily," Jessica said, echoing Bonnie's thoughts.

"She's right," Bonnie added.

She'd been about to say he wasn't a breast man but that would be lying. Still, she didn't think he'd chosen Tabitha for that reason alone. Cute and perky, Tabitha was a nurse, after all. They might have some things in common, though she was *young.*

"You know him. What's he like?" Jessica said. "What does he like?"

The other women leaned in closer to Bonnie.

"We already know the canned stuff the producers showed the public, but you can give us the inside scoop." Angela elbowed Bonnie.

"Well, Sean...Sean..." Outside, she watched him drape an arm around Tabitha's shoulders. The feelings it drew out of her weren't good.

They weren't...acceptable.

Sean was right. They'd had their chance. So why did her stomach churn at the sight of him with another woman?

You know why.

The women had followed Bonnie's gaze and there came a collective gasp from all.

"If he kisses her, I'm *so* out of here," Jessica said. "Tabitha and I are as different as a store-bought bun and fresh baked bread. If she's what he wants, then I'm not it."

"Calm down," Angela said. "He's too much of a gentleman to break the rules. Right, Bonnie?"

"Ri—" Bonnie said.

"And what if she kisses *him* first? Is he too much of a gentleman to shove her off the bench?" another woman said.

It wasn't a question, of course. No man alive would do such a thing, and Sean was if nothing else, a red-blooded American male.

How does it feel, Bonnie?

It's your turn now.

In their earlier years, Sean had to contend with the men of Stone Ridge chasing *her*. He'd had to watch as she fended off advances, as she occasionally, when she was *much* younger, let things go a little too far. She'd sometimes let a smitten guy hold her hand while she knew very well, she'd never let him kiss her. Sean had been wildly jealous at times because he couldn't see inside her heart. She'd be lying to say she hadn't enjoyed watching him squirm and bend over backward to keep her. She'd been an idiot.

The rumors that had formed about Bonnie from time to time from jealous girls weren't kind. They also weren't true, but they'd led to more than one fight and temporary break-up. She was glad now she'd gone out of her way to reassure his male ego, happy she hadn't let any fight go on for long. Then, she hadn't realized they wouldn't last forever. She'd been stupid, young, and in-love.

It felt like a lifetime ago some days.

Meanwhile, Tabitha was now leaning her head on Sean's shoulder.

"Oh, hell no! Not on my watch." One of the women said, setting her flute down. At the entrance to the garden patio, she pulled her tight black evening down around her hips and then swung the doors open. The camera crew eagerly followed.

Angela grinned. "Wonderful."

"How can you say that? This is so upsetting," Jessica said, wringing her hands. "I don't like cat fighting."

"Girl, what you doing on this show?" Angela said.

"I expected more out of a western reality show, maybe some more homegrown values."

"That's definitely what you'll get out of Sean," Bonnie said, attempting to diffuse their own situation though the drama was going on outside. "He's a man's man, through and through."

The other women were plastered up against the sliders trying to eavesdrop.

"She's saying she'd like a little time with Sean and Tabitha is hording it," one of them turned back whisper.

"And Sean said he'd like another minute," another said. "He's actually very pleasant."

Lori stepped inside. "I'm going to need you ladies to step back. You look *ridiculous*. I'm only thinking of you."

Outdoors, the action continued. Clearly, Tabitha was upset at having her "special time" interrupted. Sean stood, taking over the situation, speaking to them both.

The women were no longer repeating what they'd eavesdropped.

"I don't know how much more of this I can take," Jessica said, wiping her brow.

"This is not for the faint of heart," Angela mumbled

behind her champagne flute.

Eventually, Tabitha made her way back inside, fanning herself. "He's so hot. Did you see how he touched me? I leaned my head against his shoulder, wow! What a shoulder!"

Angela rolled her eyes. "Did you ask him anything about himself? How many kids he wants, for instance?"

Three, unless he's become reasonable.

"No, I forgot." Tabitha stared blankly. "He's so...so..."

"I *know*," Jessica said. "And when will I get my time with him?"

Eventually, Jessica did get her time with him, walking down the cobblestone path. Holding hands. All of the women got time with one exception.

Bonnie.

"You called it," Angela said to Bonnie as they all waited on the patio for the cowboy hats that would be placed in the center of the room.

Only four hats, and Sean would offer a hat to each woman he wanted to stay.

"I don't know what I'll do if he doesn't choose me," the fitness trainer from Phoenix said. While they waited, she was doing planks.

Show-off.

"Yeah, like I felt this connection," said the farm sales equipment rep from Wyoming. "The sparks were like crackling all over the place. I will be very surprised if he doesn't pick me."

Angela grunted. "I think he and I have an understanding. We happen to have a lot in common."

"If he doesn't pick me, I'll die." Tabitha, who'd rolled up into a ball on the couch, dissolved into tears. "I love him."

"Oh, honey." Bonnie rubbed the poor girl's back. Woman. Woman-girl. "You'll be alright, no matter what happens."

"I don't think so."

Angela's eyes nearly rolled right out of her head and she canted her head. "Are you for *real*?"

"Love at first sight, I think." Tabitha sniffed.

Finally, Lori joined them in the great room. "Ladies, Sean has made his decision. As you can see, there are only four cowboy hats. If he doesn't offer you a hat, tonight this is the end of the line for you. Be sure to apply for our next dating show!"

Bonnie would take Lori aside later and suggest a little consideration should be in order. Women like Tabitha would take the rejection hard.

As Bonnie wondered where they'd put all her luggage, and how quickly she could get out of here, one by one the women gathered. Bonnie moved to the back of the last row.

Sean ambled back inside the room. "Thanks for your patience. As y'all know, the men in my town are not used to being in high demand. It's more like the ladies are the ones we chase. So, thank you for being here, and considering me as a husband. It really is a great honor."

Someone sighed.

"Get on with it," the fitness trainer murmured.

"Do you have some sit-ups to do?" a wise ass muttered. "Don't let us stop you."

"Shhh," said Jessica.

Sean picked up a hat. "Needless to say, though all you ladies are quite beautiful, I can only have one wife. At least, that's what the great state of Texas says."

Lots of giggles on that one. Bonnie also wanted him to get on with this. Every minute she had to look at Sean was like a root canal to her heart. Fun times.

"So…Jessica. Would you accept this hat?"

Jessica moved forward like a gazelle on a cloud. "Yes. Thank you, Sean."

He gently placed it on her head with a grin.

Tabitha and Angela were next, all getting hats with big smiles.

All good choices, Bonnie thought, but Jessica would be best. She seemed even tempered, mature, loving, and kind. A teacher.

"And, finally..." He held out the last hat. "Skippy."

"Who's Skippy?" Jessica turned.

Everything in Bonnie stilled. *Skippy*. A wisp of a sweet memory rolled through her, causing a tender ache. She hadn't heard that name in years, a private joke between two lovers.

She moved slowly toward Sean.

One of the women gasped.

Sean held out the Stetson. "Skippy, would you accept this hat?"

"Sure."

He rather unceremoniously plopped it on her head. Not gently, like he had the others. It was a little big and wound up covering her eyes. She tipped it up to find him smiling.

Lori stepped forward and clapped her hands. "Everyone else, this is the end of the line for you."

There were tears as hugs were passed around from the women leaving, far more than were staying. Sean walked out with them, holding doors open, accepting goodbye hugs.

"*Skippy?*" Jessica turned to Bonnie, arms crossed, eyes narrowed.

"That's...um, what Sean used to call me."

"His ex makes the round?" Tabitha said, tears forming again. "This isn't fair. He already has a pet name for her."

"Like I said, *you* already have too much of an advantage," Jessica said.

"Wait a second, hold up, guys." Angela held her arms out. "I don't know how many of you actually know this, but I heard it from a friend who heard it from a friend. The producers insist on choosing at least one contestant to stay. And cause drama, right? *Who* could cause more drama than Sean's ex? Girls, have a strategy and work it. Don't be dumb about this."

As easily as Bonnie's heart had surged, it sank like the Titanic. Of course. Sean had been *forced* to keep her on. Presumably, the producers could choose a different player next week. It would be her mission to stay out of drama if she wanted to be released from the show.

On the other hand, she couldn't exactly stop being Sean's ex-girlfriend.

"HOW ARE YOU FEELING?" Lori asked Sean later, after the women had retired for the night.

"Like crap. I didn't like having to say goodbye to those women."

"That's the drill. You handled it well."

Sean had personally said goodbye to each woman because this was the way he'd been raised. One by one he shook the hand of each woman, hugging back when they did, and wishing them the best from life.

"Good *luck*, Sean," the fitness instructor said with a quirked brow. "Not everyone is here for the right reasons."

"I wish I'd had more time to get to know you," Sean said, borrowing a line from those suggested by the producers. "You deserve all the happiness in the world."

He would have said those same words to Tabitha, whom he'd wanted to send home. But the producers chose her to remain this week, saying she was clearly here for the right reasons and already loved Sean.

Plus, she cried easily and would be entertaining to watch.

Her "love" for him scared him more than it should. But Tabitha was far too young for him and he'd determined that after speaking with her for five minutes. Their so-called connection felt more like big brother to little sister. Eventually he hoped she'd see it that way too.

Jessica was very nice, a schoolteacher, and he felt a slight connection with her. Nothing earth shattering, or life altering, but...something. Might grow if nurtured. He appreciated Angela was so self-possessed and even tempered, a good balance for his more mercurial tendencies. She was incredibly down to earth and honest. She had specific goals in mind and wanted a large family. He thought maybe a connection might be able to grow there too given enough time.

He chose Skippy for the worst reason of all: he wasn't ready to see her go. Also, he selfishly wanted her to watch him as he dated all these women.

Were things going so badly in L.A. that she wanted to jumpstart her career with a reality show? He wasn't too naïve to realize women didn't always have honest intentions. According to Jolette Marie, the purveyor of all reality and thirty-day fiancé shows, some women had ulterior motives. It was up to him to see if the women were here for the right reasons and proceed accordingly.

No matter what tricks his mind wanted to play, or how much Bonnie still made lust pulse through him, *she* clearly wasn't here for the right reasons. She wasn't here for him because she couldn't be. She'd proved long ago that fame and fortune were more important than home and family. Not having been home for years said it all. She'd come back for a show which would be broadcast all over the USA.

"Tomorrow is the first group date, over at the Wade Cruz Rodeo Training Center," Lori announced, studying her clipboard. "First thing in the morning, after the ladies have breakfast, we'll give them the heads-up."

He wondered how many of them would fall off a horse

for the first time. He'd campaigned for ponies, but Wade had a good long laugh about that suggestion.

"And y'all will have Dr. Judson standing by?"

Their Podunk town at last had a clinic and a general doctor, thanks to Winona's efforts, and the ladies of SORROW. But they still had only a volunteer fire department, no police, and no certified EMTs or paramedics.

"You worry more than you should. They're riding a thirty-year-old horse that's incredibly sweet. We've taken every precaution. We have liability, after all." Lori sniffed. "Mr. Truehart made sure of that."

"Of course, he did." Sean chuckled. The man wasn't a self-made multi-millionaire from taking stupid risks.

Bonnie, of course, should look good on a horse, unless she'd truly forgotten everything.

CHAPTER 6

The next morning Bonnie woke and stretched under the silky high-count thread sheets of the massive mahogany bed. She'd been in the main Truehart mansion many times in the past, but this latest addition must have been constructed after she'd left town. The rambling Tuscan style two-story was classic Spanish stucco red tiled roofing. Several patios, fountains, and glorious and lush gardens accented every side of the home. In the distance, the rushing sounds of the river cut through Truehart land and partially separated them from the Carver cattle ranch.

She grabbed her robe and went to stand by the window that faced the beautiful hills. Below, an inviting pool sparkled with clear blue water. Nearby, a hot tub and chaise lounges scattered about. A hammock hung between two trees, and in it sat Jessica, slowly swinging her feet.

Bonnie tried to picture Jessica and Sean together, happily married, children on the way. Her stomach pitched and roiled in protest. This reaction was wrong in so many ways. She should want nothing but the best for Sean, not seethe with bitterness over how he'd dumped her. Dumped her, and then been engaged to someone else within a year. She didn't want him. She didn't *want* to want him.

Besides, she had no business dating anyone until she resolved what to do with her life. Until she decided where to go from here. She'd already wasted too much time on a dream that hadn't quite worked out the way she'd wanted. But she refused to feel sorry for herself. She'd met with early success and been a working actress for years. Not many could say the same. Starring roles came along for some, but often with years between the next gig. It was almost as if one had to pay for the luck of a huge role by having a few lean years in between. Bonnie chose steady work instead of the occasional bright and shiny role of a lifetime.

She'd never had *that* role, and here in Stone Ridge, she'd take some time and consider why. Maybe it had been bad luck, pure and simple, or perhaps her own poor business decisions. But either way, an itch grew inside daily and told her she and Hollywood were finished. Whether or not she should be completely done with acting could be another story. The desire to perform had always been in her, from the time she'd earned the starring role in the first-grade play.

She'd continued with theater in high school and later entered rodeo queen contests. At nineteen, she'd been scouted by an agency and invited to New York City. But though Bonnie may have been a beautiful girl in Stone Ridge, in New York City and Hollywood she was simply another face in a sea of others.

"Looks aren't everything, Skippy," Sean had said to her more than once.

"You tell me I'm beautiful. Isn't that why *you* love me? My looks?"

He'd been so angry he didn't talk to her for a day.

When he finally stopped sulking, he'd come by her house holding a handful of freshly picked flowers.

"Listen, baby, you won't find anyone who thinks you're more beautiful than I do. But you weren't Homecoming Queen for your looks. You won because you're kind to everyone from the least popular kid at school to the most popular. *That's* why, Bonnie."

"But why do *you* love me?"

She adored him for so many reasons. Hard-working, he was good to his mother, a good son, brother and faithful boyfriend. It wasn't his smoldering good looks which even as a teenager made hearts flutter. There weren't many single women in Stone Ridge, but every girl his age wanted a chance with Sean.

"Yeah, I should have led with that," he said sheepishly, taking her hand and brushing a kiss across her knuckles. "Sweetheart, to start with, I love your heart. How kind you are to everyone."

Why hadn't she believed him?

She would like to blame all those who'd focused on her looks from the time she was five:

Oh, my look at that gorgeous red hair! Gets it from her Mama.

Maybelle, put her in one of them modeling contests. Surely she'll win.

Her skin is flawless!

Good Lord, I wish I could eat Beulah's apple pie and still have Bonnie's body. Bless her heart.

Other kids were "smart as a whip," "good to their mama," "next President of the USA," or "a friend to everyone."

Bonnie had tried to be all of those things, too. But looks had been her main talent in the long run. So she'd chosen a profession which valued and rewarded beauty.

And she'd never really believed she had much else to offer the world.

All on her. She was now almost twice the age she'd been when she met Sean Henderson for the first time. She'd spent over a decade away from him. Her aging skin was no longer flawless. Two years ago, she'd found her first gray hair. She'd put on a few pounds and wasn't the thin girl he remembered with weight in all the *right* places. She now had a little extra padding…everywhere.

Dressing, she came downstairs and met the girls for breakfast. She found the Trueharts had lent them their cook, too.

"Good morning." Bonnie grabbed one of the cups from the coffee tray set out and poured from the French Press.

"Eggs Benedict." Angela pointed to her plate. "Delicious. Someday I'll have a cook. It's scheduled for year three of the ten-year plan."

"Mm, something to look forward to." Bonnie mixed a little cream in her coffee.

"Sean's family has a cook and housekeeper, too. Delores. But she practically helped raise the boys. She was Sean's mother's best friend."

"Really? A live-in cook?" Angela said, sounding suitably impressed.

"Yeah, but she expects help with the dishes."

"Not quite what I had in mind." Angela pointed outside to where Jessica still sat on the hammock. "Someone is a little melancholy today."

"Wonder why. I think she's the front-runner, don't you?"

"Absolutely. She reminds me of a younger version of you. Kind of a second try for Sean which might work this time. No offense."

"None taken."

"I overheard her talking on the phone last night. Poor thing. Today is some kind of sad anniversary."

"Oh? We should do something to cheer her up."

Lori entered the room with Elton and her usual blustery, hurricane-like presence.

"Hello! Hello! Morning one and all. Um, are we missing someone?" She went to the sliders and beckoned to Jessica who slowly walked to the house.

"Mornin', y'all." Tabitha sashayed in a moment later. "This is so exciting. Oh, look, coffee!"

"Are you kidding me right now," Angela said under her breath as she shot a glare at Tabitha.

Tabitha wore what came down to Daisy Duke shorts, red western boots, and a red and white checkered blouse mostly for show and not much for coverage.

Bonnie glanced down at her mom-jean Wranglers, boots, and pearl button blue western shirt.

"Can she *wear* that?" Jessica pointed to Tabitha.

Lori gave the once-over. "Looks like flesh is um...mostly covered, so yeah."

Jessica crossed her arms. "I thought this was a *family* show."

Tabitha twirled. "What's wrong with this? It's my *western look.*"

"You look smashing, but you might want to reconsider when you hear all about today's group date." Lori laid an engraved card on the table, smiled, and turned. "And... cameras rolling!"

"Oh, what do we have here?" Angela, who should keep her day job, reached for the envelope and read out loud. "Ladies, I'd like to see if you can rope my heart. See you at the Wade Cruz Rodeo Clinic where I hope to give you a few riding lessons. The winner gets the first one-on-one date."

Tabitha scrunched up her nose. "Clinic?"

"Wade Cruz is a former rodeo champ, and he teaches now," Bonnie explained.

She talked to Mama once a week, after all.

"Gee, I hope your knees don't get skinned," Jessica muttered to Tabitha.

A few minutes later, the entire crew were headed out in the Hummer driven by Lenny to the Cruz ranch on the outskirts of Stone Ridge. She knew it well, since it abutted to the Henderson property, where she'd spent many days.

The air was crisp and clear, the smell of sweet peaches ripening in the air. Hill Country was gorgeous in Autumn and how she'd missed all the wide-open spaces. No sounds of freeway traffic in the distance, honking horns, or three car pileups. No smog. Just trees, hills, and…the familiar smell of manure.

That she hadn't missed.

"That smell!" Lori waved her hand in front of her nose.

"That'll be the scent of money." Lenny insisted on leading them up to the corral, and he sauntered ahead of them.

"Hey, ladies," came handsome Wade's voice.

Wade Cruz and Daisy Carver stood just outside the corral, holding hands. Mama's latest gossip had been filled with news of those two, officially engaged and working together on the rodeo clinic. They looked so happy.

"Bonnie Lee?" Daisy grabbed her in a bear hug. "Does Sean know you're here? Does your mama know you're here?"

"Yes to Sean. No to my mama. But she will soon, I'm sure."

In fact, if Bonnie didn't call her today, she'd probably find her mother witling a switch at her kitchen table. And Bonnie hadn't had the switch to her since she was twelve.

The camera and crew set up. In no time at all, Wade took over describing what they'd learn today and bringing out the horse they'd be riding.

"This is Grace," he said, leading a beautiful paint. "She's a thorough bred and raced in the past, but she's retired now."

"She's…big," said Angela, chewing on her lower lip.

"And old." Bonnie leaned in and whispered. "She looks docile to me. Don't worry."

"Thanks." Angela smiled gratefully.

Daisy was busy demonstrating how they'd mount while Wade gathered equipment.

Suddenly in the distance, a horse's hooves could be heard advancing. Kicking up dirt and dust, Sean was literally riding in on a *white horse*. While this was a nice touch, he didn't need any help in the hero department. He looked every bit the handsome cowboy, as he dismounted his horse easily. He waved and ambled towards them, dressed in his jeans, dark shirt, and black Stetson.

"Lord have mercy," said Tabitha, swirling her hand as if she'd touched a hot stove.

She then took off at a run toward Sean, closing the distance between them, literally launching herself into his arms. He had no choice but to catch her or risk her falling on the gravel stone path and ripping up her legs.

At least, that's what Bonnie told herself as jealousy seethed inside on a low flame.

"Whoa," he said with a grin. "Pretty excited, are you?"

"Yes, yes, yes!"

And why did it sound as if she were in the throes of orgasm?

Sean set her down, stepped a few paces away, and met the rest of the group. Bonnie gently pushed Jessica forward. The girl didn't have enough confidence in herself, and with Tabitha around, for Sean to notice her she'd have to put herself out there.

Hey, Bonnie watched reality TV along with the rest of the country. She knew the drill.

"Hi, Sean," Jessica said. "I'm so looking forward to this um, date."

"Me, too," Angela said. "I studied."

"Oh, yeah? When's the last time y'all were on a horse?" Sean tipped back on his heels.

"I was probably thirteen," Tabitha piped up, having threaded her arm through Sean's. "But it will all come back to me."

"She's goin' to beat you at this if you don't get on over on his other side," Bonnie hissed to Jessica. "He has two arms."

"Huh?" Jessica said.

"What about you, Jessica?" Sean asked.

"Oh, um, I don't...I can't remember." She studied the ground and kicked a pebble with her boot.

"Same," Angela said. "Been awhile. Can't say I recall."

Bonnie smiled. Was that a slight twang Angela had suddenly developed?

"I bet it's been a while for you, as well, Skippy." Sean didn't even look at her but kept walking toward the corral, hands in the pockets of his jeans. He subtly shook Tabitha off. "I want to see if you remember anything at all."

Great. He was ready to make an example of her.

Wade had the horse saddled. Nearby stood the golf cart with the cutout wood photo of a cow used to train in roping. Which meant...she'd be roping.

A skill she'd never mastered.

"You're up, Bonnie. Let's see how Miss Rodeo Queen three years runnin' does." Wade held Grace's lead.

"Say *what*?" Angela whipped around to face Bonnie.

"It was fifteen years ago!" Bonnie said. "And you don't have to be an expert to win Rodeo Queen. So what if I barrel raced a little when I was younger? My father was a rodeo star, and I couldn't get out of it."

Too late, Bonnie realized she'd said too much. Sean slid her a slow smile, one of his wicked ones.

The women gaped at her.

"What am I even doin' here?" Jessica complained.

"Information I *could* have used," Angela said with an edge to her tone.

"I was also Miss Rodeo Queen!" Tabitha squealed as she bounced, giving everyone a wide view of fleshy skin.

Of course she was Miss Rodeo Queen.

"You know what they say…there are some things you never forget," Sean said, and then hooked his thumb at Bonnie. "Riding a horse is one of 'em."

Lord, don't let me fall and break my fool arm in front of all these good people.

"Remember, anyone not willing to participate in the challenge today is immediately disqualified and will be sent home today," Lori said from behind the camera, rallying everyone.

Or terrifying them.

This is it. I could go home right now and be eliminated. Wait. This is it!

How could the producers balk at having to give up the drama when one of their own rules came into play? She could give up right now and admit she couldn't do this. Truthfully, she wanted to see her mother instead of participating in this slow torture of watching Sean, not being able to have Sean, but watching as the wrong woman wormed her way into his life. It should be *Jessica*, the schoolteacher.

Did she have to hang a sign around Jessica's neck: *Here, Sean. This is who you should choose.* Not Miss Hotlanta. Please think with your brain.

She wanted to believe Sean was above falling for someone as bright and shiny as Tabitha, but she didn't know him anymore. The only thing she did know about him (thanks to her mother) was that in the intervening years, after his broken engagement with someone from out of town, he'd never married. However, that didn't mean he pined away for Bonnie. It only meant in a town like theirs, he might have missed out on single women his age. Because of *her*.

Bonnie felt the weight of all eyes on her as she bent and

stepped into the corral. She walked slowly to Grace, thoughts of how to play this out hurling through her brain at Mach speed. This had always been her problem, too, when it came to acting: how should she play this out? Dial up the emotion slowly, or all at once? Her problem was she didn't think fast enough on her feet.

Now, she stood next to Grace, who wasn't the tallest horse she'd ever mounted but also not the smallest. Probably a good seventeen hands or so, she'd guess.

In heaven, Daddy was probably standing by waging a bet: *I got ten dollars here says she don't get on. I'm all in.*

"I'm...uh, I don't think I..."

"You're disqualified if you don't do this, Rodeo Queen," Lori said loudly.

Both Daisy and Wade studied her expectantly, Daisy with a type of little sister hero-worship. When Bonnie turned to him, Sean openly stared. But given the passage of time between them she could no longer read him the way she used to. She had no idea what he wanted from her anymore. Stay? Go? Fall flat on her face for the world to see? What would satisfy him now?

Gee, Sean, I'm sorry I said no to living in a small town for the rest of my life and having you keep me barefoot and pregnant.

I apologize, good sir, for wanting more.

Then Sean cracked a smile. An incredulous smile, his eyes crinkling at the corners. Hands and one leg braced on the fence, he lowered his head, and shook it.

"I knew it."

Was it disappointment or triumph laced in his voice?

"Knew *what*, Sean?" Bonnie skillfully hooked her foot in the stirrup and hauled herself into the saddle. She shot him a triumphant look. "That I could still kick ass?"

Okay, so she wasn't seated the most gracefully she'd never been, and this all felt a bit awkward.

But…she *remembered*.

On top of the world. Horse and saddle. Wind. Earth. The simple things.

For the next few minutes, Wade took her through the paces and Bonnie had the horse gallop around the corral. The small amount of her long hair not covered by her hat whipped around in the breeze. A lock became attached to her lip gloss and she brushed it aside and kept going. The only sounds heard were those of hooves raking across the dry red dirt, her shallow ragged breaths, and the pounding of her heart mixing with the rough sound of the wind.

Then Wade drove the golf cart around a few times, and she tried her hand at roping. His instructions were good, but Bonnie failed every time. Whenever she rode a horse, they were one, but neither cared too much for cattle, fake or otherwise.

"Good effort!" Daisy clapped as Bonnie hopped off the horse.

"She's a good girl." Bonnie dismounted, then nuzzled Grace's white forelock.

Bonnie turned away and before she'd made two steps, Grace nudged with her muzzle.

In Bonnie's ass.

"Oof," Bonnie said, jumping forward and brushing off her butt.

"That's when you know a horse loves you." Wade joked, leading Grace back a few steps.

But louder than horse's hooves, louder than her ragged breaths, pumping heart, or motor of the golf cart were the peals of Sean's laughter.

CHAPTER 7

*E*ven if Sean didn't wind up finding a wife and partner after all this, he'd watched Bonnie ride a horse again.

He used to love watching her ride like the wind, like her life depended on it. Like her soul was on fire. The daughter of Buck Wheeler had been born to ride. He figured the girl he'd loved was long gone but he might have actually seen a flash of her today. Maybe he'd accomplished something else by keeping her through another round. She'd go back to Hollywood after all this and remember.

Hopefully she'd also go back to Hollywood picturing him with his new fiancée. With no idea who the producers would prefer in the end, he thought Jessica might be a good choice. He decided to focus on her and do his best to ignore Bonnie, no matter how great she looked.

The next three women didn't do quite as well as Bonnie had on a horse, not even Tabitha, the former miss rodeo queen from Atlanta. He supposed they had the rodeo there too, but he imagined it didn't compare to Texas.

On her way to the horse, she'd stopped by him and not so subtly whispered, "I'd rather ride a cowboy."

"That's a tired line, sweetheart." He cringed.

Anyone who dropped that line was not from Stone Ridge. He wanted to take her aside and give her a big brother talk. Respect yourself. Don't be quite so…eager. It was nearly a turn-off for him. But then again, he'd grown up chasing women, and not the other way around. Chasing Bonnie, more specifically. He simply wasn't used to this deal the other way around.

Tabitha managed to stay on the horse…barely.

"I'm going to have to edit most of this, for decency," Lori complained, after Tabitha climbed off the horse and nearly mooned everyone in the process.

Nice ass.

Too bad Bonnie's is even better.

"Might have told her to wear some long pants," Sean muttered.

"Hey, who am I, the fashion police?" Lori said.

Jessica and Angela did fine, especially since they were dressed for riding.

"Okay, ladies. Go back home and wait to hear who won this round," Lori said, waving to the Hummer where Lenny waited patiently. "Though I think we all know."

Sean ripped off his mike and handed it to Lori, who had collected all the women's microphones.

"I want to eliminate Tabitha. I have no future with her."

"We will see. Don't you want to eliminate your ex?"

"Sooner or later I will," he said. "But the timing is my decision."

"You're right, that's too easy. Anyone else would have eliminated her first and I notice you *didn't*. Unless you still have feelings, of course."

Lori slid him a significant look as in: if you still have feelings, this will make my job a whole lot easier. But no pressure. *Right.*

Sean ignored the comment. Instead, he walked over to the barn where he'd last seen Wade and Daisy head. He could use some levelheaded talk from someone who knew him. Someone who understood him. He didn't know where the hell Jolette Marie had run off to, but after this, he would seek her out. She was supposed to be his spy. A falling- down-on-the-job spy.

Inside, he didn't find anyone but Bonnie, leading Grace into her stall. He stopped on a dime because for one second, he flashed back to the first time he'd seen her, at the local rodeo with her father.

She'd turned and smiled. "Hey, cowboy."

And he'd been struck dumb.

Now the years stretched between them, sharp as glass, and neither one of them were the same people anymore.

She turned and startled. "I…I didn't see you there."

"That's obvious."

"I'm helping Wade because he had something else to do. Apparently, they just got a big hay delivery and Daisy went with him. I'm just trying to—"

He held up his palm. "You don't have to make excuses."

"If you're lookin' for *Tabitha*, she went back to the house. Probably to change into something a little more revealing."

"Damn, Skippy, you almost sound jealous."

She snorted. "Jealous? Why would I be *jealous*? I know who she is. She's young and stupid like I was, tradin' on her good looks. Those will be gone someday. You should look deeper."

"Oh, this is rich. Advice from *you* on love."

"Well, why not? I know you better than anyone else here."

He let that knowledge sit between them like a pack of explosives ready to detonate.

"And who do *you* think I should choose?" He took a step toward her.

"Glad you asked. That's easy. Jessica. She's not as sparkly and sexy as Tabitha, but she's a schoolteacher for cryin' out loud. She'll *give* you children. And she's young enough to have several."

He took another step. "What about Angela?"

"I think you know Angela isn't all that into you."

"*She's* here for the wrong reasons?" His gut burned with anger because he knew just *who* might be here for the wrong reasons.

Bonnie crossed her arms and glanced at the rafters above them. "Well...I can't say. She'd like to stick around a bit longer, let's put it that way."

With another step, he stood right in front of Bonnie, crowding her. Inches of air hung between them, with the old sensation of a live wire, sparking like the Fourth of July.

"Why are you still here, Bonnie?"

She stepped away from him and picked up the saddle she'd taken off Grace. He resisted helping her carry it. She was perfectly capable.

"You think I was going to let you make a damn fool out of me out there? No. I could have dropped out by refusing to do the event. Sure. And my daddy would have rolled over in his grave."

"Wherever he is, I think Buck would understand."

"But I couldn't live with myself. So, I guess you're just going to have to eliminate me another time."

"Or I could decide Tabitha won this event."

She snorted. "You do that. Please, Sean, don't be the bachelor who can't see what's happening right in front of him because someone has a great rack."

"You're thinking of the old Sean. I couldn't see through

you before, but now I do. All you ever cared about was fame and fortune. This is more of the same."

"Not true. I had a dream. And I wanted to *act*."

"By way of modeling panties."

The moment he'd said the words he wanted to take them back. That hadn't been their real problem but looking back with a clearer lens, it may have been the beginning of the end.

"It's just like you to bring that up." She straightened. "I thought by now you might have become a *little* more enlightened. Since you're even considering asking a former stripper to be your wife."

"Are you *judging* her?"

"Not at all. I just thought you would." She quirked a brow.

"I didn't judge you then, and I don't now. Let's get *that* straight."

"Whatever you say. You're the boss."

"You can't honestly think I'll believe you're here for me." He met her eyes, the mossy green he remembered too well. "Did all the other acting parts in the city dry up?"

"You're right, things aren't going well for me in Hollywood. They haven't for a while, and I know a visit is long overdue. I thought I'd at least be able to help you find someone if I'm on the inside."

"Ha! The last thing I want is *you*r help and advice."

"I understand." She tipped her chin. "After all, maybe you're not in this for the right reasons, either."

Those words tripped him up more than she probably realized. In the back of his mind, he'd started to wonder if the donation for the wild horses was the *only* reason he was going through with this. It was supposed to be the carrot that got him to sign on, but the real reason was to settle down. Have a family.

But seeing Bonnie here had brought back all his old abandonment issues. He didn't want yet another woman walking out on him after making lifelong promises.

"Even if I'm not, I guess I'm going to have a grand time."

"Sure you are. This is a dream come true. Beautiful, young nubile women all chasing you. You're a hot cowboy."

"I admit it is a bit of a role reversal. Must be weird for you, me not chasing after you for a change."

"No, Sean, you forget I know *exactly* what it's like when you don't come after me."

With sharp and hostile movements, she hung the saddle, then brushed off her palms.

Frustration burned, and he took off his hat, raked a hand through his hair, and slipped it back on. As expected, she was dredging up the past.

"We both made mistakes, don't lay the blame at my feet."

"Fine. I expected you to get rid of me the first night, but I don't regret being here. *You're* going to have to eliminate me if you don't want me here."

He did something incredibly stupid then. Careless. The *old* Sean did this, not the 2.0 version. Because the new man knew a whole lot better than to allow his ex to trample over his heart for the countless time. This was young Sean making a reappearance, the whipper snapper who still had a lot of faith in her.

Like a crazy man, he clasped his hand on the back of Bonnie's neck and hauled her to him. Staring into her gaze, waiting for her to stop him, he lowered his head and claimed her lips. But it almost felt as if she kissed him first, her hands on his shoulders, her mouth soft and eager. Searching. He took the kiss deeper. She tipped his hat, and it slid off and fell to the floor. She threaded her fingers through his hair, tugging. Like they were still teenagers, they managed to get from zero to sixty in a second.

Plenty of women could get him to this place of hot desire,

but only Bonnie gave him whiplash. He pulled away before he got himself too worked up and bent to pick up his hat.

"We're not supposed to do that." Bonnie chewed on her lower lip. "Kiss."

"Rule broken." He pointed. "And I'm goin' to blame this on you."

"You do that." She smiled, tucking her hands in the back pockets of her jeans. "Totally worth it. No regrets."

He'd made it to the barn's entry before he turned back and tipped his hat to her.

"No matter why you're here, I'm not lettin' you go until you regret what you did. Until you're sorry for walkin' away from me."

"I already am," she said.

Or at least, that's what he thought she'd said.

He barely heard the words and was even less certain he could believe them.

CHAPTER 8

Then

A year after Bonnie graduated from high school, she was spotted by a modeling agency scout at a rodeo in San Antonio. She'd been Miss Rodeo Queen again, second year running, grateful for the extra cash that helped after Daddy's death. To be honest, she didn't mind the attention, even if Sean wasn't crazy about it.

Bonnie was in love, deeply in love, and no manner of attention from any man would ever take her away from Sean Henderson. Every boy in Stone Ridge had chased her and she wanted no one but him. Loved no one but him. But she wanted to provide for her mother, who'd downsized from their large property to a cottage by Lupine Lake. Sadie's father owned the land and rented the cabin to them at a discount.

Her daddy hadn't died doing what he loved, but in the least remarkable way for a six-time rodeo champ: a car accident on the way to the US finals in Colorado. There was some insurance money, and savings, but not enough to keep up with the ranch more than a year without him. The upkeep on a property their size would have them in the hole within a year without her father's continued earnings.

In typical fashion, everyone in Stone Ridge helped. The men took on the physical chores her father would normally. The dairy farmer provided milk and eggs free of charge. The ladies of SORROW provided meals and organized fundraisers. They paid for Bonnie's entry fees in the rodeo queen contests. Mama got a job as a housekeeper and cook for a local family.

Bonnie worked at the General Store part-time and waitressed at the Shady Grind. There was certainly no extra money for acting lessons given by some of the great teachers she'd read about. Still, she socked away money and saved, worried she'd never get a chance to leave Stone Ridge and give her Mama the life she'd had before Daddy died.

But that particular muggy day in San Antonio at the rodeo, Bonnie saw a way out of her mother's drudgery, and her own.

"They said they would pay for the photos, Mama," Bonnie explained later the same day. "All we have to do is get ourselves to New York City."

"Oh, is that all?" Mama went hands on hips. "Might as well be the moon. We can't afford it."

But Aunt Beulah heard and thrilled at the prospect her niece might someday be a "celebrity," she organized yet another fundraiser. Both she and Mama accompanied Bonnie to New York City where they were surprised to be staying in a high-rise hotel right in the middle of Times Square. The agency took photos of Bonnie and in them she got to act for the first time in something other than her high school theater productions.

When told to "look sexy" she thought of Sean. When she had to give them "a faraway melancholy look" it was far too easy to think of her daddy. And on it went. According to the agency, Bonnie had the "it" factor and they offered her a contract with a major brand.

Mama didn't know what to do, but Beulah read the contract (all of the pages, word for word) and told Bonnie she should go ahead and sign it.

She would have done it anyway. Bonnie was hooked on the glamor of the city and thrilled these people saw her as beautiful and special. She'd been afraid she might not have what it took to be a model or an actress.

The contract was an underwear model for which she was paid more money than she made in a year at the General Store. She thought the photos were in good taste, too, even if awkward to pose for. She'd never stood in her underwear in front of anyone but Sean. These were classy photos and part of the brand's lingerie campaign for women. They were using Bonnie, only nineteen, to sell bras to women her mother's age.

She'd been home a week after New York, hanging out with Sean, telling him all about the city, when he picked up a photo on her nightstand.

"Give me that," Bonnie tried to snatch it from him, but he held it just out of reach.

"Wait a second." He studied it for a second. "This is what you've been doin' for the modeling agency?"

"Not anymore."

"You're practically naked, Bonnie!" His voice contained not a small amount of outrage.

"But I'm not. I think they're tastefully done."

He lowered the photo enough that she ripped it away from him.

"Who took the photos?"

She rolled her eyes. "A photographer. He's a professional."

"A professional creep? It pisses me off that man saw you almost naked."

"We were in a *studio*." Poor, straight-as-an-arrow Sean. "There were people everywhere."

Too late she realized this was even worse.

He scowled and narrowed his eyes. "How *many* people?"

"Not many. People for lighting, that kind of thing. Even a woman or two for make-up and hair."

"Jesus!"

She had read somewhere that boyfriends had a difficult time with these kinds of situations, and Sean the cowboy wasn't exactly the picture of modern sophistication.

"You're the only one that sees me naked, baby." On her tiptoes, she reached for his face, framing it between her hands.

"Don't try to distract me."

She did anyway, kissing him the way he liked, long and deep, grinding against him.

"You're the only one who ever has."

"Let's keep it that way." Reaching for her wrist, he tossed her on the bed and joined her.

But if Bonnie thought she had a great future with the New York modeling agency, she turned out to be wrong. The following year they went with a brunette, a seventeen-year-old model discovered in the U.K. The photos Bonnie saw online were raunchy and it was a good thing she hadn't been approached.

But it would have been nice to be *asked*.

It was the first time she realized no matter how pretty others thought you were, someone prettier could always be found.

All along she'd wanted to act, not model, and the modeling had simply been a gateway into that world. Because Bonnie had a secret from everyone who loved her:

more like her father than her mother, she liked the pageantry of the rodeo, the showmanship more than the actual skill of the event. Bonnie was different.

All of the other girls from Stone Ridge in her high school graduating class were already married. Charlotte Johansen even had a baby on the way. Bonnie loved Sean with all her heart, but she didn't just want to be a rancher's wife. At least once a week Sean talked about where they would live once they got married. In his spare time, he and Colton were staking land for each of their cabins. Riggs was off at university, and eventually they weren't all going to live together. They'd start their own families but stay right on Henderson land because why go anywhere else?

Sean didn't care there was a whole world to be experienced, not to mention forty-nine other states. Once in a while, she got to Colorado or Northern California on a cattle auction with Sean and his father. That was about as much as she'd seen of the USA until New York.

On Aunt Beulah's advice, Bonnie saved all the money she'd earned for the modeling job. And one afternoon about a year after the job in New York City, she and Sean rode their horses out for a picnic. She spread out the blanket, laid down the peach pie she'd baked, potato salad, and the deep-fried chicken Sean loved.

Sean had finished discussing his latest cattle run when she found the words to say what she'd wanted to for years.

"I want to go to Los Angeles and try to be an actor. I've got enough money saved to rent a small place for a few months until I find a job." The words came out in a rush and Sean's eyes widened.

When he immediately opened his mouth to protest, she stuck a chicken leg in his mouth, and kept talking about her plan.

He finished chewing, eyes narrowed. "How long will you be gone?"

She swallowed. "That's the thing. I don't know how long. As long as it takes to see if I can do this."

"You already know you can do it."

"I need to find out whether I can get parts in actual movies or TV shows. There's a lot of money in this business, Sean."

"Why do you need money?"

"*Mama* needs money. I want her to retire. She can't keep working as a housekeeper forever."

"She can come live with us when we get married."

"No! You're just not hearing me. I don't want her to live with us. She needs her own house. Do you think my daddy would be happy to know where we're livin' now, with her workin' so hard? You know he'd hate it. Well, it's my job to earn enough money to take care of her."

She'd decided to make it all about the money, taking care of her mother, so at least she'd sound noble. But the little secret no one knew was Bonnie wanted to get out of this small town. She had ambitions no one else seemed to have.

She wanted glamour, night life, and excitement. Bonnie was her father's daughter. He'd craved the spotlight and so did she if in a different kind of way.

"You can come with me," she said tentatively.

"To live in Hollywood?"

"Probably somewhere outside of Burbank."

"I can't go with you, baby. My parents need me. My father needs me. Riggs is going to law school, and he won't be able to come home for another few years."

"Well, that's not your problem is it?" She hated the words the moment she'd said them.

"Yes, it is my problem. And my responsibility. You know I don't take it lightly."

"I know, and that's one of the reasons I love you." She took his hand, threaded her fingers through his. "But I need you, too."

"What am I going to do in the city, anyway? I'm a cowboy."

"Maybe it's time for you to think about supporting me for a change and not what you're going to be doing all day."

Yes, she realized it sounded ridiculous, but she was desperate.

He narrowed his eyes. "I'll get bored."

"I'll keep you entertained."

"Not when you'll be going on auditions and working as a waitress."

"Only at first, until everything falls into place."

"That could be years."

"It won't be. I promise."

"Then, how long?"

They'd circled back to the original question.

But how long did a person chase after a dream? Was there some kind of expiration date?

Bonnie wasn't naïve. If she wanted a career in the industry, she'd have to start young. And if she got some traction, she could have a longer career as a character actor. People like Nicole Kidman and others started in their teens. Bonnie's timeline was evaporating. At twenty, by modeling standards, she was practically middle age.

Sean waited for her answer. He was right. She owed him at least a ballpark figure of a timeline. They wanted to get married…someday. He wanted this far sooner than she did, but either way, she'd marry Sean Henderson. There was no one else in the world for her, nor ever would be.

"How about if I try for a year or two and if things don't work out, I'll come home?"

"Two *years?*"

"I'll come visit, of course!"

Sean didn't like the idea and over the next month he did everything he could to change Bonnie's mind. No begging and no pleading from her cowboy, just examples of all she'd miss.

Fresh flowers every day from his mother's own garden.

Making love under the stars.

Slow dancing after dark in the field the way they'd done for years, the headlights of Sean's truck lighting their way, the speaker booming from inside.

It hadn't changed her mind but made leaving home even harder. Bonnie cried all the way to the airport where she clung Sean until the last minute. If he'd hoped she'd change her mind, he didn't say so.

"Do not find anyone else while I'm gone because you're mine. I claimed you a long time ago. Tell the women to find another man."

Sean kissed her temple and held her tight. "Alright, baby. Alright."

But one year later, everything would change.

CHAPTER 9

Now

"Mama?"

"Hey there, sugar," her mother said. "Ol' Lenny swears up and down he brought you home from the airport. I said he must be two cans shy of his usual six pack because you'd never waltz back into town without seein' your mama first."

"Um...well, I was going to call you."

"And your fingers broke?"

Bonnie braced her back against the slider leading to the patio of the Truehart mansion.

She clutched the handset to the landline tighter. "I thought I'd be out of here yesterday."

"You're on that reality dating show we brought to town, aren't you? Sugar, that show is something your aunt Beulah came up with to help bring more women into Stone Ridge."

"*Aunt Beulah* did? I thought this was Winona's deal."

No wonder Bonnie was here. Her Aunt Beulah had literally brought her home as she claimed she always would. This was a rotten, backhanded way to do it.

"Beulah has her hand in it, too. The whole thing was really her idea. You know how she gnaws on and on about bringing more women to town. She finally got Winona on board and everything started to come together. She wouldn't stop bugging Sean until he finally agreed."

She scoffed. "It couldn't have been that difficult to get him to agree to date all these women at once."

"He hasn't seriously dated anyone else since his engagement to Robyn, so I'd say he's about due."

The memory brought out a sharp and swift pain. "Things aren't going well for me in L.A."

"Come home, we'll bake pies."

If only it were that simple this time.

"I want to, but…I'm still on the show. Sean won't let me go yet."

"Oh, he won't let you go, will he? He did just fine twelve years ago."

"Mama, don't—"

But before Bonnie could stop her, Mama launched into her yearly diatribe:

There weren't enough women in Stone Ridge and Sean managed to chase one of the good ones out. If Sean had married Bonnie, then she wouldn't have left Stone Ridge. He wouldn't have been engaged to Robyn, a woman from Kerrville, of all places. Bonnie would have stayed close to home and hearth and given her plenty of grandbabies by now. Instead, here she was, still without any grandbabies from her only daughter.

Of course, she did have five from her two sons, but she glossed right on over that part.

It didn't matter how many times Bonnie explained that

she'd wanted more than marriage and babies, somehow Mama didn't hear it. It was easier to lay the blame at Sean's boots.

When she took a breath, Bonnie inserted, "Anyway, I hope to be out of here soon and then we can spend the rest of the time I'm here together."

"You won't be gone if Sean Henderson has a lick of good sense left in him. Who could possibly be better for him than you?"

"There's a schoolteacher. She's younger than me and could give him the children he'd like." Bonnie bit on her lower lip, regret piercing deeply.

"You could, too. Now, lookie here, we have Winona just had herself twins! She was thirty-nine at the time, sugar, two years younger than you. And then went on to have one more before she closed up shop. A girl! Plus, I read about a fifty-year-old woman who had a baby. It's science."

"It's not too late for me to give you grandbabies?"

"As long as you're happy." She sighed deeply.

This meant: *nope, it's not too late.*

"I'll get right on it."

Chuckling, she said her goodbyes and hung up with her mother before walking inside. On the filming schedule, later this afternoon they were to film individual interviews with the rest of the crew. The winner of the event would then be chosen, by Sean, for a date a couple of nights later at the Shady Grind. A "private" date which would be *filmed*. If she happened to "win" she couldn't imagine a greater invasion of privacy, especially after that kiss in the barn.

He'd pulled her to him, and she'd gone all in, reasoning and rules abandoning her in a rush. Losing her head in the process. The same electricity and heat still raged between them. The same itch of the woman she'd once been had her eager to touch him. To run her fingers through his hair and along the rough scrape of his beard stubble. The same warm and solid desire pulsed through her when he'd crushed her to him. Their kisses were hot and fierce. Fiery and explosive. Just like their relationship had been.

But hot and fiery tended to burn itself out. Best to remember this.

She still didn't have good sense around Sean. Exhibit one: the barn.

The crew had set up in the den by the massive and ornate stone fireplace. Tabitha sat on a stool in front of the camera, having changed into something a little less flashy. Emphasis on little.

"I like have this incredible connection with Sean. It's like we were meant to be, you know? Oh, gosh. He's like so ridiculously handsome. And like a real cowboy. My first boyfriend was a cowboy. I didn't think I'd be attracted to, like, an older man. At first, I wasn't sure, but wow! He's so hawt! I mean, like it's kismet!"

Older man? Now he's an older man?

"And do you think he feels it too?" Lori asked. "The uh… kismet, as you say?"

Tabitha blushed and canted her head. "I hope so…"

"Okay, let's try that again," Lori said. "There's a strange light behind Tabitha. Where's that coming from? Elton, can you work on that?"

"Can I work on the *sun's rays*?" Elton deadpanned. "I'll get right on it."

"All right, all right! Let's go again."

"I feel this incredible connection…" Tabitha's words drifted away as Bonnie went up the steps.

She found Angela and Jessica in Bonnie's bedroom sitting on her bed.

"Where *were* you?" Jessica said.

"I helped put Grace back in the stable and clean up a bit. Wade and Daisy got called away."

"And we all know how you know your way around a horsey," Angela said.

"Right. We all know who won the date. It's just a matter of time before we find out for sure," Jessica said.

"Calm down, girl," Angela said. "We need to put our heads together and find out how we can get Tabitha outta here. Who's gonna tell him she's not in this for the right reasons?"

"Do we...have to do that?" Bonnie said.

"It's in the script, isn't it?" Angela cocked her head and looked at the ceiling as if reading it.

"We should let Sean decide." Bonnie sat on the edge of her bed next to Angela. "He will figure it out."

"What am I even doing here?" Jessica whined. "I can't get his attention. Not a man like him."

Angela beckoned between her and Bonnie. "We think you're the best one for him. We can help you."

"You *can*?" Jessica went wide-eyed.

Bonnie wasn't too sure about this anymore. Sean's words were ringing in her ears: *I don't need your help.* But also, his kisses were buzzing on her lips. She wouldn't mind some more, too, if they could figure out a way to do this away from the cameras. And it wouldn't be fair to encourage Jessica when Bonnie had already kissed Sean. But the answer to that dilemma was laughably simple. She wouldn't kiss him again. Problem solved.

"Well, um...sure. We can try but Sean is so stubborn he'll do what he wants anyway."

"Most men don't know *what's* good for them." Angela pounded the mattress. "Mark. My. Words."

"I don't know what I'm doing here." Jessica said again, a stuck record.

She threw herself on the bed and sobbed. Bonnie and Angela were on either side of her immediately.

Bonnie rubbed her back in gentle circles. "Hey, it's okay. I know how tough this is, but you deserve to be here as much as any of us do. Maybe more."

"No," Jessica hiccuped through her sobs. "I mean, I don't even know why I'm *here*. I was supposed to…suppose to…get married today."

Bonnie and Angela exchanged a look.

"Um, what?" Angela finally said. "What's *that* supposed to mean?"

"It means, I had a fiancé up until a month ago. He called off the wedding which was supposed to be today!"

Oh crap.

"I want to go home," she wailed. "I shouldn't be here."

Rubbing Jessica's back, Bonnie had no more doubts: she *was* the house mother.

And perfect Jessica would be going home.

"THIS IS REALITY TV BUTTER," Angela said, as together all three of them watched Jessica give Sean the news. "Delicious."

Sitting on the patio bench, Jessica and Sean were having a quiet talk. Both miked, with the cameras rolling, an audience, but otherwise an "intimate" heart-to-heart.

"I bet this show breaks ratings when it comes out," Tabitha said, holding up one finger, then another. "We have everything. Ex-girlfriend, a jilted fiancée with regrets, age gap with a younger woman."

Bonnie bristled at being relegated simply to the status of "his ex."

"I don't think it would be fair to you for me to stay any

89

longer," Jessica said to Sean. "I'm not ready to move so I shouldn't be here. Sorry. I thought I could do this."

"That's okay," Sean said. "Break-ups are tough. I know."

"Cut," Lori said. "Okay, Sean, you really could look a *bit* more upset by this."

"Huh?"

"We need the drama. You realize now that this is never going to happen and she's a beautiful woman." Lori waved her hands in the air. "C'mon!"

"Right. But I'm not an actor." Sean straightened and tugged at his collar. "Let me try again."

Jessica smiled sweetly and at least seemed to be enjoying her moment in the limelight. Maybe there was a little bit of an actor in everyone.

Except Sean.

"I can't lie. I'm sure disappointed but you have to do what's right for you." Sean uttered the words with stilt and all the sincerity of a cattle rancher announcing he planned to go vegan.

"I think you're really special and very handsome," Jessica said.

"Thank you. I think…you're really special too," Sean said. "Too bad you have to go."

"Ah hem! Good grief, I should be the bachelor," Lori interrupted, clearing her throat. "That should be: do you really *have* to go?"

"You're right. *You'd* probably do a better job." Sean muttered, then stood and held his hand out to Jessica. "Are you *sure* you have to go?"

"I'm afraid so," Jessica said, taking his outstretched hand. "But I'll never forget you."

"Ooooh, she's good," Tabitha said. "*Nice* touch."

"Sounded insincere," Angela said.

"You think?" Bonnie snorted.

"I wonder if she and her ex-fiancé will get back together when she goes back home. I love a good reunion story!" Apparently suddenly realizing what she'd said out loud, Tabitha caught Bonnie's eye. "I mean, but not when so much *time* has passed."

They watched as Sean walked Jessica to the Hummer where Lenny stood holding the door open. The camera followed, taking first a shot of Sean standing woefully at the end of the driveway, hands in his pockets, studying the ground. Lenny drove a few feet away, then stopped the Hummer. Elton climbed in with his camera equipment, cursing when he bumped his head. He would presumably record more of Jessica's sentiments and perhaps a tear or two. Or three. The girl really could call them up.

Sean finally walked inside the house and joined them in the great room, followed by the second cameraman and Lori.

"Well, I guess it's no surprise to y'all that Skippy, uh, Bonnie won the event today. She'll be going on the date with me tomorrow night."

"Aw, really?" Tabitha pouted. "I thought I did pretty good."

"Skippy." Sean cleared his throat and tipped his hat. "Would you go out with me tomorrow night?"

"I'd love to."

"Wait a second here," Lori said, sounding thoroughly disgusted. "You can't sound so eager, Bonnie. I mean, really! If *he's* interested, you're suddenly not. How is this difficult? Am I the only one who cares?"

"No, I care! Very much," Tabitha said.

"So do I," Angela said, pointing to Tabitha. "Far more than she does."

Honestly, Bonnie resented the criticism since she was the professional here. Even Lori didn't have as many credits as she did. Yes, Bonnie had checked on ImDb.

But everything had changed since she'd arrived. She'd

forgotten this was a job and that she was here for the drama factor.

The reason for forgetting was due to one reason.

Not her lack of professionalism.

Not her lack of memory.

Not her back of talent.

Sean.

He was the reason she'd forgotten everything.

CHAPTER 10

S ean had three women left out of ten. *Three*. He couldn't see himself with Tabitha, which actually left him with two, one of whom was Bonnie.

Tomorrow night, he would go on a date with Bonnie and a *film crew*. This was a mistake. He couldn't seem to relax enough in front of the camera, couldn't ignore it and have a good time as Lori kept telling him to do. But on this date with Bonnie, he might ignore the camera *too* much and say something revealing. Their history was nobody's business, certainly not reality TV fodder.

They had to jointly come up with a neat background story they could both agree to share with thousands of viewers, including everyone in town. Like a…script.

For this reason, he made a turn on his way back home and found himself pounding on the door of the main Truehart house where Jo still lived.

She opened the door. "Hey, there. Aren't you supposed to be—"

He didn't wait for an invitation and blustered his way

inside. "Don't you 'hey' me. Where have you been? I'm going down fast. I need your help."

"I thought I should stay away when I heard Bonnie Lee was a contestant."

"Why?"

"*Why?* It wouldn't be fair. You know my feelings on this. *Bonnie* is the one you should pick. I'll never believe anyone else will do." She led him to the leather couch in the front room and plopped down, patting the seat next to her. "It's perfect."

The décor of the Truehart main house was that of a classic horse rancher. Completely different from the designer mansion women were staying in, touches of dark leather were everywhere. Photos of horses galloping wild in the range were hung from the walls.

"We had this discussion. Bonnie is the opposite of what I want."

Jolette Marie smirked and crossed her arms. "You want to tell me that's still true after you've seen her?"

He studied his hands and ignored the question. "Well… she doesn't want to be tied down to Stone Ridge. Never did. It's not going to work."

He could hear Lori's voice in his ears: *gee, Sean, are you trying to convince yourself or the audience?*

"But what if she changed her mind? That could happen."

"I'm no longer in the business of changing Bonnie's mind. I tried that."

"Give it a chance. Things are different now, I bet."

"She's an actor. I think the show brought her on to cause drama. Things aren't going well in Hollywood. That's why she's here."

It was entirely possible no one was here for the right reasons. He was here for a cause which mattered to him, and the women probably had their own causes. This was for entertainment purposes only and he had to remind himself of that.

"Bonnie won the horse-riding event, so I have to take her on a one-on-one date tomorrow night." He held up air quotes. "Where presumably we'll talk about what went wrong and how we 'feel' now."

"Oh. They are going to love exploiting that angle."

"Yeah, and I sure as hell don't want to have *that* discussion in front of a camera while everyone watches."

"No, that wouldn't be good."

"And they're seriously following us around everywhere so I have no idea where I could get her alone. If I try to do that, everyone will notice her gone."

"That's where I come in." Jo smiled sweetly and stood. "Leave it all to me."

His gaze followed Jo as she moved swiftly through the open archway of the room and headed toward the front door.

"Wait. Where are you going?"

She put out her palm to still him. "Wait right there, cowboy."

Sean waited. And waited. He waited some more, thinking of how complicated his life had become since he'd agreed to do this stupid show.

Before the ladies of SORROW managed to talk him into this fiasco, he'd been just fine living his life, free of heartache. Bonnie fixed him good for wanting any more serious relationships, so all he did was fool around with women from out of town. Not that he hadn't tried. A second failed engagement, and that was it for him. Whenever he went off to a cattle auction or some other event away from home, he could get his needs met. Neat, short, uncomplicated. Temporary. About five years ago he'd dated everyone his own age, but occasionally he did go out with someone new from Kerrville. It never lasted which was fine with him.

But Beulah wouldn't stop nagging.

Wouldn't it be wonderful to have more single women moving to Stone Ridge?

Once they get out here and see all our handsome cowboys, many won't go back home. Especially the one you choose to be your wife.

And can you honestly tell me you don't want to get married and start a family? How old are you now? Uh-huh, that's what I thought. Not a kid anymore. You best get crackin'.

True, he was no longer as young as he used to be (nobody was last he checked) but he still had some good years left in him. Truth be told, and after long days spent considering, Beulah nagging, Winona prodding, he'd decided yes, he wanted a family. If he wasn't sure this was the way to find one, at least he'd meet women willing to move to Stone Ridge and raise a family. He wanted children like baby Mary and the twins. Riggs was happier than he'd ever been.

And then he'd worked in the donation to wild horse rescue, his only required payment for taking a couple of weeks of his life off from ranching.

Sean thought he'd made the right decision until Jolette Marie and Bonnie both implied not everyone would be here for the right reasons. Some wanted their fifteen minutes of fame and a stepping stool to a better opportunity. While at first it seemed this would be Bonnie's angle, he had to consider it differently. She'd already had a career. This show was a step *down* for her and unless she saw herself hosting reality shows or broadcasting, she couldn't get much out of this.

By the time he heard Jo's truck outside and two doors slamming, he'd worked himself into a snit. Bonnie shouldn't be here. He should have sent her home already. Why hadn't he sent her packing? She deserved it after the way she'd treated him for years. Putting him last. She'd broken his heart and not the other way around.

They could have had five children by now. All that wasted time.

But then Bonnie followed Jo into the room, and his heart slammed against his ribs like a wild animal. She wore sweats and a simple Dallas Cowboy t-shirt. Her red hair was pulled into a ponytail, all her make-up removed. To him, she still looked twenty-three.

"What's wrong?" She came to him, stopping a few feet away. "Jo said you have to talk to me and it's important."

He stood. "There was no other way I could talk to you alone."

"I'll give you some privacy." Jo went out the doors that linked this room to the rest of the house and shut them.

"Did anyone see you leave?"

She chuckled. "No. Jolette Marie had her fun with this. She drew me outside by saying she was a fan who wanted my autograph. After she left, I came inside the house and told the girls I wanted to go for a walk. Lori was preoccupied with watching the dailies."

"Dailies?"

"Everything she filmed today."

He troweled a hand down his face. "I'm so out of my element with this."

"I know, but I'm here. And I can help."

"You and I are going to be on a date which will be very public. I'm...uncomfortable about this." He cleared his throat. "I even thought about choosing someone else to win the event. Like Angela. She was okay."

Her neck wiggled back as if stunned. "You have *got* to be kiddin' me. I won fair and square."

"Well, of course you did. Fair's fair. In the end I *had* to go with you."

She crossed her arms. "I'm sorry. But you could have gotten rid of me before the event."

"Yeah, and *you* could have refused to get on Grace and been disqualified. Sent home."

She tipped her head. "We already went over this. I considered it."

"You should have swallowed your pride."

"I couldn't. Even I'm not a good enough actor to pretend I'm afraid of getting on a horse. Plus, Daisy was watching me." She gnawed on her lower lip. "And maybe...I wanted to stay."

"Why?"

"I don't know why that's so shocking to you. You're a good-looking man, or don't you know it? Any woman in her right mind would be attracted to you, and I happen to have a great mind." She cleared her throat, making him smile. "If not because of the shortage of women, you'd have been married long ago and forgotten all about me."

"Who says I *haven't* forgotten about you?"

His damn face, probably, speaking for him again. There may have been an edge to his voice, but it annoyed him he could be so damn obvious when it came to her.

"Sorry, I misspoke. I meant that you would be married by now because anyone would be happy to have you."

"Anyone but you."

"Well, I was an idiot."

"I thought you said you have a great mind."

"Both can be equally true." She lowered her head.

After a couple beats of silence, Sean got to the point. "We need a story. A script of what we'll share on our date tomorrow night. It's an invasion of privacy for us to talk about what happened between us. That's our business."

"I agree. It's too personal."

"Do you have any ideas?"

"We're going to skate around the truth. Just say we were teenage sweethearts, on and off again, and—"

"So far, all true."

"Sean, let *me* be the bad guy. You did nothing wrong. You—"

"Hang on." He held up a hand. "All *true.*"

"Wait. You don't think you did *anything* wrong in our relationship?" Her cheeks pinked and she crossed her arms. "You gave me an *ultimatum.*"

"Because I wanted an answer sometime that decade." He seemed to be yelling a little bit.

"I had the opportunity of a lifetime! I asked you to wait to see if I got the show, and if it didn't work out, I'd come home, and we'd get married."

"I don't know why I didn't jump at the prospect of being your consolation prize!"

"That's not what I meant, and you know it. I loved you, Sean, with all my heart. But you had an idea of who I *should* be when it came to forever. Your wife had to be willing to stay in Stone Ridge and have a litter of children. I wasn't allowed to have dreams of my own!"

"Here we go again. No one encouraged your dreams more than I did. I was proud of you."

"Not proud enough."

"It wasn't wrong of me to want to keep you. I tried living in Hollywood, for *you*. I hated it."

"You gave it four *days* before you decided you hated it."

"I still can't believe it took me that long."

He hated arguing, made all the worse this time because he wouldn't have make-up sex, in his opinion the only solid reason for a heated argument with a woman in recorded history. But now his gut burned with anger for a different reason.

Was she right that he'd wanted her to conform to his idea of a wife? That he'd tried to squash her dreams? The thought seared him with its unacceptability. He would have supported anything she wanted to do, but her dream kept taking her away. He'd put up with it as long as he could.

"Okay." Bonnie took a deep breath and brushed her hands over her thighs. "I suppose this had to happen. We've aired it out and got it out of the way. This is good. It's something we won't have to talk about tomorrow night."

"Right." He stood. "Let me take you back to the house."

She walked behind him until the front door which he opened for her to walk ahead. Mad or not, he wasn't going to have her opening doors. He held the truck door open and waited for her to get in.

They drove in brittle silence to the mansion until Bonnie spoke up. "What are we going to say, exactly?"

"As little as possible. Canned responses like, 'we were too young,' 'too bad it didn't work out' and 'it wasn't anyone's fault.'"

"You obviously took some media training for this show."

He kept his eyes on the road but heard a smile in her voice. "Over the years, I learned a thing or two about being insincere."

"Ouch."

He pulled over a few yards from the house under the darkness of a Sycamore tree. "Tell me one thing, will you?"

"Sure." She unbuckled and turned to him.

"After all this time, why the hell am I still chasing after *you*?"

He was afraid he knew the answer. For a moment, she didn't speak, leaving him to notice how a moon ray glimmered in her hair and her emerald eyes sparkled.

"Force of habit. See you tomorrow night."

She climbed out of the truck and shut the door, but he wasn't sure she believed the words any more than he did.

CHAPTER 11

Then

Her first time in Hollywood, Bonnie worked as a waitress and shared an apartment in Burbank with other struggling actors. They split the rent, PG&E, and groceries. They recited lines with each other, kept up on the trades, shared subscriptions, and sometimes went to the same auditions.

She texted Sean daily, a running commentary on her life in the big city. The smog. All the cars and constant traffic. But also, great food of every ethnicity, within blocks. Warm and dry weather. Not much rain and certainly no hurricanes or snow.

The beach only a short drive away.

He thought her life sounded mostly horrible, but if this made her happy, he understood. Bonnie missed him terribly and begged him to move with her. They could get an apartment together and live a different kind of life. A more metropolitan and sophisticated life. He'd get used to it, she assured him. Eventually, they'd get married. Sean resolutely declared in every text that being a cowboy meant he couldn't live in a big city. Instead, she should come home to their clean air and wide, open spaces.

And then one beautiful morning a few months later, Bonnie answered the front door to find Sean standing there, with a backpack.

"Okay. You win," he said, and took her into his arms. "I'll try city life."

The next week was a delicious blur of happiness for Bonnie, who introduced Sean to her friends. They went out to eat and Sean admitted the burgers were great and so was the Mexican food. The sweet iced tea, however, was garbage. She had to agree.

"Oh my god," said her roommate, Katie, who would later go on to have a starring role in a sitcom and forget she ever knew Bonnie. "You weren't lying. He's a real cowboy. He held the door open and said "ma'am" to me. Ma'am!"

"It's not an insult. He says that to all women, young and old. If you're not a child and you're a woman, you're a ma'am."

"It's adorable."

When Sean walked into a room, anywhere, heads turned. Even here, one more handsome guy in a crowd of them, he stood out. Tall, broad, and built like a cowboy, he didn't hesitate to open doors and help anyone in need. Once, he'd tried to help a man whose car had stalled in the middle of an intersection. The man thought Sean was attempting to steal his BMW. Instead, Sean had pushed it off the street, jumpstarted it, and gone on his merry way.

Later, he told Bonnie people in the city were "weird."

"I know, it's different, but you'll get used to it like I have."

"What am I supposed to do for a living? Anyone hiring ranch hands?"

"It would be quite a commute."

"I feel useless every day. Meanwhile, I have plenty of work waiting for me on my own ranch."

Neither would say the truth out loud: this wasn't going to work.

Bonnie didn't want to believe it and she fought with every cell in her body to *make* it work. She wanted to keep Sean happy and keep him with her. But they couldn't have sex every minute of the day (though admittedly they did try) and Bonnie had work, acting classes, and auditions. Her life was quite full without him, but that didn't mean she wanted him to go home.

Then Sean received a phone call that changed everything.

He turned to her, face gray. "My mom has cancer. I'm going home."

"I'm going with you."

"Yeah?" Sean picked her up in his arms and held her so tight.

There was never any question that she'd have to go home. Sean needed her. Bonnie packed, let her roommates know, and asked for time off from her job at the restaurant. When they wouldn't give it to her, she quit.

She held Sean's hand on the airplane. From the time they landed in Texas Bonnie was by his side. They took Marge to doctor's appointments and helped Calvin handle the stress of hospital bills and medication.

So did the entire town, of course, most importantly the ladies of SORROW. They held fundraisers, organized the delivery of meals, and held the family up in prayer.

But even so, only six weeks after her diagnosis of pancreatic cancer, Marge Henderson died peacefully at home surrounded by her family.

All the Henderson men were devastated, but none more than Sean.

"She didn't deserve this. All her life she did nothing but

help people and this is what she gets." And even though she never saw him cry, his eyes were often red.

She loved him so much it hurt.

"I love you," Bonnie said. "Forever."

She didn't say it to offer comfort but because the truth hit her hard and swift. She'd grown up while living in California away from family and faced a few hard and painful facts. Even if they didn't last, Bonnie would love Sean for the rest of her natural life.

"Then you'll marry me, won't you?"

"Are you sure you want to get married?"

"I've wanted to marry you since I was sixteen. I'm sure."

"Then of course I'll marry you."

"I love you, Bonnie Lee." He picked her up and spun her around, smiling for the first time in weeks. "You're my whole world."

Did she agree to marry him because she felt sorry for him? Yes, on some level, she did. She wanted to please Sean. Always had. But like a needle burrowed under her skin, her ambition wouldn't let go. More than the fast-paced big city life and even more so than acting, Bonnie couldn't give up. Meeting with success in a competitive field was the challenge of her lifetime. Only Daddy and his love of the glittery rodeo and competition would understand. Giving up felt like failure. Giving up felt like a loss. Giving up was unthinkable.

But she stayed.

For two years, she tried to pretend she lived a life of satisfaction in her hometown. She got her job back at the General Store and waitressed part-time at the Shady Grind because where else would she work? Her friends in Burbank got a new roommate, of course. Life went on for everyone else. She helped Sean move past the pain of losing Marge and Riggs came back to help run the ranch.

She and Sean decided not to plan the wedding yet, of

course, because they had to get over Marge's loss first. Sean also wanted to save up for a ring and do this "right."

He was traditional in every way, her cowboy.

And as her luck, or the timing of the universe would have it, Bonnie heard from a dream agent she'd queried a year ago. He offered representation. Producers were casting an Irish mafia show and she'd be perfect for the tough as nails youngest sister of the crime family. She'd be required to audition, of course.

Shocked, Bonnie asked her mother and Aunt Beulah what she should do now. "I've tried for so long, and now when I'm back home everything starts to happen for me."

"That's the way of the world, sugar," Aunt Beulah said. "God's timing is not our own."

"You're going back, aren't you?" Mama stood and clutched the knotty kitchen table, her eyes watery.

"Now, Maybelle, you can't hold Bonnie back if this is her dream."

But Sean was also her dream.

"What about her intended?" Mama went hands on hips. "And what would her daddy say about all this?"

"He would say that his daughter is a jewel, and if Sean loves her, he'll wait." Beulah smiled with pride. "The show sounds *wonderful*."

It wasn't like her aunt to encourage any woman to leave Stone Ridge, but then again, the allure of fame and fortune never failed to stir Aunt Beulah's pot.

"She'll be back after she films the show, right Bonnie Lee?"

"He's not going to wait forever," Mama said. "There are *other women* in Texas."

"I know."

"How long will you be gone this time?" Sean asked once she told him the news.

"I don't know."

"You said that last time and you only came back because my mother died."

"Sean, be reasonable. I can't put a time limit on how long it will take me to achieve success. It's a competitive industry."

"So, we're not getting married."

"Not until I audition for this part and if I don't get it, I'll come back, and we can get married."

"And if you get the part?"

"It could be a while, I guess. Depending." She gnawed on her lower lip.

"On the success of the show. I'm supposed to wish you failure so I can marry you...*someday*."

"No! I love you and I won't ever marry anyone else."

"I love you too, baby, but I'm tired of being your second choice. Tired of being last."

"You're not *last*. I want you to come with me, but I won't ask anymore because I know you won't."

"I tried."

Bonnie went home and auditioned for the part. When she got it, Sean was the first person she called.

"Congratulations, baby. I knew you could do it. You're going to make the most amazing kickass mafia sister ever."

"The show might only run one season, so I'll be home before you know it."

"Sure."

But the show was a hit and renewed for two more seasons. When she told Sean, he was honest.

"I'm really happy for you. But please...don't call me again."

"Sean, you don't mean it! We're not over. I'm coming home soon, you'll see."

"I need to let you go. You're not mine anymore. Maybe you never were."

She didn't honestly believe him because they'd broken up and gotten back together many times before.

But eventually, Sean stopped responding to her text messages or taking her calls.

Her heart shattered in a million pieces when, a year later, she learned Sean was engaged to another woman from out of town. He hadn't bothered to tell her, and she'd only learned of it from her mother who was full of "I told you so's."

He'd meant it this time. She'd burned her last bridge with Sean.

It was over.

Calvin Henderson never recovered from the loss of his wife. When he died of a literal broken heart two years later, Bonnie came back for the funeral. She stayed away from the Hendersons, having already sent flowers and her condolences to Sean. The brothers, straight and tall, endured their loss together.

Bonnie endured hers alone.

At the airport, she said her goodbyes to her mother and Aunt Beulah and hopped on a plane back to California to get back to work.

She would face living the rest of her life without Sean and somehow be okay with this.

And it almost worked.

CHAPTER 12

Now

*B*onnie pulled on the top of the gold and glittery revealing dress. No matter how hard she tugged up on the material, this top wasn't going to fit over her girls, or cover them *properly.*

This situation might be fun for Sean, but she didn't want the rest of America to see her boobs al fresco. She'd never done any nudity in films, and why start now on reality TV?

"This gown...doesn't...quite fit."

The wardrobe person fussed over Bonnie. "We have your measurements and ordered it to spec."

"So...it's *supposed* to look as if I'm presenting my breasts to the world as a peace offering?"

Lori peeked inside the bedroom. "I'd like to record a few of your thoughts before leaving tonight. Your excitement, anticipation, hopes, yada, yada, yada."

"I have a few *thoughts* about this dress, but I'm not sure I can keep it G-rated." Bonnie tugged some more.

"C'mon, you look like Christina Hendrick."

In her early years, Bonnie had worked for the beauty as a stand-in and some believed her to be a dead ringer. But Bonnie didn't see it. Christina was far more sophisticated and talented.

She swept her hands over her cleavage. "This would be fine in Hollywood, but believe me, it won't go over well in Stone Ridge."

The producers had rented the Shady Grind for the evening and a private concert for their date. Just Jackson Carver with his three-piece back-up band, Sean, her...and a film crew.

At least they'd aired their grievances with each other. No surprise, Sean didn't take *any* of the blame for their break-up. Shocker.

A crew member came rushing up the stairs. "Sean called the house and said he'll be late, and he apologizes."

Lori pulled out her phone and studied it. "Why didn't he text me?"

"He probably did, but reception out here is spotty," Bonnie reminded. "It will be better in town. My mother said a year ago they ponied up the bill for WIFI all through downtown."

"We'll have to get the shots of you two arriving together later. Let's get going, I'll get your thoughts on the way. We have to finish the set up."

Not long after, Bonnie and the crew were on their way in the Hummer, Lenny driving again, suited up in a black tux tonight.

"Lenny, where on earth did you get a tux?" Bonnie tugged on his black tie.

"Winona ordered it for me." He brushed down the lapels. "Fancy, right?"

"Yes, sir." Bonnie gave him a kiss on the cheek. "You look like an upscale Sam Elliott."

"Exactly what I was goin' for."

They passed the sign at the entrance of Stone Ridge, one that had hung in Stone Ridge for decades:

Welcome to Stone Ridge, established in 1806 by Titus Ridge
Population 1,030
Women eat free every Tuesday night at the Shady Grind

"IT USED to say women eat free every night," Bonnie said. "That's changed."

A few yards later, a new sign:

Women are especially welcome

LORI CHUCKLED. "Elton, are you getting film of all this signage? This could really add flavor and color to the show."

Lori whipped out her phone once they got into town and read her texts. "I don't understand. Sean is late because he had to pull a cow out of the mud? What does that even mean? Is that some kind of small-town colloquialism I'm not aware of?"

"Nope, he really is pulling a cow out of the mud. It happens sometimes. When they get stuck, it's not easy to move them. It usually takes a few grown men."

Lori gaped. "And what about this phone tree he

mentions? Where's the tree shaped like a phone? That would be *great* to get on film."

Bonnie had a tough time holding back the full-on belly laugh.

"No, sorry, a phone tree is a rather old-fashioned concept from the days of landlines. One person calls another, and then that person calls the next person on the list, and so on. It's a system they've used for years. We rely on each other in a town this remote. It sounds as though someone needed help, and Sean got a call."

"But he had other plans!"

"I'm sure he hated to break them, but when someone needs a helping hand, he's not going to be the one to say no to his neighbor."

"How quaint." She elbowed Elton. "Let's get a short interview recorded. Tell us how you're feeling, Bonnie, and don't hold back. I want the excitement of blossoming love, hopes, dreams. Give me everything you got."

"I'm excited," Bonnie said to the camera. "And a little nervous, too. It's been a long time since I've been on a date like this with someone who…someone who I have growing feelings for. Sean has some really wonderful women to choose from, and I'm lucky to be the one here tonight."

"Nice," Lori said. "I believed every word of it."

Once they arrived, Lori and the crew went inside to set up the lighting and camera angles. Bonnie waited in the car with Lenny, her stomach growling because she'd been so nervous, she couldn't eat before leaving.

The stress diet. In the first year away from home she'd lost ten pounds without even trying. Even so, there were calls where she'd been asked to "lose a few" for the role. Silly Hollywood, making a regular sized woman feel fat and a young woman feel old.

Silly you, for letting them.

Lenny turned in the driver's seat. "How are you doing with all this, Missy?"

"Oh, I don't know." She sighed.

"Sean treatin' you right?"

"Of course, he is."

"I wouldn't think it any other way. He's always loved you, that young man. I thought he'd never get over the heartbreak when you left."

"I wasn't sure I would, either."

"Take deep breaths, would ya? You look nervous as a long-tail cat in a room full of rocking chairs."

Bonnie snorted. "Point taken."

But she wasn't nervous, exactly, simply anxious that her feelings would be written all over her face, reflected in her eyes and displayed for the entire viewing public to see. She'd have to call on all her acting abilities tonight and appear to be a woman *beginning* to fall in love with Sean.

Not a woman who'd apparently never fallen *out* of love with him.

The very thought seared her heart with fear. She had to pretend to be along for the ride when in reality pain struck every time she thought he wanted Tabitha and all her bright and shiny newness.

He'd kept her in the contest because the producers asked him to, for the drama. Not for her, but because she was the hired actor. Everything else was nostalgia but she could easily walk out of this show alone, having to watch Sean start his new life with his new fiancée. She'd already done that once, but from the safe distance of a thousand miles.

The very idea had a pebble lodging itself in her throat.

Pretend. Pretend. Pretend.

"Here's the whipper snapper now," Lenny said.

Bonnie caught sight of him rushing out of his truck, his gorgeous dark hair tousled and disheveled. She wouldn't be surprised if he'd hopped out of the shower minutes before. He was dressed in a black suit so sharp the studio must have had it tailored to fit. As she watched, he fiddled with his tie using his truck's side mirror and ran a hand through his hair before he plopped his black Stetson on. This was the most primping she'd ever seen him do.

Sean waved to Lenny and tapped on the back-passenger window of the Hummer.

Bonnie rolled the window down. "Hey."

"Sorry I'm late."

"I know. You're never late. It must have been important."

"Guess there's a first time for everything. You used to pitch a fit whenever I dropped everything to help move a cow."

"I was *sixteen*."

As if just now noticing her dress, he scanned the exposed flesh and quirked a brow. "Damn. Thanks for the show, Skippy."

"Not my idea."

She decided not to remind him that Tabitha put on a daily show for his benefit.

"You've always been a little shy about showing me your best assets." Sean grinned.

Lenny cleared his throat. "Uh, son? Watch it now."

"Oh, sorry, Lenny." Still, he winked at Bonnie.

"You're not at all sorry," she whispered.

"Finally, he's here!" Lori blustered outside and clapped her hands. "Let's get this show on the road. I want a nice clean wide lens angle of them coming inside so we can see their amazed faces. And I shouldn't have to say this, guys, but you had better look amazed! I don't care what you really feel. Amazed and astonished is what I need."

Sean opened the door to the Hummer and offered his hand. "Ready?"

Together they walked inside the opened doors of the Shady Grind Bar & Grill. Bonnie didn't have to fake her amazement. She hadn't been here in years, but her memories of the bar before Jackson Carver bought it were of a plain old honky tonk. Tonight, white fairy lights lit up the otherwise dimly lit room. Colorful flowers were artfully arranged throughout. Toward the back of the room stood Jackson with his band, smiling as they walked in like "the chosen" ones.

Jackson immediately began to play a private concert, his first choice a love song. He sang one of his hits, The Only one for Me, coincidentally or not, about lovers who'd lost touch over the years.

"Dance?" Sean held out his arm and walked to the center of the room where Lori had taped their mark.

She joined him, carefully placing both hands on his shoulder. Touching Sean. This was dangerous business. He held her, not too close, hands on her waist, watching her, probably waiting for a cue. Oh, yes, she knew him almost better than she knew herself some days.

"Nervous?"

They weren't individually miked for this portion, so they wouldn't be heard above the music playing. "A little. All these eyes on us."

"Relax and try to think of something else."

That's rich, Sean. Show up looking the way you do and how can I think of anything besides jumping your bones?

"Something else? Like what?"

"Like…laying on a blanket outside watching the stars." He met her gaze. "Or pretend we're dancing alone outside, the headlights of my truck our only light, the music coming from my junky speakers."

He'd mentioned the ways he'd tried to keep her from

leaving. The ache wound itself around her heart and she swallowed the pebble lodged in her throat.

"Or maybe I can pretend someone I love brought me flowers every day for weeks. And how it made me feel like the most loved woman on the planet."

"Yeah. Just like that."

"Sean, you—"

And then it happened.

As if no longer able to ignore the laws of physics, her right breast bust right out of her gown like a Jack from its box.

She plastered herself against Sean's body, literally using him as a human shield. And sweet baby Jesus, he smelled so good. She almost forgot her breast was loose.

"Wardrobe malfunction," she whispered into his neck.

"Huh?" But then he looked down and his eyes widened. "Wow, Holy Jolly Rancher."

"We have to get their attention somehow so I can stop the madness."

"I don't see the rush," he said smugly, tugging her closer. "Just stay right where you are. I'll protect you, little lady."

"That's not funny." But okay, it was a little funny. "I'm uncomfortable."

"Cold?" He grinned. "If anything shows, they'll cut it. This is a *family* show."

"So they say, but on the other hand Tabitha gave you a half moon."

"Yep. You're definitely jealous."

"You mean a little like you were when you saw the photos of me in my underwear?" In her irritation, she pulled back a bit and met his eyes.

He only tugged her back into place, plastering his body to hers. "To borrow a line from you, I was *young*."

"Okay, I can't do this anymore."

"Why? Getting a little turned on?"

That was beside the point. But yes, her exposed nipple rubbing against Sean's chest was causing all manner of tremors and tingles.

"You're right, I'm a little cold, or at least a significant *part* of me is. Plus, I don't want Jackson to see me. He's on a riser and might get a bird's eye view."

"He's too busy playing his guitar and doesn't give one hoot about your nudity."

"I love how much fun you're having with this."

He slid her a slow grin. "Can you blame me?"

"That's it," she said, and started her effort at making motions toward the crew.

They went mostly ignored and so she gently pushed on Sean, using him for cover, moving them out of the frame just as Jackson finished his song. But he pushed back some, having his fun, letting her get only a few inches at a time. They shuffled along finally leaving their mark.

"Cut! What in God's name are you doing?" Lori yelled. "Don't they teach you how to dance in Texas? You look like you're trying to wrestle with him."

"I have a wardrobe malfunction!" Bonnie hissed.

"Elton, do me a favor and close your eyes? You too, Jackson?" Sean called out.

"Um, sure, buddy." Jackson turned and so did his band mates.

"*This!*" Bonnie moved back enough to show Lori her exposed breast.

"Well, damn! Why didn't you say something?" Lori yelled.

Sean tried to move away from her, but she wrestled him back.

"What are you doing? I at least need you to block me so I can try to shove my boob back inside the dress."

"A man waits all his life to hear those words."

And so it was that Bonnie used Sean's body to block her from the crew and Jackson's band while she turned and shoved the stray girl right back in where she belonged.

Only then she realized a small crowd had gathered outside to watch their filming from behind a barricade.

And the entire crowd, including Bonnie's mother and Aunt Beulah, watched as Bonnie shoved her breast back in the dress.

CHAPTER 13

"Oh, Jesus," Bonnie muttered, shimmying against his back.

"What now? You okay back there or do we need a surgeon?"

Funny and smartass comments were his fall back whenever caught with Bonnie out in public, her breast exposed.

First time for everything.

She turned to him. Bonnie was quite fair, but occasionally she resembled a bleached white sheet, this being one of those times.

As far as he could tell, everything um, had been repositioned. His roving eye took it all in. "You're good."

"Look behind me."

A crowd had gathered behind the barricade set up, presumably to watch them filming, and all the fun "Hollywood" action. In the crowd, Lenny stood, eyes shut, using his hand to cover Jeremy's eyes. Sadie Carver held the hand of her toddler son, the other hand covering her mouth. Beulah and Maybelle looked to be roughly a thousand different shades of outage.

"Well, um, check this out. Look at all the signs," he tried. "Go, Bonnie Wheeler for the win!"

She's his first love, another sign held up by Jolette Marie.

Don't be an idiot, pick Bonnie!

Hometown girl in it to win it!

"I can't *believe* this. My mother will be so proud. No nudity, ever, until now." She plunked her forehead to his chest.

His arms went around her, drawing her close, simply to offer comfort. "It wasn't filmed, and if so, it won't be seen by anyone else but me, and well, a few of your closest friends."

"Mmmauh," she mumbled unintelligibly into his chest.

"Say that again?" He pulled her back by the nape of her neck and met her eyes.

"Never mind."

For several long seconds, they simply gazed into each other's eyes. And something outrageous and unbidden split open and clicked into place.

She's here. Now. My second chance, if I don't blow this.

Hold up, cowboy. Wouldn't that be third or fourth chance?

Damn it, who's counting?

Lori joined them, interrupting the staring contest. "Wow, good going guys. Other than the gown thing, and by the way, I'm *so* sorry. But you looked *amazing.* We're getting this romantic vibe all over the place and we're getting it on camera. Great, great work!"

"Yeah, it's almost as if we were together before," Sean muttered before reality slapped him in the face. "Though I suppose you're acting."

"No, Sean, I'm not. This is the worst acting job I've ever done if you want to know the truth."

He scratched his jaw. "How's that?"

"I'm supposed to pretend I'm falling in love with you, Jackass!"

"I thought you were doin' just fine there. I *almost* believed it."

Her neck jerked back as if he'd slapped her and her eyes were suddenly wet.

Sure, maybe he was being an ass, but also protecting his heart from another roundhouse kick. No one could blame him. He might want a second chance with Bonnie, but he wouldn't do this without a *guarantee*. An extended warranty plan. He was thirty-seven years old and he wasn't going to wait for Bonnie to settle down. And the idea to pressure her into staying and having a family still wasn't an acceptable one. He'd tried to keep her many times before, and it never worked.

He couldn't forget that she'd likely come here in the first place only to revive her sagging career. If she'd changed her mind, how did he know it wasn't temporary and in the spirit of competition? Bonnie always loved winning, even if at times it appeared the spit and sunshine had leaked out of her.

She was still beautiful to him. Her type of beauty was ageless and sometimes, like the day she'd come over with Jolette Marie, reminded him of the young woman he'd adored. But something in her eyes told him she'd been through a rough patch and he'd never know the half of it. She'd once told him the industry was ruthless but then she'd gone right back to the punishment.

"I need a break!" Bonnie rushed out the back of the bar, ignoring Lori, and everyone else. "Deal with it."

"Alright, geez, take five everyone!" Lori bellowed.

"We'll be back," Jackson called out from the stage.

Lori joined Sean. "What the hell's wrong with her? You two had a vibe going there, don't lie to me."

"She didn't like the dress. It showed a little too much... you know." He ran a hand down his face. "Oh, man. I'm so out of my element."

"I know, I know." Lori patted him on the back. "But you're doing just great, cowboy. You should see Twitter. It's exploding. I've been leaking little reels of the show to whet their appetite. You're every woman's dream cowboy. This show is almost as good for westerns as *Yellowstone*."

"Twitter?"

"Right. You've never been much for social media. Well, you have a million new followers as of today, Sean Henderson!"

"I do? What *for*?"

His previous followers of note included Jolette Marie, because she was into that sort of thing, Jackson, Winona, Riggs, and the San Antonio cattle rancher's association.

She waved her arms around. "For this, of course! You didn't think this would remain a secret, did you? Once you were announced as the cowboy and the teaser reels started posting, it went nuts."

"I left my phone at home."

Lori handed him her cell. "Check it out. You should be proud. Oh, do me a favor and don't show any of this to Bonnie? I need to talk to her first."

With that she walked back to Elton and left Sean to check Twitter. He fell down a rabbit hole of tweets and comments and links. Though he didn't embarrass easily, some of the comments under his new profile photo made him cringe.

FlashMein2022 said: Hawt, hawt, hawt!

GetReelz2tonight: Mama, where can I get me one of those?

Clearly, he'd never be able to post to Twitter again. No big loss. His old tweets about cattle, wild horses, and what he'd be having for dinner were long buried. Should he respond to any of these new comments? No. No, he'd leave it alone. Later, he'd figure out how to take his profile down.

All of this upset him enough but then he followed a cookie trail to Bonnie's profile. The photo of her in the role she'd played on three seasons of a popular Netflix series, now ended, remained on her profile. An amazing shot of a powerful woman. She'd played a kickass character on that show, the youngest sister of an Irish mafia family. Yes, he'd watched along with everyone else.

Bonnie's Twitter was now filled with hashtags about her coming appearance on Mr. Cowboy. Only a few of them were positive. His gut pitched and roiled as he read.

Some genius had posted:

She's too old for him.

The replies went downhill from there.

She was too old for him? She was *his* age! What the hell was wrong with people, anyway? He nearly threw the phone until he remembered it belonged to Lori.

Stomping toward her, he placed it her outstretched palm.

She scowled. "See what I mean?"

"Yeah, let me be the one to talk to Bonnie."

"They're just jealous, but still…damn, people suck."

"Tell me about it."

HE FOUND Bonnie standing not far from the dumpster in the back. The picture this presented of incomparable beauty next to trash said a lot about social media.

A dumpster fire if there ever was one.

People throw rocks at things that shine.

Yeah, he'd heard that song lyric before and no one shined brighter than Bonnie Lee Wheeler. Not for him, anyway.

"You okay, Skippy? I'm sorry I was an ass."

"You weren't. But I see why you believe I'm acting."

"Well, you are an actress."

"Regardless, I think the real reason I came back is because I wanted to see you again."

"Why?"

"You *know* why. I missed home. I missed...so many things." She met his eyes, and to his utter amazement and shock, they were wet.

"Stop it. Don't you cry."

"I won't." She brushed off one cheek with the back of her hand.

"Hell, are we going to do this all over again? Go back forth because we can't seem to stay away from each other unless we put some serious miles between us?"

"*You're* the one who put miles between us."

"Here we go again. Let's not to this." He held up outstretched palms in the universal "stop" sign.

"You're right," she said, turning to him. "I am acting. I'm trying to *act* like I don't I regret everything about my life for the past twelve years. Like I don't regret putting my career ahead of family, love, ahead of...everything. Where did that get me, exactly?"

"You've had a great career."

"And I don't have *anything* else." Her shoulders were quivering. "This is too painful for me. Please ask the producers if you can eliminate me this week. I know they've forced you to keep me along for the drama, but I can't take this anymore. It's not fair to either one of us for them to play with our past this way."

"The producers asked me to keep *Tabitha*. Not you."

"Oh." The knowledge seemed to slide into her in slow bits. "Then...why did you...why?"

"Why do you *think*?"

"I have no idea. I thought maybe you wanted me to see how much you'd moved on. But you didn't have to do that. I already knew you'd moved on when you were engaged to Robyn. You were done with me."

"I was angry that you gave up on us. Or maybe I was angry I gave up. I don't know which it is anymore. I'm all turned around. The point is, I was not going to chase after *you* anymore, but when you showed for this, I realized…" He rubbed the back of his neck. "There's still something here, isn't there?"

He asked it like a question, but he understood it as a statement.

She nodded. "Yes. For me, there is."

"But I don't know if I can trust you."

"I can't blame you." She met his gaze. "Where does that leave us?"

He shrugged out of his jacket and slipped it on her shoulders. "You want to get out of here?"

Her eyes widened but she did not hesitate. "Yes."

The idea they would do this, just walk away from tonight, and their commitment to this show, stoked a fire in him. He took Bonnie's hand and they slipped out the back, rounding the corner of the outside building. The small crowd of people were still staring toward the bar, no doubt waiting for more action to begin. Fortunately, he'd parked his truck on the other side of the street. Walking slowly and stealthily, he bent low, using the truck to block the view.

He opened the driver's side and let Bonnie in first.

"We have minutes before they see us leaving."

She slid in easily, hunkering her body low.

Sean climbed into the driver's seat, hurriedly closed the door and started up the truck. As expected, almost in tandem, everyone turned to see Sean driving away in his truck. He gave a little salute-style wave toward Lenny's gaping jaw.

Bonnie sat up. "We are probably in such trouble with Lori."

"Do you care? She's got to learn this deal isn't a dictatorship."

"Right? I like her but she's so…devoted."

"Marti Jr. I call her." Sean chuckled. "She's ambitious."

"She's going to have us drawn and quartered. I feel like we've just 'borrowed' your father's truck again." Bonnie chuckled.

"Hey, I'll have you know I've been driving my own truck for years now."

"Where are we going?"

"I have something to show you."

He hadn't known whether he'd have a chance to show Bonnie what he'd been working on in the intervening years. She'd been starring in commercials, a feature movie or two, in addition to that hugely popular mafia series that started her career.

He, among other things, built their dream house. When they were younger, Bonnie had in mind exactly the kind of house she wanted them both to live in someday. A ranch style farmhouse with a wraparound porch. A swing where they'd sit and have iced tea at the end of the day. She'd sold him on this idea, and eventually it became his own. Sometimes he could literally visualize the two of them sitting on the porch swing with their children.

He pulled down the long lane at the entrance to their property, but she still sat quietly beside him. No questions. He liked the change to a quiet kind of acceptance between them. They'd fought so long and hard he'd forgotten what it had been like to get along.

Pretty damn glorious, as he recalled.

He kept driving up the hill, past the main house where Riggs and Winona lived, to his own home. When he reached it, he shut the truck off but kept his headlights on and gripped the steering wheel till his knuckles turned white.

"I took my time and dragged my behind for years, but when Riggs got married that lit a fire under me. I wanted my own house." He finally turned to her. "What do you think?"

"You built it." She reached for his hand and covered it with her own. "The house I loved."

"It was our dream house." He heard the nostalgia threaded through his voice. "All it needs now is the swing."

He squeezed her hand. "Want to come inside?"

They searched each other another moment, gazes locked. They both knew the minute they crossed the threshold they wouldn't be able to keep their hands off each other. It had always been that way between them. Hot and fiery. Electric.

"Yes, but I better not."

He nodded. "You're right."

"Technically, Sean, you're dating two other women besides me."

"I am not."

"Yes, you are." She smiled patiently. "That's the deal we both signed on for. I don't feel right about what I know we'd do inside when there are two other women still here."

"Okay, guess you're right. But I haven't done anything with those two other women. No kissing. Nothing."

"Well, you put your arm around Tabitha."

So, she'd noticed that on day one. Gratifying to realize she'd been jealous even then.

He snorted. "True. I guess in some countries that means we're engaged."

"Don't even joke about that. And you caught her in your arms when she ran at you."

"I couldn't very well drop her, could I?" He unbuckled his seat belt and pulled her close. "Damn, I'm sorry, Skippy. Now you know what it was like for me all those years when every man in town chased after you."

"I'm sorry you had to go through that."

"You always came back to me."

"Except the last time." She leaned her head on his shoulder.

He nodded, remembering. But he wouldn't think about that right now. Instead, he turned on the radio station to the country channel and went around the passenger side to help her out.

She took his hand and shrugged out of his jacket, leaving it on the seat. An up-tempo newer song ended, and *Grow old with Me* came on.

"I'll keep you young forever," Sunny Sweeney sang.

"Damn, I was hoping to swing you around."

"You're just going to have to hold me close."

And he did, his hands low on her back, head resting on top of hers. She was a dinky thing next to him. Her hair smelled liked coconut and flowers.

"This time the speakers aren't junky," Sean whispered near her ear.

"No, now we're the ones who are old."

"Speak for yourself. I'm not old, and we're the same age."

"It's different for men."

"How so?"

"You men get to spread your seed well into your eighties. Look at Michael Douglas."

"I'd rather not, thanks."

"My baby making days might be over. And I know how much a family means to you. You should know that about me."

"True, but there are many ways to create a family. Look at Angelina Jolie."

"I'd rather not, thanks."

He chuckled. "Winona had twins when she was forty. It's possible."

"You were always the eternal optimist. Thank you for that. No wonder I was obsessed with you for years."

"*Obsessed,* huh?"

Like the universe understood they were floating too close

to painful memories, the music over the radio waves switched to a faster beat.

"Now this is what I'm talking about." Sean lightened the mood as he swung Bonnie around.

Every few beats he'd pull her back to him, then swing her back. She kept up with him, smiling, her hair whipping around in the light breeze. This night was nearing perfection for him. Good music, good woman, the sounds of the crickets in the background.

"Are you trying to wear me out?" she gasped.

"Hell, no. I'm just praying for another wardrobe malfunction. This time when there's no one else around."

She grinned. "Don't worry. I've got my girls packed in there really well this time."

"Now you tell me."

Another slow ballad came on next, and Sean pulled her close in the circle of his arms. He bent to press his forehead to hers and they stayed that way for a while, her hands around his neck, his resting low on her hips.

He didn't know if an hour or two had passed. Time stretched out before him and he refused to think about anything else but this empty field in front of his cabin.

Right here, right now, he *could* die a happy man.

Right now, Bonnie wasn't the woman who'd left him.

She wasn't the one who'd stomped on his heart.

She wasn't the woman who'd put him last and expected him to take it like a man.

She was the woman who'd come home.

CHAPTER 14

*H*eadlights lit up the driveway to Sean's cabin and Bonnie blinked in the bright glow of the approaching Hummer. She should have known this moment wouldn't last. Couldn't. It was too perfect.

Alone with Sean, she remembered too well why she'd fallen in love with him. He had a way of pulling her out of whatever dream she'd been caught up in and taking her somewhere even better.

"They found us. I should have never given Lori my address." Sean shaded his eyes against the lights.

Lori climbed out of the back and stomped to them. "Well, well, well. What have we here, kids?"

"I'm sorry, Ma," Sean said.

"It's my fault. I was upset, and Sean tried to calm me down."

"*Please* don't let the Twitter thing get you down," Lori said, hands splayed. "People are idiots."

"Wait. What about Twitter?" Bonnie glanced from him to Lori, and back again.

Sean winced. "Um…I was going to talk to you about that."

"You didn't tell her?" Lori bellowed. "I thought you were going to tell her!"

"There wasn't time. We had other…stuff to discuss."

"Tell me what?" Bonnie fisted his shirt bringing his attention back to her.

"It's nothing to worry about. Don't look at it now." Sean brought his fingers around her wrist. "I guess you're not going to be the fan favorite."

"That doesn't exactly surprise me, but something tells me it's a lot worse than not being favored to win this competition."

"Lucky for you two," Lori interrupted and for once Sean was happy about it. "I shot some B footage of Jackson and his band while you two were off having your fun. We can head back to the bar now and get a little more footage of you two dancing. Some scenes at the candlelit table talking about life and what your plans and hopes and dreams are. Yada, yada, yada. I'll splice it together and save the day. It's what I do. Then we'll call it a night. This is good stuff, guys, but I hate to reiterate and sound like a nag: I need all of this *on film*."

"Right." Sean scowled.

"Let's do this," Bonnie said, letting go of his hand and kicking back into professional gear.

To please Lori, Bonnie and Sean drove back to the bar where they danced again, this time with music piping through speakers. Apparently with the angles Elton would use, it didn't matter the band was long gone from the stage.

So was their outside "audience."

She was far more relaxed in Sean's arms after their intimate talk. Lori didn't have to pose them or tell them what to say or do. They followed rules and didn't kiss for the camera, but their faces tipped to each other with only centimeters between them. She could feel his warm breath on her bare skin and see the one green speck in his amber eyes.

"Okay, let's call it a night!" Lori announced after the slow torture.

Next, Bonnie would need to call her mother before all hell broke loose. She'd rather do it from the comfort of the Hummer, downtown, where she had cell reception. The memory of Mama's shocked expression, along with Beulah's far more censuring one, would follow into her dreams tonight.

Because her mother and Aunt Beulah had a recurring argument every year after Bonnie had made the lingerie commercial:

Mama: Beulah, you were wrong. Admit it!

Beulah: I was not wrong. Bonnie Lee made enough money in a few hours wearing lingerie than some make in a year. It got her acting career started. No harm done.

Mama: I thank the good lord daily my daughter didn't wind up in pornos.

Beulah: Maybelle, have you lost your cotton-pickin' mind?

And on and on it went.

Bonnie would never tell her mother, or Aunt Beulah, but in those first few years the commercial had, as much as possible with someone so young, typecast her.

"You're the girl from Topanga's first huge campaign! They took branding in a whole new direction. I assume you're okay with nudity?"

"We've seen most of your body, so we don't need to see any more for now. The part has just one small nude scene..."

It took years to be taken seriously, when she'd waitressed and auditioned, then gone to acting classes at night. Eventually, her acting teacher recommended her for a small part on a hugely popular long-running TV series.

She'd had one line: "Oh my gosh, is that really you?"

But she was wearing all her clothes when she said it.

When she'd come home with Sean after his mother's

illness, she'd almost given up on her dream. Then she'd been asked to audition for *Kavanaugh's Way*. She hadn't ever done a nude scene.

No nudity, until tonight.

Now, she had so much to deal with all at once. Something on Twitter she didn't really want to know about, her mother and Aunt Beulah, and last but not least, Sean.

Her feelings for him were so deep they must have never gone away. His smile, his touch, his arms tight around her were everything. For so long, she'd accepted she couldn't have him. He'd found someone new and she'd tried to move on. In many ways she had. She'd had boyfriends, all of whom never even slightly compared to Sean, and friends, who tended to come and go depending on how hot a commodity she was.

But she'd never come close to what she'd once had with Sean. Tonight was a reminder of the simplicity she'd missed. The same things which had once seemed corny and cheap as a younger woman now seemed sweet and nostalgic. They rang true and real.

Or maybe it was all Sean, who made everything dull a little brighter for her. He always had.

After parting with Sean, and before leaving downtown, Bonnie called her mother.

"I can explain."

"Can't wait to hear this."

"It was a wardrobe malfunction. The designers put me in this small gown. I complained, and just as I knew it would happen...well...and so I was trying to fix it when...you know. Y'all really shouldn't have been there anyway!"

"I wish I hadn't been. But good Lord Bonnie, everyone saw you, until Sean blocked you. Thank goodness for that boy's height."

"Yes, and don't worry, the nudity won't make it on the show. This is a *family* show."

"Will you now tell me what on earth is going on with you and Sean?"

"You know what's happening. I'm in a contest. He..." she remembered the moment Sean told her *he'd* kept her on, not because the producers asked him to. "hasn't decided what he's going to do with me."

"Oh, he hasn't decided, has he?" Mama snorted. "You tell that boy if he doesn't make an honest woman out of you I'll ring his fool neck!"

"I will not, Mama. I signed up for this. As soon as this is all over, I'll come home and stay with you a while. We'll bake pies and drink iced tea."

"But what if Sean picks you?"

She hadn't allowed herself to consider it because she didn't believe Sean would risk asking her to marry him in front of a huge audience. He'd want to do it privately, after already feeling assured she'd say yes, or he wouldn't do it at all. They both had too much riding on this.

"I don't want him to pick me. Maybe I want him to have everything he wants. Sean wants a family and I doubt I can give him that now."

"And what do you want, Bonnie Lee?"

The question of the decade. "I'm figuring this out."

"Just don't get your heart broken again, sugar."

"No, ma'am. I don't intend to."

A little more placating Mama and Bonnie promised to speak again soon.

And then, even though she knew better, Bonnie checked social media.

"She's not good enough for Sean."

"Bonnie had her chance and blew it."

"Hello? Speaking of wrong reasons, anyone notice Bonnie is a member of the Screen Actor's Guild?"

She, Bonnie, was the old hag who'd come to reclaim her career in the spotlight.

Seriously, she'd come to reclaim her career with a *reality show?*

No one seemed to remember Bonnie had a decent career before the Irish mafia show ended. She'd been perfectly cast. After that, redheads fell out of favor and so did Bonnie. It was time for someone new to come up the ranks. She'd sought solace in friends like Eric, who looked up to her because she'd had a successful run. Even if the big parts had dried up, she'd had her moment, which was far more than some could say.

But she just didn't care anymore.

Well, maybe a little, because it stung to be called old. Thank goodness her mother was not on social media. She'd want to take a switch to all of these people. Why did it seem like kindness and compassion had no place left? It had been erased from every consciousness. Behind a screen, some forgot these were real people whose hearts beat, and whose blood rushed through their veins like everyone else.

"You're looking at Twitter, aren't you?" Lori said a few minutes into their drive back to the ranch.

"Sean asked you not to look, and you didn't listen."

"Well, no." She threw her phone down. "Now I wish I had. No good ever comes of it."

"Unfortunately, I have worse news."

"What now?"

"I've been uploading the dailies to the cloud and well..." She sighed and held up air quotes. "Not enough drama according to the producers. You and Angela get along like besties, and Tabitha might be aggressive, but she's not a bully or anything."

"And that's a problem *why?*"

"These types of shows thrive on that sort of conflict. Myself, I hate pitting women against each other."

"You don't know how happy I am to hear you say that. Y'all said this was a *family* show."

"We have to do something." Lori waved her hand dismissively. "Don't worry, I'll figure this out."

Once back at the mansion, Bonnie found Angela waiting for her in the living room, sitting on a couch, her laptop perched on her knees.

She glanced up. "Hey, how did it go?"

Bonnie plopped down next to her. "Wardrobe malfunction."

As Bonnie told the story, Angela dissolved into laughter that verged on tears. "I bet Sean loved that."

"He's always been a breast man." Bonnie chuckled. "Where's Tabitha?"

"She went to bed after doing her interview." Angela rolled her eyes. "Lots of tears that Sean didn't choose her for the one-on-one and she can't possibly get to know him if they don't get some alone time. I don't understand her. Is she for real or putting on an act?"

"For her sake, I hope she's acting."

And the thought of Tabitha and Sean getting "alone time" made Bonnie's gut pitch. She'd never truly appreciated how difficult it had been for him to watch as other men continually tried to take her away from him. He'd been in more than one fist fight over the years, all due to staking his claim. But...he'd been young. Now, he understood there was a whole world out there filled with beautiful women who would see Sean for exactly who he was: a truly honorable, loyal man with integrity and strong character.

Who, of course, also looked pretty incredible in a pair of jeans.

"Let's face it," Angela said. "I'm on the chopping block. They'll want to keep Tabitha."

"You think so?" Bonnie reached for Angela's hand and squeezed. "I'm going to miss you."

"I'll miss you too, Skippy." She chuckled. "How on earth did you get that nickname, or is too private?"

"No, it's quite boring. I like peanut butter. A lot."

"It's a weakness for many of us."

"I once ate an entire jar by myself."

"Big deal."

"In a few *hours.* My mother came home and wanted to know what happened to the peanut butter. She'd planned on making cookies for a bake sale. So, I did what any good daughter would do. I helped her look for the jar."

"You never found it, did you?" Angela smirked.

"A mystery unsolved to this day. I went down to the store to get another one for her. Sean has never let me live it down."

"Now that's a guy after my own heart."

"Every year for Valentine's Day he gave me a jar of Skippy peanut butter, the largest jar he could get his hands on."

"Better than chocolate."

"Well, he gave me the chocolate and flowers, too."

"Aw, man He's pretty wonderful, isn't he?" Angela's gaze was filled with sympathy.

Later, Bonnie retired to her bedroom upstairs, where her thoughts ran to Sean. The moment he'd shown her the home he built something in her heart stretched and unfurled. It settled deep in her bones. She had no doubt.

He'd never forgotten her, and she'd *never* forgotten him. Sean had created the standard by which she judged all other men.

And despite all the memories she already had with him, tonight, they'd made some new ones.

. . .

THE NEXT DAY was another group date challenge which everyone had expected Jessica to win. Now, it was anyone's guess.

In today's event, Sean's "women" would demonstrate how good they were with children by spending time with a group ranging in ages from two to ten.

"I love children," Tabitha said as they waited outside for Sean to arrive. "That's why I became a nurse."

"Not a teacher?" Angela pressed.

"I could have done either." Tabitha tipped her chin. "But nursing pays better."

"I myself have visited schools with early childhood lessons I've prepared on the importance of financial stability early in life," Angela said. "I wouldn't exactly say I dumb it down, but I break it up into manageable chunks."

"I'm pretty good with arts and crafts," Bonnie tried.

"Bless your heart," Tabitha said.

Sean pulled up in his truck, and the crew began to film.

Today he wore casual jeans, his ever-present boots and hat, and a tight T-shirt that emphasized his muscles. Gulp.

"Good morning, ladies. As y'all know, I'm looking to add some branches to the Henderson family tree. I want children. Lots of them. And so today, we're going to see how you all do around a group of kids."

"I love kids!" Tabitha squealed.

Was there anything Sean could say that she wouldn't love? Bonnie worried she would another run at Sean and had a half a mind to block her this time.

"Of course, so do I." Angela straightened and stuck out her chest. "*Everyone* should love children. This is America."

"I believe the children are our future." Bonnie pressed her lower lips together and fought a smile.

Sean winked at her, not missing the reference to her favorite Whitney Houston song. "We're going to our local charter school so we can meet up with the teacher, Sadie Carver. I don't know what she has planned for us, but I'm sure it will be fun."

This time, Sean drove them all in his truck. One guess as to who made shotgun.

"Which school are we going to?" Tabitha asked from the front seat.

"We only have the one," Sean said.

"You have one school in the entire town?" Angela gasped.

"For now," Sean said.

"When I grew up here, we didn't have a school at all," Bonnie said.

"Oh, you poor thing, that explains so much," Tabitha said. "Is that why you went into acting?"

"We were bussed to the next town for school," Sean said a bit defensively. "Both Bonnie and I were in the same grade."

"Oh. How sweet."

Sean cleared his throat. "Anyway, I'm glad my nephews, niece, and my own children will be able to attend grade school right here."

Tabitha remained quiet the rest of the ride.

CHAPTER 15

*W*hen they arrived at the school, which Bonnie recalled used to be the original Trinity church building, Sadie stood at the entrance. She wore a blue and yellow dress that hit just above the knees and cute brown western boots. She was as pretty as Bonnie recalled and had grown up quite a bit in twelve years.

"Hi, guys!" Sadie waved happily. "Are y'all ready to hang out with the kids? They're so excited! When the parents heard Sean wanted this challenge for the show, they volunteered to bring the kids. We'll do anything for our Sean."

"Aw, now, sweetheart. Thank you." Sean put an arm around Sadie which Bonnie saw as completely brotherly.

She was married, after all, to one of the sexiest most rugged cowboys in town.

Tabitha crossed her arms and jutted her hip out. "Let's get this contest going. I'm going to win it. You won't believe how good I am with children. They *adore* me."

"The babies, in the NICU?" Angela asked. "And how can you tell?"

"Ha! I'm an aunt to four." She held up her splayed hand showing off four fingers.

Bonnie wasn't exactly an expert with children. Because she was the youngest of her family, she'd had none of the family experience at home. But Bonnie had been a big sister to many, and it was her nature to nurture others. She'd played a young mother on the set of her last series pilot and wound up feeling a deep attachment to her young co-star. Jolette Marie had relied on her for years, since she hadn't had a real mother figure. All the younger women asked for advice and she'd given it to them. She'd remind them to respect themselves first and be kind to everyone.

As a teenager she volunteered for Sunday school along with everyone else. She'd always wanted children, of course. Someday. But one morning she woke up and someday had come and gone. It didn't seem possible anyway, when every man she met was an actor who wanted fame more than family.

But every time she saw a baby in a grocery store, she nearly wept with envy. It was her biological clock ticking, something that could not be helped. Science. She tried to assuage it every now and then with a jar of peanut butter.

They all followed Sadie into the one-room school room. All the pews had been removed and in the large space there were sections of small tables and chairs. Sadie taught from kindergarten to sixth now, every year adding a grade since they'd started the school.

"Welcome! Children, please say hello to our cowboy and these lovely ladies," Sadie announced.

"Hi!" The children waved.

There were mostly boys, not a shock, with two girls in the group. Sadie introduced the children, including her own little Sammy, whom she'd brought along because Lincoln was busy at their ranch.

There was Jimmy Ray, a tall cute kid who seemed to be a leader among the boys, Bobby Joe, and a handful of other boys. The only girls were Ellie and Naomi.

Sadie explained and pointed to the events she'd set up. A section for story time, with a large comfortable chair and throw pillows on the floor. Another section had bottles of glue and plenty of glitter, and in another section the "pancake project" which involved a hot plate.

"Alright, kids, the grown-ups are in charge. Remember to always have a grown up with you in the cooking section. Safety first! I'll be just outside with Sammy if anyone needs me."

Bonnie headed straight to the glitter and glue.

She folded red construction paper and drew a crescent shape, then cut one out to demonstrate. And noticed for the first time that her hands were no longer shaking. She didn't even remember the last time they had. Probably the day she'd boarded the plane to Texas.

Within minutes, she had a group of boys surrounding her. Angela, over at the book nook, had all the girls. And Tabitha, stuck with the cooking project, couldn't gather any interest. Instead, she chose to follow Sean around like a shadow.

Some of the younger boys were taking their kinetic energy out on Sean, grabbing onto his pants leg, forcing him to walk with them hanging on. Nothing seemed to faze him.

But Tabitha kept trying to talk the wild boys into behaving, and when that didn't work, she became flustered.

"Just…just settle down, boys! Do you want to climb off Sean's back now?"

Even Bonnie knew better than to ask a kid to stop doing something they were obviously enjoying. Re-direction was the only way.

"Not really," said a little boy, holding on to Sean's neck. "This is fun."

"It's fine." Sean walked over to Bonnie's table, where glitter, hearts and glue would never again be separated in this lifetime. "All the boys, huh? Some things never change."

"Ha, ha." She grinned up at him and he winked.

This seemed to greatly disturb Tabitha's mojo because she grabbed Sean's elbow. "Sean, can we talk, please? Alone?"

"Yeah, sure."

She shepherded him to one corner of the large room where Bonnie couldn't hear a thing. Holding up a book, Angela glanced over the top of it at Bonnie and slid her a significant look. The entire exchange was being filmed, but though Bonnie had no sound she gathered it wasn't going well. Tabitha flayed her arms around, gesturing wildly, occasionally reaching up to place a hand on Sean's shoulders. If his shoulders got any tighter, they'd snap like a branch. When he crossed his arms, Bonnie realized he'd lost his patience with Tabitha. And Sean was a patient man. Bonnie ought to know.

Whatever they were talking about seemed to be more reality TV butter because Lori was watching it all, a huge grin on her face.

"Hey, everybody! Look what I made!"

A little boy held up a pan on which he'd apparently cooked a pancake all by himself. His arm dangled perilously close to the hot plate, and he had the pan tilted so that sooner or later, the laws of physics would cause it to fall to the floor.

"Oh, hey, buddy." Sean rushed over to the unsupervised child. "Let me help you with that."

"This is my station." Tabitha followed Sean.

"I'm sorry," Sean said to the little boy. "Someone should have been supervising this station to help you."

"That's my fault," Tabitha admitted. "Let's make another one together!"

"I don't want to make another one. I want *this* one!" the little boy shrieked.

"Good Lord." Tabitha covered her ears. "Why are you getting to upset, you little brat? I'm trying to help you!"

If looks could kill, Tabitha would be lying on the floor with a knife in her back, courtesy of Sean. Angela had stopped reading, and all the girls were staring at Tabitha.

"That's mean," Ellie said.

"Yes, it is." Angela agreed, cracking open another book. "Now, for my next story."

"Miss Bonnie, could I have some more glitter?" Jimmy Ray asked, oblivious. "I want to make another heart for my mother."

"Who's the first one for?"

"My...uh, never mind." His cheeks flamed. "I just need two."

"Never be ashamed to have a sweetheart," Bonnie said.

Out of the corner of her eye, she watched as Tabitha dissolved into tears.

"Miss Bonnie, don't you love Mr. Hend—I mean, Mr. Cowboy?" Bobby Joe asked.

"Oh, um, well...sure. Of course, I love him. Growing up he was pretty much my best friend." She sprinkled glitter on a heart.

"My mom said y'all are perfect together and she hopes he chooses you," Jimmy Ray said. "She also fell in love with my daddy when she was in high school."

Bonnie glanced around the room. Chaos reigned supreme. One boy was hopping on a foot around the room, another was trying to wrestle a throw pillow at the reading station away from Naomi so he could use it in a fight against another boy. Sadie balanced Sammy on her hip while she supervised Ellie making a pancake. Sean stood just outside the entrance, patting Tabitha's back. Comforting her.

Guilt sliced through her. Sean really had been her best friend, and she was keeping something significant from him. When she'd arrived, it didn't matter whether or not he knew she'd been hired for the show. She expected to be gone immediately and he'd never *have* to know.

But now, everything had changed. Social media was blowing up with suspicions she was here for the wrong reasons. And he'd apparently ignored it all and had taken her word. Either that, or he simply felt sorry for her. But it wasn't pity she'd seen in his eyes last night.

She may not have come here for the wrong reasons, but it would certainly look that way to Sean, unless she could be the first to explain.

Sean, here's the thing. I took the job because I had no place to go. And yes, I wanted to come home. I wanted to see you even if I thought you wouldn't want to see me.

Her feelings for Sean were still not clear. She kept second guessing herself because she couldn't possibly still love him after all this time. Maybe the tenderness was born out of nostalgia. Out of affection for the memories. They'd basically grown up together. He'd taught her how to love, and it was possible she'd never loved anyone else quite as deeply as she had him, once upon a time.

But she'd come here to simply consider her options and it hadn't taken long. She was done with Hollywood. No more auditions. No more dying her hair a different color to get a part or be forced to accept work as the spokesperson for Oopsie Underwear. She'd get back to basics again, maybe performing in regional theater. Somewhere along the line, she'd let chasing fame become more important than craft.

Now, she wanted a quiet life in her hometown surrounded by family and friends.

. . .

145

BACK AT THE MANSION, after they'd cleaned up, rested, and had dinner, Lori announced, "Sean will decide the winner of the event tomorrow. In the meantime, we have a shocking surprise."

"What *surprise*?" Tabitha said.

"Someone from one of your pasts wants to talk."

"Oh, c'mon!" Angela's palms went up. "We're not on live TV. Tell us already!"

"I want to get an honest reaction when he shows up. It's best for the show." Lori crossed her arms. "If you take a look at the contract you signed, you'll see that we reserve the right to film anything that comes up. Such as jealous exes come back to stake their claim."

"Great," Tabitha whined. "If he shows up now and tries to ruin this for me, I'll kill him."

"Um, we were supposed to be completely single when we came here," Bonnie said. "Do you have something to tell us?"

"No, I broke up with my ex a while ago. I told him I was doing this show. And now that things are going so well with Sean, he'll want to ruin it for me."

"Going so well?" Angela pressed. "What planet are *you* from?"

"Sean hugged me and told me it was all going to be okay."

"Because you were out of control sobbing and he's a gentleman," Angela said.

"It's because we have a *connection*." Tabitha snapped her fingers. "And you two hate me because of it!"

"I don't hate you," Angela said, tipping her chin. "I feel sorry for you."

The doorbell rang in the middle of their dramatic exchange.

"Here he is now," Lori announced. "Elton, we better be rolling."

"We are," Elton said with a weary sigh.

"Make sure all the hidden cameras are on in all the rooms of the house. I want to catch the expression of every nuance and emotion. This is good stuff."

"Hidden *cameras*?" Bonnie said. "Since when?"

"Read the fine print," Lori said, heading to the door. "How can we have a reality show otherwise?"

"You better not have filmed me naked in my bedroom or I swear I'll sue!" Tabitha turned in a circle, searching the ceiling and corners, shaking her fist.

"They can't do that, Einstein, it's a family show," Angela said.

Bonnie would have said something, too, but her eyes were riveted to the front door because someone from her recent past had stepped inside.

CHAPTER 16

*E*ric.

Dressed in all his struggling handsome actor splendor, he strutted inside like he'd been invited here.

Damn it, maybe he had.

"Oh, thank God." Tabitha sighed with relief.

"Who is *this*?" Angela whispered in Bonnie's ear.

Bonnie didn't answer, she simply marched straight to Eric. "What are you *doing* here?"

If the producers wanted drama, she'd give it to them.

Eric's eyebrow quirked. "I didn't like the way we left things."

"Oh, you didn't like the way you cheated on me and forced me to move out?"

"No one forced you to do anything. I would have come home to you. You know I always do."

"Always? Eric, we dated for ten months."

"Can we talk outside?" He slid a smile at everyone in the room, his hands spread out.

See? I'm completely reasonable, ladies. And these are not veneers.

148

Tabitha nearly wilted at his smile and Angela glared at him.

Lori indicated with sweeping motions of her hands, that taking this "outside" would be a nice set change.

"Whatever." Bonnie stomped to the patio, swung open the French doors and then slid them shut.

Elton hid in the bushes with his camera.

She crossed her arms and faced Eric. "*Why* are you here?"

"I've come to fight for you."

She snorted. "Um, *what?*

Okay, so reality TV show acting happened to be the toughest work she'd ever done. She had no script, and everything that came out of her mouth sounded sophomoric. Stupid.

What she wouldn't do for a solid script with good dialogue! Never again would she watch a show and think "good acting." Damn good *writers*, for crying out loud, putting the words in actors' mouths!

"Why is that hard to believe I want you back? You're a good-looking woman."

She jutted out a hip. "I'm good looking. That's all you got for me?"

"What? I thought we got along great!"

"I feel sorry for you if you think we had a good relationship. It just shows me you don't know what the real thing looks like."

He rolled his eyes. "Regardless, you weren't supposed to come into this show when you still had a relationship."

"Eric, look at me." She pointed to her eyes, then his. "We didn't *have* a relationship. I left you and we were *done*."

"Via text message! I need closure. You have to admit it happened fast. And I personally think we *could* have had a chance, if we'd just stuck it out and done the tough work."

She shook her head. "I don't even know what I'm supposed to say to that."

Clearly, Eric was here to further his acting career. He must have not gotten the part in "Vic's" show. The real question remained whether she wanted to let the viewing public know this could be the *only* reason he'd show up. Some small innate sense of self-preservation within her didn't want everyone to know the way Eric had humiliated her. She held back from accusing him on camera for this reason alone.

But did she want to risk Sean wondering if she'd come here with a broken heart, simply using him to feel wanted and beautiful again? No. It was bad enough she'd been originally hired as the plant and was being paid to be here.

She desperately didn't want Sean to know about Eric. He wouldn't understand.

"Eric, I want you to leave."

"You don't mean that." He needed his full fifteen minutes of fame, after all, not five short minutes. "We have a history."

"A short one."

"Look, I know you're here for your ex. The cowboy you used to talk about. But do you *really* think he's going to choose you over some of the other women? You're not a sure thing, Bonnie."

"We're down to three, and he hasn't gotten rid of me yet."

"Maybe he just feels sorry for you. He's going to get rid of you sooner or later."

"So, I might as well just come back with you? You're ready to be my consolation prize? Is that what you want to be?"

He straightened and tugged on the collar of his shirt. "I wouldn't quite put it that way."

"If I come back with you, it will only be because I gave up on getting back the best man I've ever known."

Here's some of that butter, Lori. It helps that I believe it.

This is my reality.

He held his palms out pleadingly. "But I'm *young*. I can learn to be a better man."

"Wow, okay. Eric, you don't care about me. If you think about it, you'll find your truth." She took a deep breath. "I'm not sure you've ever loved anyone."

"Well, I'm not sure you have, either."

Either Eric wasn't acting, or he'd become a better actor overnight. He fisted his hands, his words sharp and brittle.

"Oh, but I *have*. Very much."

AFTER THE CHAOS of the day's group date event, Sean headed to the Shady Grind for a cold beer. He needed the break. After all that chaos with the children, he needed to relax and unwind. He hadn't expected a school full of kids to be easy but he sure hadn't been prepared for the biggest child there to be a twenty-five-year old woman. When he agreed to let the producers choose the winner, he'd never imagined they'd bring on someone who so obviously wasn't ready to be in a serious relationship. Tabitha cared about one person and one person only: Tabitha.

If they asked him to propose to her, he'd honor his contract, but they'd break up the next day.

Tonight, he found the bar filled with women, most the former contestants from the show, and some he didn't recognize.

Levi rang the cowbell they'd had installed over the bar. "Hey, Mr. Cowboy! Drinks on the house!"

Sean accepted claps and fist bumps and slowly made his way to the bar.

"This is something, right? I had no idea this was going on."

"All thanks to you. The women were encouraged to stick around for some kind of 'after the show' thing. Most of them are staying in Kerrville but they come down often for Ladies' Night."

"Plenty of lonely cowboys to go around."

Levi slid him a beer. "Heard the school event didn't go too well."

"Nope."

He was supposed to consult with Lori later and pick a winner but between Angela and Bonnie it was a toss-up. Unless, of course, he asked his heart, which never made logical decisions. It was Bonnie, of course. Always Bonnie. The woman who'd told him she couldn't give him children. He couldn't decide if she truly believed it or if she gave it as an excuse to opt out. But as an adopted foster kid, she of all people should realize he wouldn't mind adopting. Maybe even fostering some kids.

But Bonnie, as always, was a puzzle. He'd watched her with the children and saw nothing but the patience and compassion Jolette Marie had reminded him about.

One of the show's contestants, the fitness trainer, Kristan? Kristen? Kiersten? found a stool next to him. "How's it going? I heard you've narrowed it down to three. And of course, by process of elimination we've already figured out who they are."

"Hmm." Sean didn't want to say much, considering there were enough opinions on the subject.

According to everyone, including his brain, he *shouldn't* pick Bonnie.

"I hope you wind up with Tabitha. She's a sweetie, isn't she?"

Sean took a swallow of his beer and avoided answering.

"Either way, I'm happy I came. It's been *such* a great experience."

"Well, I sure hope you stay awhile, darlin'." Levi winked. "You owe me a dance, Kristan, don't forget."

"Oh, Levi, you charmer."

"Who are you goin' to pick, pal?" Levi asked.

"Jury's still out."

"He's not supposed to say," Kristan said. "It's in the contract."

"Though we'll all be able to figure it out way before the show airs." Levi gave the bar a wipe. "Depending on which lucky lady winds up sticking around for good."

"Until then, we wait." Kristan gave Levi a flirty smile. "And have fun waiting."

One guess as to whose bed she'd wind up in tonight.

Meanwhile, Sean would go home to his lonely bed again. It wasn't as if he hadn't *tried* to get Bonnie out of his system. He'd dated plenty, every eligible woman his age in Stone Ridge. He'd moved on to Kerrville. That's where he'd met Robyn with a y. She was everything Bonnie Lee wasn't, and he'd eventually asked her to marry him, making sure the news got back to Bonnie, because he was still an eighth grader when it came to her.

But he didn't love Robyn enough, it turned out, and she saw right through him.

They were watching Kavanaugh's Way one night and she teased him about his crush on the youngest sister of the Irish mafia family.

"I think we should make a list," she said. "Celebrities we can get a pass on if we ever meet them in real life. We're allowed to cheat with no guilt. Henry Cavill is at the top of my list. I'm guessing that redhead is on yours."

He became so defensive that it led to a fight. "She's full of herself. Of course I wouldn't pick her."

Because Robyn wasn't from Stone Ridge, she didn't know about Bonnie until someone else told her Bonnie Lee Wheeler was a hometown girl. "Sean's first love."

That had spelled the beginning of the end for him and Robyn with a y.

Sean finished his beer, then joined Beau Stephens for several games of darts most of which he won handily. At first, he didn't recognize the buzzing in his back pocket, then realized he had cell reception.

From: Marti, Jr. aka Lori the bane of my existence:

Where are you? I tried your cabin. We need you back on the set pronto! HUGE development!

Great. What now? Had Tabitha pitched another fit? He couldn't take much more. She'd pulled him aside to share how hard it was for her to share "her boyfriend" with other women and how he could be a little more understanding. He should maybe not put his arm around the pretty school-teacher to make Tabitha jealous.

When it came to Tabitha, everything was about her.

Later, he'd had to comfort her after she wound up insulting a child. But he couldn't let a woman cry in his presence, so he'd been stuck being the proverbial good guy again.

Some days he was sick of himself.

"Duty calls." He held up his cell. "We have some kind of emergency."

"I'd love to have that kind of an emergency," Levi muttered.

"No, you wouldn't. I can't even kiss any of these women."

"You're a saint!" Levi clutched his heart.

Not so much a saint as a sinner. He's already kissed Bonnie once and he would have done a lot more than kiss her until she put the brakes on. Just the typical story of Sean chasing Bonnie, a new version now. She should be chasing *him*.

Feeling dread roll through him at the thought of seeing Tabitha again, Sean drove back to the mansion.

Lori met him outside.

"What's up?"

"It's a shocking complication."

"Would you stop talking like a commercial and tell me what's goin' on?"

"Honestly, we didn't seek him out. Swear to you. He came to us, saying he and Bonnie hadn't really ended their relationship and you should know."

Cold dread spiked through him and he wanted to punch a wall. "And what do you want *me* to do about this?"

"This is a development we hadn't expected. Bonnie is in the patio trying to get him to leave."

He scratched his jaw. "Wait. She *wants* him to leave?"

"Good God, keep up! She claims she broke up with him, he says she didn't." Lori held up her palms. "Who to believe?"

"I get it. This is some of that drama y'all live for."

"Yes, and I think we need to get you on film talking to Bonnie about this latest shock."

Sean strolled toward the patio and went through the outside wrought iron gates covered with Spanish moss. Bonnie sat on the patio bench, head in her hands, while some wily guy paced back and forth.

"And in conclusion, for these compelling reasons, I should be given a second chance."

He sounded like a lawyer reciting his closing arguments. This guy must be another actor.

"Please. Just go," Bonnie said.

"I can't. This is my opportunity to fight and I can't let you go."

"Yes, you can. If you try really, really hard."

"Hey," Sean said, coming closer.

Bonnie stood. "*Sean.*"

"Oh, hey. The man of the hour." The dude held out his hand. "I'm Eric, Bonnie's boyfriend."

Sean did not shake his hand.

"No, he's not. He's my ex-boyfriend." Bonnie said. "Actually, Eric, didn't we decide we were roommates? That's what I remember."

"Let's not get caught up in semantics." Eric waved a hand dismissively.

"Well, it's nice to meet you Elvin, but you can go now. I think Bonnie and I need to talk."

"*Eric,*" he corrected, straightening. He slid a nervous look in Lori's direction, who remained off camera. "Um, I think I get a little more time?"

"That's too bad. You're not getting it."

"Dude, if your relationship is rock solid, I'm nothing for you to worry about."

But there had always been something to worry about for Sean when it came to other men and Bonnie. He was possessive with a capital P. Apparently, some habits died a hard and painful death.

He took a step forward and forced himself to speak calmly. "I'm not worried. You should still go."

"I can't."

"But I'm asking nicely."

"Why can't we all discuss this like adults?' Eric turned to Bonnie.

"You don't know *how* to be an adult!" Bonnie said.

"Is that another crack about my age?"

"This doesn't concern you, Elliott." Sean gave him a slight tap to his shoulder simply meant to encourage him to start walking. "You should go now."

"It's *Eric!* Are you stupid or what? And what if I don't want to leave, big guy?" The man shook his shoulders and his arms, adopting a 'come and get it' stance, and giving Bonnie a self-satisfied smile. "Huh? What about that?"

It reminded him of a kid: *how am I doing? Good job, huh? Convincing?*

"Eric, please don't. Just go. *Please*, you idiot."

Sean counted to twenty. Then twenty-five. Thirty. He was a grown man who didn't get in fist fights anymore. Not even with supremely annoying men. Always took the high road. Always.

"I don't know why you want her so much," Elliott said. "She's not as pretty as she used to be."

He could take a whole lot, damn it, but he would not take anyone insulting Bonnie.

Sean's fist went flying so fast even he didn't see it coming.

CHAPTER 17

"*M*y nose! Did he break my nose? I'll sue!" Eric sat on the couch and covered his jaw with the ice pack Tabitha had given him. "This is my *face*. I work with my face! My livelihood!"

"I barely touched you," Sean said, sounding deceptively calm.

This was not quite true. Bonnie saw the whole mess coming and she'd tried to warn Eric. Sean had a mercurial temperament, and he did not back down from any conflict. She almost felt sorry for Eric, because though he'd come here to get some screen time but had no idea he'd be dealing with anyone like Sean. He was accustomed to men who used stand-ins for their fist fights, wore Spanx to award ceremonies, waxed, and enjoyed dual mani-pedi days with their girlfriends.

"I'll take the fist fight out of the final cut." Lori crossed her arms and sent Sean a censuring look. "This is a *family* show."

Sean snorted. "Right."

"You should take the whole thing out," Angela said. "I'm

sorry to say I think this was all a little exploitative of the show."

"Oh, you think?" Lori smirked.

"Really? You're going to cut my *scene*?" Eric lowered the ice pack.

"You poor thing," Tabitha said to Eric, rubbing his arm and repositioning the ice pack. "But I thought it was kind of sexy."

"Yeah?" Eric sat up straighter.

"I was talking about *Sean*."

"It wasn't sexy!" Sean stood. "I lost my damn temper. I'm really sorry, Elvin. But you should apologize to Bonnie. Then we'll call it a day."

"Sean—" Bonnie warned. "It's *okay*."

Had it hurt? Said by anyone other than Eric, maybe. But she considered the source. He was a struggling, often unemployed, actor trying to muscle his way into a tough business. Trying to find his place by taking every opportunity offered to him. Most of the time, she sympathized.

"No, it's not okay," Sean said.

"Well, of course, I'm sorry, Bonnie. You're the most beautiful woman I've ever known. Plus, you're awfully nice, much nicer than anyone else in Hollywood. And I blew it." Eric almost sounded sincere as he bent his head and shook it.

"I accept your apology."

"Great, now we can all be friends again," Lori said.

"Except I still need to talk to Bonnie alone," Sean said, turning to Lori. "*Without* cameras."

The way he said it left no doubt there would be no wiggle room. With that he took Bonnie's elbow, and guided her outside. They walked past the patio and toward the expansive grounds of the mansion. Sean walked them past the pool and chaise lounges. Past the line of Sycamore trees near the edge of the property. He finally let go of her and walked a few paces ahead, lowering his head, and taking in a deep breath.

"Let me explain," Bonnie said, feeling a sense of desperation rising in her.

He shook his head. "What am I doing? *Why* can't I just let you go?"

"Please, listen to me. I didn't come here to make Eric jealous. I didn't come here to revive my career. I came here for you."

"I'm supposed to believe that?"

"Have you ever known me to lie to you?"

"You think he just came here to get some screen time?"

"I have no doubt. This is another acting opportunity for him. Eric doesn't care about me."

"What about *you*? Do you care about him?"

"Only as a friend. If you really want to hear the sad state of my love life after you, I'll tell you. I was lonely when you gave up on us. You were the one who got *engaged*, not me. I was *devastated*, Sean. Devastated."

"Yet you seem fine."

"I recovered but I'm not *fine*. Every day I'm afraid I'm going to lose you all over again. You certainly have plenty of choices. And I know I'm probably not the best one."

He turned, his eyes dark and flashing heat. "Why do you keep saying *I* gave up? You're the one that chose between me and your career."

"But I didn't want to choose! You *forced* me to choose."

"We're going in circles again." He ran a hand through his hair and groaned.

"I know. We do that."

"Aw, damn." He held his hand out to her and when she took it, he drew her into his arms. "I'm still trying to find a way to keep you here. I don't know if you realize this, but I agreed to let the producers choose the finalist. They'll listen to my input but in the end, it's their decision. So, whether you stay or go, it may not even be my choice."

A chill went down her spine. "Why would you *agree* to that?"

"I obviously don't have to get married to whoever they choose. But I have to propose. They agreed to make a donation to the wild horse foundation I'm trying to start. A big one. Riggs worked it into the contract."

"Oh." The realization hit her with the force of a punch.

"I'm not going to stay with anyone I don't love. This is a *show*. Not my reality."

"I've acted in dozens of productions over the years. I honestly didn't know reality TV would be quite like this. It's not at all reality, is it?"

"It might sound strange, but I didn't care. Winona talked me into this. I was all about having fun, a good time, and if I wound up finding a wife, great. Until you showed up and changed everything."

"Angela was right. They've exploited both of us. And I don't know if I can stand by and watch you propose to someone else, real or fake. I already had to hear about Robyn, which nearly killed me."

With the explosive knowledge now between them, Bonnie knew it was time for her own revelation.

"Listen, I n-need to tell you something."

Just do it, Bonnie. Tell him. He'll forgive you. This is Sean.

"I was hired to come here. The producers are paying me."

His fists clenched and unclenched, his jaw rigid. "What did you just say?"

"Let me explain. At first, I turned it down. I assumed you'd get rid of me the first night."

"I should have known." He turned on her, eyes flashing heat and anger. "You came here to hurt me, isn't that right? That's all I am to you. Another acting opportunity."

"No, look at me. I didn't know they were choosing *for* you, and I thought I didn't stand a chance with you."

"So, you thought you'd go for door number two, the money? A job?"

"No, I came here to get *away* from Hollywood!"

"Good, and I'm back to being your consolation prize again." He turned his back to her.

She pulled on him, trying to get him to face her. "I'm giving the money back. I don't want it. And I'll leave here tomorrow if you ask me to. Screw what the producers want. Sean, you didn't deserve this. But I care about you. I would never hurt you intentionally."

"I don't know how I'm supposed to *believe* that."

With those sharp and cutting words, Sean turned and stalked back to the mansion alone.

A sense of complete loss gripped her all over again. She'd ruined this, too, because her dreams were forever in conflict with each other. For one brief second, she'd allowed herself to believe she could have a second chance with her first love. But that would never be true, would it, because she'd waited too long. She hadn't the courage to face him again until now. Too late.

And even though a film crew was waiting, Bonnie stood alone and watched the sun set over the hill in shades of red, blue and gold.

CHAPTER 18

S ean was kissing Bonnie again, against the rules, sure, but ask him if he cared. It felt amazing to be with her again, earth shattering to hold her in his arms, to know she'd come home to him again. It didn't matter why, just that she had. With the way she kissed him, her entire body in it, he wouldn't complain. He reached under her top feeling warm soft skin and traced the edged of her silky bra.

"I'm all yours," she said, removing her top and straddling his hips. She wore a black bra similar to the one in the ad campaign she'd posed for long ago. "Please, Sean, make love to me."

She didn't have to ask him twice. They rolled around in the tangle sheets, burning them up with their blazing heat.

"I've got to go now," Bonnie said suddenly, pulling out of his arms. "I have an audition."

She was fully dressed, wearing a short dress and heels.

He blinked and rolled up on one elbow. "Now?"

"You wouldn't hold me back from my dream, you would?" She canted her head and smiled.

No. He wouldn't. She was beautiful and deserved everything she ever wanted out of life.

"How long will you be gone this time?"

And just like smoke dissipating over a fire, she disappeared.

He woke with a start, clutching nothing but air. Someone was pounding on his door.

What the hell?

He hopped out of bed and threw on a pair of jeans, running down the steps two at a time. This could be another emergency with one of Riggs's and Winona's children. A few months ago, Cal had a high fever. They called in the reserves then, both Delores and Sean. He'd rocked and held Mary, giving her a bottle and later pacing the floor with her. Delores took care of Joe. Riggs and Winona, panicked, drove Cal to the clinic in the middle of the night.

Sean threw open the door to find Winona. "Is one of the kids sick again?"

But she simply smiled and didn't ask for an invitation as she waltzed right past him. "The kids are fine. Put on a shirt."

"You're lucky I put on *pants*. I was sleeping." He reached for s shirt from the pile of laundry he'd left on the couch.

"At six *o'clock?*"

Normally he had ranchers' hours but lately he'd taken advantage of the fact his chores were being done for the next few weeks. A little perk of being on Mr. Cowboy and some extra sleep never killed anyone.

"What do you want?

She took a seat on the sofa and crossed her legs. "I'm sorry but I can no longer take the guilt."

He squinted. "Huh?"

"I didn't want to tell you, but now I feel like I have to."

Sean grumbled then went to the kitchen to make coffee. Winona followed him.

"What do you have to tell me? That I should have never signed on to be Mr. Cowboy? Do I have to remind you this whole thing was your idea?"

He pulled out a filter from the cabinet and started shoveling store-bought canned coffee into it.

Bonnie hated the stuff and called his use of it "criminal." He wouldn't tell anyone, but there was a reason he'd never switched to the fresh ground coffee Delores served. For years, he took secret pleasure in irritating Bonnie, even long distance.

"Sean, you have to understand. I didn't think it would get this far."

"Spit it out, Winona!"

"Okay, okay. I agreed to hire Bonnie for the show."

"You did?"

"Well, of course, it was Beulah's idea to begin with. And I wasn't supposed to tell ou. She wanted to get Bonnie back home. The parts have dried up for women her age, she needed the money and...well..."

"Yeah?"

"Beulah has this mistaken idea that it's *her* fault you and Bonnie didn't wind up together."

"Well, she's wrong about that. And if you're worried Bonnie is going to mess with my head, don't. She's out of the picture."

"That's not what I'm hearing. Lenny said you two took off alone and got away from the cameras."

"Yeah, before I knew why she'd really come back. She told me the truth."

"She did? Oh, phew! And I've been feeling so guilty keeping this quiet."

"Information I could have used before I made a damn fool out of myself, but never mind. She's here for a job. Not for me. Got it."

"You shouldn't be all that surprised she took the opportunity. After all, they're paying you, in a way."

"That's different."

"Is it, though?"

"Once they agreed to the contribution, I didn't see the harm. I figured if I hadn't found the right woman by now, maybe I'd let someone else try. The worst that could happen is another broken engagement."

"And then Bonnie showed up."

"The producers obviously want Tabitha. She's selfish, full of herself, not great with children."

"Well, at least you don't have to marry her. Either that, or she'll grow on you. Look at me and Riggs! And who knows, maybe you'll find someone new in the women who stuck around. I hear the fitness trainer is very nice."

"Yeah." He couldn't argue with that, even if she was currently sleeping with Levi.

"Either way, you could come out a winner in the end. It's time some wonderful woman noticed how fantastic you are."

"Ha! You used to hate me."

"You used to hate *me*."

Ugly rumors had swirled around Winona when she'd first arrived in Stone Ridge. Sean worried about Riggs. Sean thought she'd end their marriage of convenience soon after the twins were born. She'd go back to Nashville, taking the kids with her, and break his brother's heart. Sean knew all about being left behind by the woman you loved, after all. He could give graduate courses on the subject.

But Winona had saved Riggs life when she aimed at the man who'd pulled a gun on him, holding a damn shotgun in her hands. After that, Sean nicknamed her 'the singing Annie Oakley' and forgiven all.

Next, she'd given him nephews he'd teach how to ride a horse and a little angel niece he'd guard with his life.

"Glad we don't hate each other anymore. If you don't hate me, what are you doing here bothering me?" He flipped the switch and started the brew.

"No matter what happens after the show, I want you to wind up with the right woman."

"I don't need your help but thanks."

"You do need my help. This contest was to bring more women. Beautiful women who were dying to meet you once they saw your photo. You're a real catch, Sean, but I'm afraid you're still stuck on Bonnie."

"I'm *not* stuck on Bonnie," He held up air quotes. "She somehow manages to get my attention. I think it's force of habit."

"You agreed to this. And look at it this way: if they choose Bonnie, you'll get to break it off with her later and give her a taste of her own medicine."

"What exactly do you have against a woman who pursued her own dreams of an acting career? Didn't you do the same with your singing career? Isn't that a little judgy of you?"

"I wish I could have met Riggs when I was sixteen, but I didn't. You can bet if I had I'd have never walked away from him."

"You don't know that." He scoffed. "You have no idea how hard it is to be in love when you're *too* young."

Sean didn't know how to explain, either, that his perspective had shifted. He realized on some level he hadn't given Bonnie much room to grow. The only thing that had mattered to him was his own timing and he'd wanted to get married right away. He had ignored Bonnie's very real dreams, which when he considered it, he should have supported better.

"Sean, she's beautiful and I know first love can be tough to get over, but don't let her hurt you again."

"She won't." Sean took two mugs down from the cupboard and poured.

Winona accepted the mug of coffee. "And I know how tough it is for women our age in the industry. When I met

Riggs, I still had somewhat of a career, but I chose him and our family over my everything else. I don't want Bonnie to come crawling back to you because she's come to the end of the line in Hollywood."

Sean didn't want that, either. Much as he thought he might still have strong feelings for Bonnie he'd also never again settle for being her second choice. He'd already been last too many times with her. But Bonnie was right. He'd been the one to put the miles between them because he couldn't accept she didn't want to settle down at the age of twenty-three, get married, and have a houseful of children. When he was younger, he thought she'd rejected him and everything he stood for. A rejection of who he was at the core. A slap in the face.

He might have overreacted.

"Don't worry. What *you* need to know is maybe I've also changed from the man who wanted everything in his own structured time. Plans didn't work when I tried to shove them into place where they'd fit. That didn't work for Bonnie, and it sure didn't work when I tried to replace her with Robyn."

LATER THAT DAY, Sean headed over to the mansion to announce the winner of the school event. The producers' heavily weighed Angela for the win, and Sean didn't disagree. She'd had the attention of every little girl as she read to them patiently, but on the other hand Bonnie had all the boys. Still, the way he felt about her today, he welcomed letting the idea of letting her go.

When he walked in the front door, he met Elton on the way out, carrying some of his equipment with him.

"Oh, hey man," Elton said. "Nice working with you."

"Uh, you too. What's going on?"

"Talk to Lori."

He found Lori in the kitchen on the landline, pacing back and forth. Bonnie, Angela, and Tabitha were seated at the counter.

"Sean!" Tabitha ran to him and grabbed him a hug. "Something is going on. We have no idea what it is. Thank God you're here."

"This is unacceptable. We have a contract," Lori said. "Yes. Yes, of course. I understand, but—you—now, listen here."

He moved to Lori's elbow, which meant having to shrug Tabitha off him to walk.

"I think we're cancelled," Bonnie said.

"Cancelled?" Angela squeaked. "How can we be cancelled? I gave up weeks of work for this gig. My listeners are waiting to hear from me. My colleagues are picking up the slack. What do you mean *cancelled*?"

"I don't know about reality shows, but this happens in the business sometimes. Entire series pilots get filmed, never to be seen again. I've made four of them."

"But this show has been heavily advertised, for weeks!" Angela said.

"I took time off work for this, too!" Tabitha said. "All I want is to get married and have plenty of babies. That's my dream."

When it came out of Tabitha's mouth, the words made Sean inwardly cringe. These were the words he'd longed to hear for so long, but damn if they didn't sound the same coming out of the wrong woman's mouth.

"That's show biz," Bonnie said.

Lori hung up the phone and strode to Sean, hostility emanating from her every pore.

"Don't tell me," Sean said. "We're cancelled."

She crossed her arms. "Not exactly."

"What does that even mean?" Angela stood. "I *demand* an explanation."

"Alright, alright. Calm down. The show is merely postponed. We have a problem with one of the distributors. Once we work it out, we'll pick up where we left off. In the meantime, I've got to get back to California."

"I know you don't think I'm going to stay here waiting for you to come back and resume this show." Angela waggled a finger. "I have a life."

"We all have lives," Tabitha said.

"You can stay here in the mansion and enjoy the free food and accommodations. It shouldn't be longer than a week. Maybe two, tops."

"Two *weeks*? Well, I'm going to need some equipment so I can do my podcast from here," Angela said.

"Fine, I'll have Elton set something up for you."

"I guess I'll go home and stay with my mother for a while," Bonnie said. "She's been waiting for me to visit."

"What about me?" Tabitha held out her arms. "What should I do?"

"Soak up some color," Lori said. "Get to know the place where you might someday make your home if Sean should choose you. Make friends."

"Good plan," Angela said. "And I might consider interviewing you for my podcast if you'll dial back on the drama."

"And folks, needless to say: tweet daily and often, hashtag Mr. Cowboy. Nothing confidential like whose already been eliminated, but little tidbits here and there about how much fun you're having in Texas cowboy country. Yeehaw. You know the drill."

"But what about Sean?" Tabitha's gaze slid up and down his body, and he felt like a slab of meat.

"Needless to say, no one here is *dating* Sean until we get back to *filming.*"

With that, she finished packing, hopped in the Hummer, and the whirlwind that was Lori "Marti, Jr." was gone.

CHAPTER 19

"*S*ean, you really don't have to drive me," Bonnie protested, as he hauled one suitcase after another to his truck.

He'd barely looked at her when he'd walked in the door today, and now he was trying to get her where she wanted to be.

Angry with her or not, Sean was still trying to help.

"I don't think your mother would like it much if I leave you to find your own way to the lake."

"I could wait for Lenny to come back from taking Lori and the crew to the airport."

"You're not going to wait for anyone. I'm taking you." He threw the last suitcase in the bed of his truck and held open the passenger door for her.

Bonnie hoisted herself inside and took one last look at the Truehart mansion. Tabitha stood near the window treatments, arms crossed, giving her a disgusted look.

Even before they approached Lupine Lake, Bonnie could smell the ripe scent of peaches in the air, the light airy smell of lake water wafting through the trees. As she got closer, she heard the rippling sounds usually caused by a duck landing. She'd always loved the stillness and quiet of Lupine Lake, even if moving to one of the cabins after her father died was a step down for the mighty Wheelers. Her mother never treated it that way, though Bonnie assumed it was purely for her benefit. Mama called their move an adventure, living near the lake a thrill, even if it was just a small lake. The cabins were "cute" and plenty of room for two. Bonnie, inspired by her mother's attitude, didn't realize for some time that most everyone in town felt sorry for their sudden shift in fortune.

It took a while to realize she and her mother were "charity cases" the ladies of SORROW and others funded. Bonnie was humiliated to be so needy. Later, she'd allowed them to pay for her entry fees into rodeo contests because she always paid them back with the winnings. She'd been sending money home to her mother for years, part of the reason she couldn't buy a condo in L.A. The other reason was she'd never gotten over the sticker shock of California real estate.

You wouldn't believe it, Mama. A home here costs a million dollars, with no land. You couldn't even fit Daddy's old horse trailer on it.

Bonnie always assumed she'd buy a home when she came home to Texas, full of money, pride, and success. A nice big spread with plenty of acreage.

She turned to Sean, whose features were still rigid and chiseled in anger. He'd hardly spoken a word to her the entire drive.

"What are you going to do with your time off?"

A sharp early autumn wind ruffled his dark hair and her heart tugged. There came the old ache, a love so sharp and swift it almost hurt.

"Don't worry yourself. I'll keep busy."

She didn't allow his hostility to derail her.

"I'm sure Mama and I are going to do a lot of baking. Maybe some canning, too. And I'll sleep in my own bed. Gosh, I've missed that lumpy mattress. I'll go through some of my old stuff I never did send for. There's probably stuff I've held on to for too long."

Like you.

He didn't respond but drove his truck across the rows of cabins to the lane that faced the eastern corner of the lake and their cabin. Her mother's truck was missing.

"It doesn't look like Mama's home."

"You still have a key?" Sean shut off the truck's engine.

"No, but I know right where to find one."

She found the rock in the shape of a frog among the Hyacinths and held up the key with a smile. A little dirty, a little bent, it still fit inside the keyhole after a few honest jiggles and opened the door to...home.

It smelled like peaches inside. And Mama still had the most horrible taste in décor. The mama and her duck's ceramics were still on the windowsill in the kitchen. The curtains were dingy yellow, white, and worn to a crisp. But warm and cozy. Bonnie loved every little bit of it.

Mama, why didn't you at least buy new curtains? Or a new throw rug?

Knowing her she'd probably saved all the money for a "rainy day."

Sean brought in all the luggage. He stood close, smelling like soap and leather, and she wanted badly to kiss him. Hug him. Beg him to forgive her, then take him to bed. But this wasn't possible when she had decisions to make, and a life to overhaul. How could she, at her age, make decisions based solely with her heart?

No. It was time to take a step back, re-evaluate, and decide on a course for the rest of her life.

He reached, gently traced the outline of her ear, then tugged gently on her earlobe. Hope shot through her, new and bright, because this was an old move, one that took her back to reminders of how gentle their love could be.

How quiet and calm at times, when they weren't shattering each other's hearts.

"I'm still so damn angry."

"I know."

"You should have told me sooner. How can I ever trust you again?"

"I don't know."

"That's a bad answer."

"It's the only one I have. Thanks for the ride. I'm going to unpack and take a nap on the old worn and lumpy couch until Mama comes home and puts me to work."

"You know where to find me if you need me." Still kind, even while angry. He took a few steps toward the door, then stopped and turned. "I might be mad, but I don't hate you. I never could."

She watched from the window as he tipped his hat before he drove off.

Then she curled up on the couch, threw the afghan blanket over her legs, and fell asleep within minutes.

Heartache, it worked out, was exhausting.

"AUNT BEULAH WILL BE along for dinner shortly," Mama said later as she and Bonnie worked in the kitchen. "She can't wait to see you."

"And I can't wait to give her a big hug." Bonnie pitted a peach, then put it in a bowl with the others. "You explained the whole wardrobe malfunction?"

"Of course. She understands more than I do how these things happen. You don't know this, but she's become good friends with that Winona James. You know, the singer Riggs Henderson knocked up?"

Bonnie chuckled. "Is that a new saying for you? *Knocked up?*"

"My goodness. Guess my words got a little looser since you've been gone." She shrugged. "It's not so different from knockin' boots. Knock boots, well, you might get knocked up. Anyhoo, you know how hard we've all been workin' on bringing more women to town. This contest was Beulah's brainchild. At first, she wanted to have an email bride exchange, but don't you know, these men of ours are picky. They want to meet the women in person first. They're demanding for someone so lonesome."

"Seems reasonable to want to meet a woman first."

Bonnie had been wondering about something else since she'd been offered the job on Mr. Cowboy. "Did Aunt Beulah tell the producers of the show about me? I assume she did."

"It was one way to bring you home."

"Oh brother! She put together a reality dating show to bring me back home?"

"And a lot of other young ladies too."

"She could have just *asked* me to come home."

Mama went hands on hips. "You would have done that?"

"Maybe."

"Hmph. Is Sean behaving himself around you?"

"You know he is. He's a man of Stone Ridge, isn't he? Opening doors, comforting sobbing women."

"When have you been sobbing?"

"Not *me*. We have a young lady who's quite taken with Sean. She claims to be in love with him at first sight."

Mama guffawed. "What a kick."

"I don't think it's *funny*. She isn't right for Sean."

"Uh-huh. How could she be, when you are?"

"I didn't say that."

"Well, you were thinkin' it." Mama hip checked Bonnie.

"Whether I'm right for him or not is debatable. Even if I wanted to come home and be barefoot in the kitchen, we both know what the odds are of having children at my age. And that's what he wants more than anything."

"Not this again."

"It's true."

"Nothing is written they must be biological children. Those Henderson boys were closer to Marge and Cal than their actual blood family. You can't tell me biology makes a family. *Love* makes a family."

"Mama, that's so very enlightened of you."

She snorted. "Imagine, and I've never been in California longer than a week."

"Yeah, you hated it as much as Sean did."

"Woohoo!" Aunt Beulah's voice called out as she bustled in the kitchen. "What is that *wonderful* smell? I smell peach pie! C'mon over here, Bonnie Lee, and give me some sugar!"

Bonnie went into Aunt Beulah's open arms. "I'm sorry about the other night."

"That's just fine, now. Winona assures me your malfunction problem won't ever see the light of day."

"Thank the good lord," Mama said.

They settled into cooking and baking, the sister's favorite way to connect. Aunt Beulah jabbered on about how many women were still looking for work and places to rent in Stone Ridge. Enough that Sadie's father and his son, Beau, both carpenters by trade, were trying to build more cabins on Lupine Lake as fast as they could.

"You don't have to tell me. I hear 'em banging every mornin' about the crack of dawn," Mama said, setting the table.

"It's a wonderful thing, all this commerce and business," Aunt Beulah said. "All I wanted was to marry off some more

177

of our men, and it looks like I've revitalized the entire town."

"It's amazing how hard men will work when you motivate them," Mama said.

"Uh-huh," Beulah agreed. "That's right, sister."

The spread before Bonnie was more food than she'd seen on one table in years. Chicken fried steak, barbeque ribs, potato and macaroni salad, two peach pies, fried okra, green beans, Beulah's famous three-alarm chili, queso, and of course a pitcher of sweet iced tea.

"What? No pecan pie?" Bonnie joked.

She ate a little bit of everything, feeling almost as if her stomach had permanently shrunk from all those years of watching and counting every calorie she put in her mouth.

"I heard you told the producers all about me," Bonnie said, taking a second slice of pie. "You didn't have to do that. Work would have come along eventually."

"You've had a long dry spell," Aunt Beulah said. "And besides, no harm done in Sean gettin' a good look at what he's missed all these years. He was a daggum fool to let you go."

While it wasn't quite that simple, she didn't want to get into the weeds with two of her favorite people in the world. "At least I always had your support. It meant a lot."

"Was it worth it?" Beulah asked, the question shockingly sincere.

Bonnie heard no recriminations in her tone, only an honest question.

Was it worth it?

"I don't know." It was an equally honest answer. "But I hope to find out while I'm here."

A knock came on the front door, and Bonnie sat up straight, hoping it would be Sean, coming to get her. Coming to tell her they should give up on the stupid show, rip up their contracts, and just get back together.

All three women eyed each other, and spoke without words:

Did you invite someone?

Are y'all trying to fix me up?

Has Sean finally come to his fool senses?

Mama stood. "Who could that be?"

A few minutes later, Mama led Joe Bob Smith into their kitchen, holding his hat. "Good evenin', Bonnie Lee. Miss Beulah. I heard Bonnie was here and I wanted to come say hello."

"Hello, Joe Bob," Bonnie said.

"Please don't get up. I see y'all are in the middle of supper. I'll come back another time."

"You will do no such thing." Mama pulled out another place setting. "I will not let a man of Stone Ridge leave my home without a meal."

"Um, well. That's kind of you."

"Here, now, sit next to Bonnie." Aunt Beulah moved her place setting over. "It's just like old times, when Bonnie Lee had more young men come courting than Maybelle had chairs in the house."

"You're just as beautiful as ever," Joe Bob said, taking a seat.

"Thank you."

A sliver of guilt slid down Bonnie's spine. Joe Bob was the boy who'd had a car when he was sixteen. Bonnie broke up with Sean for about a day before she came to her senses. Most teenage girls were not the wisest people on the planet, but Bonnie had been especially dense. Until she realized she could go after what she wanted herself, she'd only too easily accepted gifts from lovesick boys.

"How's Chantilly doing?" Bonnie asked. Joe Bob and his wife were married shortly out of high school.

"She left about a year ago," he said. "Me and the boys are getting along a bit better now. Their teacher is a great help. She took my boys under her wing and of course like every young boy they have a crush on pretty Miss Sadie."

Oh no. Poor Joe Bob.

"I'm so sorry about Chantilly," Bonnie said, patting his hand. "I always liked her."

"Here's a man with a ready-made family." Mama pointed her fork at Joe Bob between bites. "Two wonderful boys ready for a mother to love."

Bonnie cleared her throat. "Well, they already *have* a mother."

"True, and I don't expect anyone to take her place. Chantilly sees the boys from time to time." Joe Bob accepted the bowl of fried okra from Mama. "But I'm looking for a partner. Someone to fall in love with all over again."

"Didn't you two date a while?" Aunt Beulah asked.

Bonnie gave her a small kick under the table. "About a day, was it? He had a car. I'm sorry, y'all, but I was *sixteen.*"

"This is true." Joe Bob laughed. "But the car sure wasn't enough to keep you."

"Had it been, I'd really have to hate myself."

Another knock on the door, and this time Jeremy strode into the kitchen. He handed her a bouquet of red roses with a smile.

"Welcome home, Bonnie Lee."

I used to change your diapers Bonnie nearly said out loud, but that wasn't quite true. She'd changed his younger *brother's* diapers. Jeremy had been four and used to run around in his "big boy" Batman underwear proud to be potty-trained. He probably wouldn't appreciate how Bonnie remembered this.

"How sweet of you, Jeremy!" Aunt Beulah said. "I'm sorry

we didn't cast you as the bachelor, but good to know you're not holding a grudge."

"That's alright, ma'am, this might work out better for me if I can wind up with Bonnie." He winked.

"Well, now, we don't know who our bachelor will choose in the end. It could still be Bonnie," Aunt Beulah said but she had a mischievous smile on her face.

"Or not," Jeremy said.

"I'll get another place setting," Mama said with a sigh.

It was only then that Bonnie realized why they'd cooked this much food. Not much in Stone Ridge had changed.

Word got around fast.

Mama was still the queen of hospitality.

Cowboys were hungry and lonely.

And apparently, Bonnie was still a hot commodity here.

CHAPTER 20

$\mathcal{T}$wo days later, Sean drove the truck with the trip hopper feed dispenser hooked up, spreading feed for the cattle every few feet. As a kid new to ranching life, their father had the brothers do this chore together. When it came to feeding cattle, Sean had used a whip to keep the cows off Colton while he tried to feed them. They kept knocking him down in their eagerness.

For the horses, Sean would drive the pick-up truck around the pastures since he was fourteen, and Colton would sit in the bed and shove hay out every few feet for the horses. Afterward, they'd kicked back with a cold beer they'd sneaked out of the fridge.

He missed those days. Wonder what the hell his Colton was up to now? And in what part of the world. He was not great at keeping in touch, but Sean could use the idiot's advice right about now. Like him, Colton had never married. There had to be a reason for that.

Why hadn't Sean's relationship with Robyn worked out? His problem, he guessed, was that he'd still been hot-headed. And Robyn had pushed too hard about Bonnie. She'd wanted to know too much about stuff he hated talking about. And when he stopped answering questions about Bonnie altogether, Robyn suspected it wasn't because he had nothing to say.

He had far *too much* to say on the subject.

Too many unresolved issues with Bonnie. Robyn wasn't wrong. Bonnie brought up memories still too sharp and cutting. Like most women, Robyn was far wiser than him. She broke things off even before he had a chance to realize he should have never asked her to marry him.

This kind of mind-numbing work of driving and dumping feed, the cows crowding the truck in their eagerness, did nothing to put the pause on his overactive imagination. He had way too much time to think, that was the problem with this chore. His thoughts kept running to Bonnie and what she'd do with this time off. They kept wandering to concerns on how fast the single men discovered *Mr. Cowboy* was on a weird hiatus, and all the women were to stay away from Sean. Including Bonnie.

Maybelle was a kind and God-fearing woman, who seemed to believe Sean should have nailed Bonnie's feet to the ground to keep her home. She wouldn't be turning away any cowboys who might want to take advantage of the wide berth they'd just been granted.

There were other women here now, but none quite like Bonnie. He had first-hand knowledge that he wasn't the only man to have figured this out.

The question is: *what are you going to do about it?*

He was driving back from the northern pasture when he saw Riggs and Winona near the stables. A few seconds later, Riggs walked out holding the lead to their smallest horse, Oreo, a sweet docile gelding who'd been retired from ranch work for years.

Winona carried one of the twins, from here Sean couldn't

tell which one, and they walked to the corral. The boys were still young, but Riggs had it in his mind to train them to be fearless cowboys, the sooner the better. Cal had already demonstrated an affinity to horses but had to be supervised carefully because like most toddlers he didn't understand horse-spooking rules. Once, he'd nearly given Sean a coronary when he'd gotten a wild burr and crawled under their most ornery horse.

Taking the truck to be refilled, Sean pulled over, then ambled over to the corral. Watching the boys grow up had become one of the single joys in his life. He watched, one foot braced on the rung of the fence, arms draped over the side. Riggs paced Oreo with the lead, warming her up. She was saddled and ready for a rider. Winona stood inside the corral holding who he could now clearly see was Calvin.

"Is he ready?" Sean called to Winona.

"I'm not at all sure," Winona said, chewing on her lower lip. "Riggs thinks it's time for a first ride."

"Don't worry. You know my brother wouldn't do anything to put the boys at risk."

"Oh, I know." She sighed. "But I sometimes think he forgets they're still babies."

Not exactly babies anymore, but he imagined to a mother they always would be. Even when standing in line at the recruiter's office with Colton. He recalled Marge's tears at seeing Colton's crew cut. He'd wanted to sign up for the service from the time he'd been ten.

"You boys don't understand. To me, you'll always be the little boys who showed up and needed a mother. You don't seem old enough to go into battle."

They never would have been old enough, Sean imagined.

"This way we can say he was born to the saddle," Sean joked, trying to ease Winona's obvious distress.

Winona stuck out her tongue. Apparently, she didn't find the humor.

Riggs beckoned to her. "Bring him over, baby."

"Which baby do you want? Me, or him?" She walked over to Riggs.

"Both of you." He tenderly took both of them into his wide embrace, kissing Winona's temple.

The image of them standing in each other's embrace made Sean's world stop for a moment. It was beautiful, their later-in-life romance and family, and had given Sean hope when he thought he mind wind up alone for the rest of his life. He guessed this is why the ladies of SORROW had twisted his arm to be their Mr. Cowboy. Even if he'd tried to pass the whole thing off as a chance to horn dog after some gorgeous women and get a grant for his foundation, he'd frankly had his fill of all that by now. And they'd sensed it in him, may have noticed the way his gaze lingered on Riggs' little family.

But Riggs hadn't planned on any of this genuine happiness, it had all sort of dropped in his lap quite literally by accident.

He supposed it had happened in a similar way for Sean on the day he'd first *noticed* Bonnie. Nothing he'd wanted, having his heart held hostage for the rest of his life. Not at all part of any grand plan.

He resented it, honestly, because at some point he'd realized he had no real choice in the matter. Unfortunately, he'd love Bonnie for the rest of his life even if they had to spend their lives apart. It wasn't as if he hadn't tried to move past her. He was still trying to do that now, taking one step forward and ten back. Bonnie would never be happy here without the acting she'd become addicted to early on. And he would never leave Stone Ridge.

She'd kept him in the dark about the reason she'd actually

come here. Not for him, no matter what she said now. On the other hand, he certainly hoped she could have had a better opportunity if she'd waited for one. She'd once told him how sporadic show business was. One day on top, the other nobody remembered your name. So, maybe she had come here at out of some sense of curiosity about him. He'd likely have done the same, were the roles reversed.

She claimed to have been devastated to hear of his engagement and may have realized then it was too late. He'd wanted her to give up, after all. Wanted her to stop playing with his heart and let him go. She never had and he'd had to force the issue when he saw they would never work. But that was then. Now, Sean understood the way he felt about Bonnie was rare.

He watched for several minutes as the little family before him introduced Calvin to his first ride. He rode in Rigg's lap and squealed with delight.

Sean ducked under the fence and came to stand beside Winona as she watched from the sideline.

He draped his arm around his spark plug of a sister-in-law and chucked her jaw. "You okay there?"

"I didn't honestly think he was serious about this. Cal is just a baby. What if he falls?" She covered her face with her hands.

"If they go any slower time will stop."

"Ha, ha." She turned to him. "Distract me. Is it true they might cancel Mr. Cowboy?"

"All we know is we're on a short break, and the women are to stay away from me. No dating while they're not filming."

"Sounds ridiculous. They can't tell you what to do."

"You and Beulah are the ones to blame for this whole thing."

"And I don't regret it. Everyone in town has a business that has benefited from all this attention."

"We just have to make sure they don't wind up changing Stone Ridge too much."

It would be nice to have fast food closer than thirty miles away but on the other hand, he'd witnessed firsthand what business could do to traffic. Around here, a traffic jam happened when someone's cow wandered on to the road. Three car pile ups were unheard of and he'd like to keep it that way.

"Don't worry, it won't be too much progress too soon. Beulah will put the brakes on that."

"I suppose soon we'll have to incorporate the town. Have a city council and a mayor."

"All that is years away." She crossed her arms, a serene smile lighting up her face. "Just look at them."

And he did, father and son, circling the corral like they would many more times in the future.

It was a damn beautiful sight.

That evening after dinner and a shower, Sean cracked open a cold beer and spread out on his leather couch in front of the flat screen. He would watch the game in peace and quiet. He patted the space next to him for Beer. It was a strange name for a dog, sure, but he'd adopted Beer when he'd found him on the side of the road with four others in a Miller Lite box labeled "FREE." After finding homes for all the others, he wound up with the runt of the litter. Beer looked like a cross between a Border collie and a Beagle, had a cowlick the size of Texas, one ear permanently folded, and ran a little sideways. Other than that, he was a good dog.

By now, Sean had become accustomed to the single life, through no fault of his own. There were good parts of being alone and watching a game without interruptions was high on the list.

When a commercial came on for Mr. Cowboy, Sean leaned forward with interest. He'd only seen it once the time at the Shady Grind.

He pointed at the screen. "Check this out, Beer. That's your old man right there."

This was a different commercial that the first one. Quick photos of the women he'd met flashed across the screen in all their many glamour shots. A few cuts from their group date, and the date with Bonnie, Jackson singing with his band. Short clips of their interviews with the women, most of them gushing over meeting a "real" cowboy. Angela. Jessica. Tabitha. *Bonnie.*

Not surprisingly, he'd lost his anger somewhere between yesterday and today.

In her clips, she didn't gush about her first time meeting a real cowboy. She didn't mention, either, her late father had been the real thing. Instead, she focused on the men of Stone Ridge:

"The men here are loyal, hardworking, and family-oriented. Any one of us would be lucky to wind up with a man like Sean."

Who will win Mr. Cowboy's heart?

Tune in for the first season of this new western reality show where there are no rules to finding love.

He nearly threw something at the screen. "What the hell? No rules? Y'all have all kinds of rules."

He couldn't even see Bonnie because of their stupid requirements. If not for that, he would be over at Maybelle's right now, dragging Bonnie out to the lake or to his ranch. He didn't see any reason they couldn't hang out together while she was still here.

Yeah, exactly. No reason under earth.

And he knew *exactly* what he had to do next.

CHAPTER 21

For two days, Bonnie stayed home and baked pies. Single men kept dropping by unannounced, making her wonder if Mama had put out an ad. If Bonnie wanted them to leave, she had to be polite, and look busy. So, she baked until they left, taking a pie with them.

It helped that baking brought her back to a pleasant time in her life. Before her father died. Before she felt responsible, even in some small way, for her mother. And before she realized that perhaps the only way to make a real difference was to follow her heart and pursue acting.

The scents of peach, apple, pecan, the crusts buttery and flaky, wafted through the small cottage. The entire kitchen was covered in flour dust as she rolled out crust after crust. Dropped them carefully into pie tins, pinched the sides in place. The peach filling was thick, sugary sweet and she shoveled gobs into each pie.

"I appreciate the donations to the bake sale, but you can take a break now," Mama had said just this morning before leaving for work. "Go into town and have lunch with one of your many suitors."

Bonnie had simply smiled, shook her head, and waved her away as she danced around the kitchen, listening to music through her ear buds.

She happened to enjoy the repetitive work because it relaxed her. Her mind flowed freely when her body was physically engaged with a task. This morning it had been Chris Stapleton and ABBA, but now, she listened to Angela's podcast for the first time.

"Don't let anyone say you can't make more money than your husband or significant other. It's a girl's hang-up to accumulating wealth. A barrier. There has to be a mind shift. I used to believe I couldn't possibly make the same amount of money my father did. Believe me, I had flawed thinking. I'd put up my own obstacles to financial freedom. No *man* can give you true financial freedom. That's come got to come from you, girl."

Bonnie wished someone had told *her* this a decade ago and maybe she wouldn't have felt so guilty about wanting to be successful. About wanting her own life, and her own money. She rolled the next crust a little too thin as she took out some of her frustrations out on the pliable dough. Even Mama, who'd been the recipient of Bonnie's hard earned money, had once mentioned that she shouldn't ever make *too* much money, or a man wouldn't necessarily want to marry her. So, it was good to be a working woman, so long as you didn't out earn your partner. Because, God forbid.

Flawed thinking.

Bonnie rolled up the crust into a ball and pounded it a few times with her fist.

Stone Ridge was a bit of a throwback to the old-fashioned days but there were women here now like Winona, and Eve, Jackson's veterinarian wife, who probably did well operating the only clinic in town. Bonnie wished Angela would consider moving here to help bring their few older women into the new millennium.

Or maybe you can do that.

Sure, she could, but everyone here knew her only as Bonnie Lee Wheeler, Maybelle and Buck's daughter. Sean Henderson's ex. The "actress."

She went to Hollywood, don't you know. Never came back. She's gone full tilt L.A. Uh-huh.

Well, damn it, she'd posed for a major ad campaign at nineteen, performed in numerous theater productions to acclaim, acted in a popular series, and one low budget independent film short listed at the Cannes Film Festival.

Please! She was so much *more* than Sean's ex-girlfriend.

"Today, my guest is Tabitha Eden, a neonatal intensive care nurse from Atlanta. Now, we are *not* going to discuss anything related to Mr. Cowboy because we all signed non-disclosure agreements. Tabitha, welcome to *Girl, you Should be a Millionaire*. What's your financial health score?"

Hey, what about Bonnie? She had a few things to share on financial security, such as there *wasn't* any in show business! Get used to living on one paycheck for months until the next one comes. Sometimes, you simply pick the wrong business. One of financial *insecurity*. She wondered what kind of advice Angela would give Bonnie.

Girl, you better quit show business.

Okay, this was too depressing. Bonnie shut off the podcast and went back to ABBA. She danced around the kitchen, putting another pie in the oven and setting the timer, all while singing her heart out.

Dancing queen, feel the beat of the tambourine. Oh, yeah! You can dance...

Bonnie sensed more than heard someone behind her, but before she turned, firm hands were on her shoulders. She startled and whipped around to find Sean giving her a slow smile. Slowly, she wiped her hands on her apron and removed one earbud which paused the music right in the middle of the best part.

He hooked a thumb toward the door. "Door was cracked open."

"Was it?"

"With a taped sign." He held up a piece of paper for her to read.

In Mama's neat cursive writing, Bonnie read:

If you're a gentleman caller, come right on in and stay awhile. Bonnie Lee is baking pies and she could sure use a distraction.

"Are you *kidding* me right now?" She snapped it out of Sean's hands. "Um, *you're* not supposed to be here."

"Who said?"

"The rules, for one." She removed the other earbud.

He wasn't angry anymore and then she remembered: no matter what, Sean couldn't stay angry at her for long. Nothing had changed there, and she added it to the list of steady and reliable parts of her life. Sean would always, *always* be her friend.

And even if she had to stand up for him at his wedding to another woman, damn it, she would be there for him.

"We already broke one rule, what's another?" Sean reached out and tweaked her nose, then held up his finger. "Flour."

She brushed off her nose and pointed. "We c-can't do this. You can't be here. I'm supposed to stay away from you."

"No one said I had to stay away from *you*."

Oh good, more flawed thinking.

But he looked so amazing here in her little kitchen, looking every inch the cowboy. He wore jeans, a flannel shirt unbuttoned to reveal a black T-shirt underneath, his ever-present hat, and work boots. His jaw and chin were dusted with a day or two's worth of beard stubble. Sean was famous for forgetting to shave, she was certain because he knew how women loved beard stubble.

"You need a break from baking pies."

She squinted her eyes at him. "What did you have in mind?"

"For starters, I want to show you my cabin."

"But—"

"Hang on." He held up a palm in the stop sign. "Technically, I'm not dating anyone right now."

"Oh, right. I guess that's true."

"No more group dates, no more ridiculous cocktail parties. Just you, me and catching up."

"That totally makes sense. I don't think anyone would fault us." She was already untying her apron and shutting off the oven.

"Unless you'd rather bake but honestly, it's been a beautiful September so far. You don't want to miss the rest of it by staying inside."

"I thought I was going to see your cabin."

"Quick tour, then we go outside."

Even better. She couldn't be seriously tempted by him if they went outdoors, could she?

"Well, what's it going to be?"

"Fine, I'll come, but you have to take a pie."

A FEW MINUTES LATER, Bonnie stood in front of the cabin she'd seen only once before. This time, she took it all in with the benefit of daylight. She wondered if Sean had hired a landscaper. Colorful flowers like bird of paradise and columbine were strategically placed, giving the house what a realtor friend once referred to as "curbside appeal." A young pecan tree, a live oak, and a magnolia tree surrounded the home.

And of course, the beautiful wrap around porch, empty of any swing or chairs.

"It looks much better than it did in the dark."

Actually, she thought the landscaping had decidedly feminine touches. She waved her hand. "Did your ex-fiancée help with all this?"

"No, Winona helped. I didn't start building until after Robyn broke off the engagement."

So, *she'd* broken it off. Not Sean. Otherwise, he'd be happily married and raising his two point five children, no doubt.

He opened the front door he'd left unlocked and waited for her to walk inside.

"Also, there's a dog."

"A dog?"

"Beer."

"No, thanks," Bonnie said, stepping inside. "It's a little early for me."

Sean chuckled when a black and white sheep dog hopped off the couch and ran to meet them.

"No, *that's* Beer."

She stopped so quickly Sean bumped into her. "You named your dog after your favorite beverage?"

"I found him and his siblings on the side of the road in an old wood Miller Lite crate."

"Oh, poor baby." Bonnie squatted to pet the dog.

"Thanks, it was rough going there for a while, but I found homes for all of them."

She smirked. "I meant poor baby *Beer*. What a rough beginning."

How classic of Sean to rescue abandoned dogs. Dogs. Wild horses. One of the things she'd loved most about him hadn't changed.

"Had I known you had a dog I might have felt safer about

coming inside the other night," she admitted, rising to meet Sean's gaze.

He slid her an easy smile. "Why? Beer's a great wingman. He knows when to disappear."

"Don't go anywhere, Beer." She patted Sean's chest. "I don't trust this guy."

It was the wrong thing to say. She might have had less of a reaction if she'd stabbed him with an ice pick.

"You *don't*?"

"I'm kidding," she said, even if there was a smidgen of truth to the statement.

It wasn't *him* she didn't trust. It was her heart, and what it might do if it had wings. "I don't trust *myself* around you."

"Yeah, makes more sense."

"Okay, mister, don't let *Mr. Cowboy* give you a big head."

He ignored that. "Want a tour or you want to keep yakking?"

"A tour would be nice."

"C'mon, Beer. Let's give the lady a tour." Beer trotted behind Sean. Sideways.

"You must sound ridiculous calling him inside."

For the next few minutes, Bonnie watched an alternate life play before her eyes. Her possible future. This might have been the home she'd be living in, had she made different choices.

Upstairs, three bedrooms and a master one with an attached bathroom and a sunken tub she'd guessed Sean had never used. The home was modest, but also didn't hold back on anything. Downstairs, the kitchen was state of the art with granite counter tops and blonde cabinets to match.

Would she be baking in this big home, too, or wiping running noses and changing diapers? More importantly, how would she and Sean be doing? Still crazy in love or on each other's last nerve because she'd given up on her dream?

Would he love her or resent her for getting a faraway look in her eyes and secretly wanting to be somewhere else?

Don't think about any of that right now. Just be in the moment.

Still, the past stood between them like a solid brick wall.

"Let's go outside." Sean held open the slider leading to the backyard.

He didn't have any fencing and land seemed to stretch ahead of them for miles. The beautiful green and gold of Hill Country. Beer ran ahead, yarking, chasing after some critter or another.

"He loves it here," Bonnie said. "Look at him go."

"Runt of the litter on his second life. Dogs aren't like cats with nine lives. They only have two."

"Two?"

"Just like people. Why do you think they're man's best friend?"

"Sean, we only get one life. Not *two*."

"I realize that, Skippy. Read between the lines. I'm talkin' about chances. Two chances in life."

"Only two?"

"If you're lucky." He offered his hand to her.

Together they walked hand in hand, following Beer and his silly puppy antics. He chased after the fluffy white tail of a wild rabbit, then gave up and went for a bird that had the audacity of landing on his pasture.

"Sean? Tell me why didn't it work out with Robyn. I mean, you were engaged, and I know you don't take that sort of thing casually."

"She didn't think I was ready to commit."

"That's the most ridiculous thing I've ever heard! Did you tell her you were ready to commit at eighteen?"

"Not ready to commit to *her*," Sean clarified.

Her stunned heart slammed against her rib cage. "Oh. *Oh*."

He gave her a sheepish look from under lowered lids. "It was a mistake. I rushed into things. Just wanted to get on with having a family, building a life. It doesn't work that way."

"No, it doesn't."

"What about you? Did any man ever come close to stealing your heart?"

"Other than you? No, I was career focused for years. I dated some here and there, but mostly actors. They were the only men I ever met."

"What about Edwin? Did you love him?"

"*Eric.* And no. As a friend, sure I did. Don't laugh, but I sort of took care of Eric. Took him under my wing. He was so hapless at times, kind of like a lost puppy."

"Jolette Marie reminded me how even though you said you never wanted kids, you were always looking out for her and those younger than you."

She stopped in her tracks. "Wait a second. I *never* said I didn't want kids."

"Okay, sorry. I thought—"

"I didn't want children when I was *twenty-three*. That doesn't mean I didn't want them at some point. I just...I thought it would be before now. It didn't work out, I guess."

"I'm an idiot."

"*Why?*" She squeezed his warm hand.

"I pushed you into making a choice. I should have waited and been patient."

"Oh, Sean. It wasn't entirely *your* fault."

"Can you tell me for sure we wouldn't have wound up together if I hadn't broken up with you? If I hadn't stopped taking your calls and waiting for you to come home?"

"But you were right in many ways. I failed to put you first and that's important in a relationship."

He didn't answer, but kept walking, holding her hand, keeping an eye on Beer.

"Hey, buddy. Beer! He doesn't usually go that far ahead of me. Something must have his attention."

Bonnie laughed. "I was right. You sound silly calling him. Beer! Come here, I need you! Please be cold when you get here."

"Ha, ha." But Sean let go of her hand to walk a few paces ahead. "Ah, there he is just up ahead."

No sooner had Sean spoken than the unpredictable Texas sky opened up and dumped a deluge of water.

CHAPTER 22

"Beer! Beer!" Sean called. "Just my luck to have a dog too dumb to come in out of the rain."

"It's fun for him. Some dogs love the water." Within minutes, Bonnie's hair dripped like she'd been in the shower. She held her hand low on her forehead to block the raindrops from her eyes. "Beer! Gosh, I wish you'd named him something else. *Anything* else."

"Just go inside. No need for us both to get soaked to the bone."

"No, I want to help."

Thunder boomed and the storm rolled in. They both called out the name of Sean's favorite beverage for what felt like hours but was probably only minutes.

Eventually, Sean walked deeper into the woods and yelled at Bonnie to go back.

Shivering from the cold, she gave up and ran to the house.

Inside, she dropped puddles of rainwater on the gleaming hardwood floors. She found towels in the bathroom downstairs and wrapped her hair in one. Twisting her shirt, she wrung it out over the wash basin. Slipping off her boots and jeans, she wrung those out too, then tried to wrestle the pants back on, but they'd shrunk two sizes. Instead, she wrapped a towel around her waist.

After a few minutes, she peered out the window. Anytime now, they'd show up, soaked. Sean would be perturbed. Understandable. A dog *should* come when called. She got towels ready for both of them. But when a few minutes later there was still no sign of them, Bonnie wondered if she should use the telephone tree. *The telephone tree for a stubborn dog?* But what if Sean was in trouble? What if he needed her, and she was inside, warm and comfortable?

Panic seized her, tightening every muscle, and she wondered if she'd come this far, come home again with her tail between her legs, only to lose him for good.

But no, it was simply rain, an autumn shower, and no self-respecting Texan would be intimidated by a little water. Still, there was a river nearby, and what if...okay, no.

On the wrap around porch with no swing, Bonnie cupped her hands around her mouth and shouted Sean's name. Over and over again she called the name of the man she'd loved since she was old enough to understand what love meant.

Please, please, please. Come back and I'll tell you everything.

Just give me one more chance. Please.

She wanted to marry him and live the rest of her life here, and what did it matter if she couldn't give him children? They'd adopt, or they'd foster children. Or maybe IVF. Something. These were small details in the grand scheme of things. The important thing was she wouldn't let him go this time. She would fight for him.

And for that, she needed him to be alive. She picked up the landline and dialed Aunt Beulah.

"Hey there, sugar."

"I want to active the phone tree."

"What's *happened*?"

"I'm...over at Sean's getting a tour of his new house and—"

"What on earth are you doing over there? I thought you were going to play this hard to get!"

"I don't know what you're talkin' about, but I want some help over here. Since it started pouring, Sean hasn't been back for several minutes. He's out there in the woods, alone, looking for Beer."

"Dear Lord above! How many did he have before he went lookin' for some in the woods?"

"No." Bonnie face palmed. "His dog, Beer. That's his name."

"You want me to alert the men to come help Sean find his *dog*?"

"Okay, I know it sounds silly, but—" Just then she heard the front door slam shut. "Never mind."

Sean stood in the foyer, tall and rigid, holding Beer in his arms. Muddy and drenched, they both looked like maybe they'd been for a dip in the river, but thank you God, they were alive.

She grabbed the towels and ran to them.

"He was caught in a patch. That's why he didn't come when I called." Sean squatted on the balls of his feet and set Beer down.

Together they patted the poor puppy dry while he whimpered and whined. Bonnie reached to grab another towel when Beer shook himself off, hurling rainwater on everything within a few feet. Floor and walls. Bonnie's eyes and nose.

Both she and Sean jumped back, their gazes met, and they burst into laughter.

"I saw that coming," Sean laughed as he continued to mop up the mess, wiping off mud and rubbing Beer dry.

"I was worried about you two."

"Why? It's just a little water."

"I know, but I...I just...when you didn't come back for a while..."

"You thought I got lost on my own property?" He squinted, his long, wet eyelashes practically curling.

"No, of course not." Now that she thought more on it, her paranoia about this moment made no sense at all.

Unless she framed it in another context.

Like an old memory, slicing sharp and deep. The overwhelming sense of loss when he'd cut her off and stopped taking her calls or responding to her text messages. When Mama called to tell her of Sean's engagement. When she attended his father's funeral and saw him and his new fiancée together. Embracing and supporting each other through the grief.

That should be me, she'd thought, and Mama's words haunted her: *I told you so.*

Bonnie hadn't just lost her lover; she'd also lost her best friend.

How had she dared to imagine he'd always be hers? Total hubris. She'd learned her lesson and earned a shattered heart in the process.

She watched him now, his clothes plastered to his body, outlining his hard and tough physique. Not only did he rescue dogs, horses, and people, he did it while built like a cowboy.

"What's wrong, Skippy?"

Oh, right. She seemed to be crying a little, and she wiped the tear which had rolled down her cheek.

"I love you."

He blinked at the sudden words and straightened to his full height. His eyes darkened, his jaw stiffened. For a moment, she thought he'd lose his temper and ask her whether she thought this was a good time to realize this fact. But she couldn't help the timing. Her dreams had never been in line with his, and their timing left a lot to be desired. That hadn't changed. But love had never been the problem.

He took her hand, pulled her up to stand without words. Then he tugged her upstairs.

"I'm sorry about the timing. I know, it's not the best. But I mean it."

He stopped abruptly at the top of the staircase. "Beer, make yourself scarce."

The puppy, who'd been following them upstairs, seemed to understand as he turned around and went back to the couch.

"Oh my gosh. You were right."

"We both need a warm shower." In the master bedroom bath, he turned on the shower head and bent to adjust the knobs.

His gestures were so deliberate, so mechanical. Almost hostile.

"Are you *mad* at me?"

He might want sex, but she wasn't going to have angry sex without knowing what they were fighting about. She expected a hug, kiss, or at least some type of reciprocation.

Words. Acknowledgement of her bleeding heart. Sean had never been short on either.

"No."

The single word answers were so uncharacteristic for him that she tipped her chin and hardened her resolve. "If you want to kill me, just *say* it."

He faced her, his gaze softening. His fingers curled around the baseline of her neck. "Why would I want to kill you? I love you."

The words pierced her with joy and her eyes went watery all over again.

"Then why are you angry?" She took his hand from her neck and brushed a kiss across his knuckles. "What did I do?"

"I'm not mad at you, Skippy. I'm mad at myself. Because *you* had to say it first.

Because I was too damn proud to come after you when I changed my mind. Because I tried to run you off the show and only kept you around to make you jealous."

With each 'because' he took off a piece of his clothes. The sopping wet corduroy jacket, the flannel button-up, the long-sleeved T-shirt underneath. His jeans.

"Because I wasted too much time. Including all the days since I've been back." Joining him, she pulled off her blouse and dropped the towel from around her waist.

His gaze heated as he slowly peeled her panties down. "No more wasted time."

Their naked, damp, and clammy bodies entwined for a long, deep kiss before Sean stepped into the shower and she followed him inside.

Then, nothing but warm water, soap, and a peeling away of all layers. Slippery, they grappled for each other, trying to hold on.

A metaphor for their relationship if there ever was one.

Finally, Sean used his arms to brace her against the hard granite wall. His beard stubble scraped against her neck and her breasts but none of it hurt. It felt like branding, like he was claiming her all over again. Then he went lower and lower, going to his knees, kissing every part of her burning flesh.

"You're still so beautiful," he murmured against her thighs.

She felt far more than beautiful with Sean. She felt seen. Corny? Maybe, but only he had ever bothered to look under the façade, and past all the walls she'd built to protect her heart.

Her beauty had faded, but the love she had for Sean had never even dimmed.

"I love you so much it hurts," she said, pulling him to stand.

"I know what you mean."

He pulled her tight into his strong arms, and a thick and heavy sweetness wrapped around her heart.

"This is my second life," She whispered against his neck.

"Mine, too."

He gave her a slow and wicked smile, his hands lowering to her ass, his kisses slow, hot, and lazy as he took his time plundering her mouth.

When they came up for air, Bonnie threw back her head, arched her back, and let the warm shower spray her hair clean of rainwater.

Sean turned her and did the same for his head, then shook his hair like a dog and laughed.

After that, they both stopped laughing for a very long time.

SEAN HAD FANTASIZED about this moment for years, and though sometimes his expectations never quite met with reality, Bonnie had always been his exception. Her body was still beautiful and firm, with curves in all the right places. He'd always loved a woman's hourglass shape. Her long legs were firm and wrapped around his back. She surprised him, her aggressiveness and eagerness gratifying.

He protected them both, then thrust into her over and over again, so eager himself that the headboard smacked against the wall. Bonnie cried out in pleasure, arching her back, lifting her legs higher, her body tightening around him. He couldn't hold back his own release for another second.

Breathing hard, he tucked her sweaty body next to his. "*That* hasn't changed."

"It's the one thing that hasn't. We always could burn up the sheets."

"More like the blankets on the bed of my truck." He pressed a kiss to her warm temple.

"Or a blanket thrown over the meadow."

"We had to be creative. We're grown-ups now, and we can do it anywhere we like."

"Including the shower stall."

"So, I got a little over-eager." He rubbed her back. "Did I hurt you?"

"My back is a little bruised but nothing I can't handle. Worth every second."

"Hey, just because I have a house doesn't mean I won't invite you to my truck bed again."

"I'll bring the blanket."

She buried her face in his neck. "I missed you so much."

Outside, the rain continued to slam against the windows, hammering the roof. "I don't know how to break this to you, Skippy, but I think we're stuck in here for a while."

"Why? You're afraid of a little water?"

"No, but I'm taking my opportunities when and where I find them."

"You were always the smart one." She kissed his pec, then sighed. "What are we going to do now, about the show?"

"I'm guessing we broke every rule."

"*Broke* is not a strong enough word. And rules? Let's toss that word out too."

"I don't care. Do you?"

"No, but I don't want this to be bad for you. You know, 'bad bachelor' makes his way through the women before he chooses one. Tries them all on for size. That's how rumors get started."

"It almost sounds like you had firsthand experience."

"You don't want to hear about it."

"Maybe I do."

"Only if you promise not to get mad."

"I'm so happy right now I doubt anything could get me angry."

"Remember those photos of me modeling underwear? The ones that made you so jealous?"

"I was *young*."

"I know. But you weren't completely wrong. For a while, everyone saw me as the 'underwear girl' and assumed I'd do nudity. I almost got typecast."

"But you kept at it. You never did any nudity."

"You've watched all my work?"

He smiled sheepishly. "Of course I did. And I had to drive to Austin to see the independent film."

"Did you watch the mafia show regularly?"

"Sure, we all did. The whole town. Even Riggs. You kicked ass on that show."

"I loved playing a dangerous woman. The writers we had were geniuses. It's some of the best work I've ever done."

"Why did they cancel the show?"

"We couldn't get the headlining actor to sign up for another season. They considered killing him off and letting me take over the family business, but in the end, they scrapped it."

"Or I would probably still be watching it."

"It means so much to me that you supported me all these years, even from a distance."

"I always wanted you to be successful."

"Some old boyfriends would have wanted me to fail. But you're not most men."

"The whole reason I let you go is because I didn't want to hope you'd fail. Coming home to me meant you'd failed."

"I wanted it all. Someone should have told me it's a myth."

"You can have it all, just not at the same time."

"Ah. You're so wise." Her palm pressed to his chest, she felt the slow rise and fall of his breaths. "Tell me more about these wild horses. When did this become such a passion?"

"A few years ago I was down in New Mexico at a cattle auction, when someone told me about a group of horses they'd corralled. A foundation gathered them up, and cowboys came from all over to adopt them. If you can break the horse, you can have him for free. Tank was my first wild horse."

"Did you break him?"

"With Levi's help, yes, we did." His voice took on a distant tone. "I wish I could make a home for all of them, but we don't have enough land. So many of them suffer because they have nowhere to graze. They're dying without food and water. Not enough people know about the plight and others assume that it's best to let the wild horses roam free across the land the way they have for hundreds of years."

"And that's wrong?"

"It's cruel. They're dying and there's no reason for it when we can save them. For a few years now I've wanted to start a foundation to provide enough space, feed and water for wild horses. They don't all have to be broken and they don't all have to work but it's cruel to let them die out there alone."

"It's such a worthy cause. I never knew."

"Guess we all have dreams."

"I'm sorry my dreams were so big."

"Don't ever be sorry about that, baby."

"I'm proud of what I accomplished but I'm also sick of giving so much else in my life up just to be successful." She played with the soft hairs on his chest. "What's going to happen to us?"

"I don't know." He took her hand and kissed it.

"We have to take this a day at a time."

"It won't always be easy. You're going to get bored. I'm going to lose my temper sometimes. I'll have to pull a cow out of the mud every now and again. Beer is going to come in smelling like cow patties. We're going to fight."

"And then we're going to make up. My favorite part."

"Correction." He rolled on top of her, pressing her into the bed. "That's *my* favorite part."

CHAPTER 23

The rain abated, then came down again for hours. Bonnie spent the day wrapped in a tangle of sheets, catching up on years of missing Sean's strong, firm body pressed against hers. Finally, they came up for air, and talked about everything, including the short time they'd lived together in L.A. They both carefully avoided minefields on the subject of how unhappy he'd been.

She heard firsthand how difficult the years after their father died had been for the brothers. Colton decided to enlist in the Army and hadn't been home in years, stationed overseas. The two youngest brothers were always close, and the emotion in Sean's voice when he spoke about Colton was palpable. It occurred to her that he'd had two significant people snatched out of his life. Four, if you counted his parents.

Later, Sean made a fire, and they ate popcorn and watched old movies while dressed in very little. She wore Sean's bathrobe and nothing else underneath, delighted it smelled like him. Woodsy and freshly cleaned. Sean had pulled on a pair of jeans but didn't bother with a shirt. They were keeping each other warm.

Beer sat at their feet, begging for scraps. Every now and then Sean threw him a kernel which Beer caught mid-air.

When Casablanca ended, Sean used the remote and switched to *Kavanaugh's Way*, season one. "Here we go."

"No! I never watch myself." She wrestled the remote from him.

"You *never*?" He held it out of reach. "Why not?"

"Why would I? It makes me cringe."

"So, you've *tried*." He went her a wicked smile. "What's it like?"

"Um, *cringe-worthy*. I silently criticize and sit in judgment of every move I make. Every word I say."

"You were damn good. I think you're being too harsh."

"That's nice of you to say but Sean, remember, I played the youngest daughter in a crime-syndicate family. She was bitchy, unhappy, and raging with anger at the world."

"And?"

"I lived every day in her skin. After a while, I realized it wasn't just *Meghan Kavanaugh* who was miserable. I was, too."

"Yeah?" He set the remote down.

Drawing her into his arms, he caressed the soft hairs on the back of her neck, causing an all-body tingle.

She curled into him. "I had everything I'd ever wanted, or at least thought I wanted, and I hated my life."

"I'm sorry, Skippy." The words were soft, tender, and her heart tugged in a sweet ache.

And even though he'd been the one to cause that misery when he'd given up on her, she'd forgiven him right at his father's gravesite. Nothing in life had been easy for Sean, not from the moment he'd been born into the world to parents who chose their addiction over their children.

"But...I've got to be honest with you here." Sean stroked

her spine in slow up and down motions but sounded deadly serious.

"What is it?"

"I thought you were *hot* on that show. Sexy as hell."

Relieved, she chuckled. The show had nearly made her a sex symbol, which had never been her goal. Every week she'd fought with the director and wardrobe to be fully clothed in her scenes. The closest she'd ever been to nudity was a silky red bathrobe.

"You didn't get jealous watching your ex-girlfriend with other men?"

"I had lost the right to be jealous." He tugged on a lock of her hair.

"If anyone had a right, it was you. I got delusional mail from boys jealous I'd slept with the FBI informant on the show. They thought I was *their* girlfriend, and how dare I?"

His eyes narrowed. "You mean stalkers?"

"I had a few but nothing to worry about. Worse were the women who hated me for 'being mean.' to the men." She held up air quotes. "The guys who kill their rivals are fine, but when I did the same, I was bitchy."

"*Bitchy* when you shot the man who'd framed your father for a mass murder?"

Surprise thrummed through her and utter delight to know she'd been in his life in some small way. He wasn't exaggerating.

"You really did watch the show."

"Every episode." He cleared his throat. "It may have cost me a relationship."

"Robyn?"

"We used to watch the show. She didn't know about you, but once she found out, she accused me of cheating by proxy." He shook his head slowly.

"That's ridiculous. You're not a cheater, never have been."

"No, she was right. My body never cheated but my mind and heart did. I'm not very enlightened. It took me a while to realize I watched the show to feel closer to you. But it was one of the reasons. Because I never got over you."

She crawled into his lap and framed his face in her hands gazing into his amber irises. "Please know this. There has never been *anyone* else for me besides you."

Outside the rain had slowed, and the fire's flames kicked up and crackled with heat. The scent of wood filled the air.

Sean's calloused hands slid down her bare thighs. "Damn I feel lucky."

IT WAS ONLY MUCH LATER that Sean realized he hadn't just broken one rule. He'd violated an entire contract and it didn't sit well with him. His actions were less than honorable. He was supposed to be Mr. Cowboy, allowing the show to find a woman for him to fall in love with and bring home to Stone Ridge. Instead, he'd reunited with Bonnie Lee. But hell, it was the producers who had brought her here.

How was he supposed to propose to someone else when he'd fallen back in love with Bonnie? Everything had changed, except the contract.

He should really talk to his brother, the lawyer. Riggs had reviewed the contract for him, after all and written in the option for the large grant.

"I'll talk to Riggs today," Sean said, as he pulled a t-shirt on.

He had chores he'd neglected by engaging in marathon sex.

"Riggs? Why?"

Bonnie, still half-dressed and wearing only her bra and panties, gave him a hard-on just by looking at her.

"He reviewed the contract. I don't want to propose to

whoever they choose now. I didn't know you'd be here when I agreed to this."

"And I'm at least in violation of doing far more than kissing you off screen."

"We both are." He bristled at the thought of not living up to a promise he'd made. "What can they do to us? Burn us at the stake?"

"No, but they can sue us."

"If I do anything to risk our ranch, I'll never forgive myself."

"They won't come after your ranch. Look, I have an idea." She stepped behind him and wrapped her arms around his waist. "We'll keep us a secret. No one has to know."

"I don't want to keep us a secret."

He fought the urge to be pissed at the suggestion. She was only trying to help.

"Me, either. You think I want to see Tabitha keep fantasizing about you? I want her to know right away that you're mine no matter who you propose to."

"Okay, yeah. I was right. You were jealous. *Are* jealous."

"Of course, I am, dummy! I was 'acting.' I'm jealous every time you even look at another woman."

"You're a damn good actress. So, I'm supposed to make you miserable by pretending Tabitha or Angela have a chance with me?"

"Yes, because they do. You don't know who the producers will choose. But I'll know the truth. And I won't be miserable." She hesitated a beat. "Well, I'll try not to be."

"I guess you're right. It's not like I'm even *kissing* anyone else."

"Don't even joke about that."

"C'mere." He tugged her into his arms. Smooth soft and silky skin under his hands made him want to forget about ranch chores.

He wondered if he'd get anything done when she moved in with him. But he was getting ahead of himself. They had things to resolve first.

The doorbell rang and Bonnie startled. She pulled out of his arms, grabbed her jeans, and pulled them on. "You have company."

"Probably Riggs or Winona." He took the steps down two at a time, Bonnie following.

But it wasn't Riggs. Not Winona.

Tabitha.

"What the...?" Sean cursed. "It's freaking *Tabitha*."

"Oh, no! She can't know about us." Bonnie rushed back up the steps and made crazy motions with her arms. "Get rid of her."

"Sure." Bonnie upstairs, Sean opened his door, and tried to pretend a visit from Tabitha was the most natural thing in the world. "Hey there. What are *you* doin'? You're not supposed to be here."

"I won't tell if you don't." She didn't wait for an invitation but pushed her way inside. "Lenny dropped me off and he's waiting down the lane. I thought you might want some company. I know I do. I just finished Angela's podcast earlier today and now I have nothing else to do."

"Well, I have chores."

Tabitha ignored that, too. "Do you have some coffee? I love some coffee on a rainy day."

"It stopped raining."

"Even so. It's still wet out there." Walking further into the house, she scanned every room. "This is nice. I think I could raise a family here."

He cleared his throat. "Look, I'm busy."

"Just one cup of coffee and then I'll go?" She stuck out her bottom lip in a pout which made her look twelve. "I know you don't want to be inhospitable."

"Just one cup." He stalked over to the machine and pulled out a mug from the cupboard.

Evidence of his and Bonnie's random kitchen foraging after sex was evident everywhere. Paranoid, he quickly threw the popcorn bowl in the sink and rinsed the two cups they'd used earlier.

"Milk and sugar?"

He turned to ask and Tabitha had removed her top and stood in her frilly pink bra.

"Just milk." She smiled.

"What the hell are you doing? Put your shirt on!" he yelled and threw the kitchen towel at her.

"I know we can't kiss, or anything else." She licked her bottom lip. "But I thought I'd at least give you the chance to view the merchandise."

"Jesus! Tabitha, you don't even know me."

Was he shouting? Yes, he was. With Bonnie upstairs.

"But I want to get to know you." She stepped closer.

"Then you'll have to wait until the contest resumes. I signed a contract and I want to honor my word."

Liar, liar, pants on fire!

He winced. Upstairs, he heard something drop. Something...large. It might be a lamp, or a...he didn't want to even consider what Bonnie might be breaking.

"What's *that*?" Tabitha quickly pulled her shirt back on. "Is someone else here? You didn't tell me you're not alone!"

"I am alone. It's probably my...cat," Sean lied. "She...likes to push things off tables to piss me off."

"My cat is the same way! They'd probably get along. Can I meet her?"

"Another time. You...you better go. I need to feed her before she breaks everything I own." With two hands on her back, he firmly but gently pushed Tabitha toward the front door.

"Phew, for a second I thought you were cheating on me."

"I can't *cheat* on you, Tabitha. We're not together."

"Technically we were dating just a few days ago."

"Right. I was dating *three* women, not just you." He held open the door.

"If you're bored, Angela is looking for people to interview for her podcast while she waits. She's probably going downtown to start asking around."

"Sorry. A rancher is never bored." With that he shut the door in her face.

He turned to find Bonnie standing at the top of the stairs, arms crossed, hip jutted out.

"How does *she* know where you live?"

CHAPTER 24

*I*t took another hour for Sean to assure Bonnie that he hadn't invited Tabitha over, at any point, and remind her that finding out where he lived would be as easy as asking Lenny.

And to think men outside of Stone Ridge went through this kind of jealousy thing all the time.

Once again, they agreed to be discreet, but Bonnie swore she'd find a way to sneak out again soon.

An awkward silence passed between them when he drove Bonnie home to her mother's house. Lupine Lake was now the busy site of new construction on the south end of the lake. Bonnie asked him to take the long way around to her cabin and avoid all the trucks and activity.

"You can't walk me to the door," Bonnie said when he pulled up to the house.

"The hell I'm not," Sean said, coming around to open the passenger door. "Your mother will tan my hide if I don't say hello."

"She might tan your hide if you do."

"I'll take my chances." He offered his hand and walked with her up the short staircase.

"Okay, this is good." She said at the top step. "You don't have to come in."

"I'm coming in to say hello and that's all there is to it."

She sighed and threw open the door. "Mama, I'm home, and look who I ran into!"

Sean quirked a brow and Bonnie shrugged.

"Hey, Miss Maybelle. I read the sign. Bonnie needed company, you said so."

Maybelle lowered her eyeglasses and peered from over them. "Uh-huh. Thank you."

"My pleasure." He offered Bonnie his hand. The same hand which had caressed every inch of her soft body not long ago. "See you when the contest starts up again."

She shook his hand, giving him a wink. "Yes, see you then."

Then, back to her mother, Bonnie mouthed, "tomorrow night."

"Good *day*, young man," Maybelle said, clearly meaning 'please leave now.'

"Ma'am." He tipped his hat, then quickly squeezed Bonnie's hand and was out the door.

This whole sneaking around thing wasn't going to fly with him. Not for long. He'd roll with it for now but when Lori got back, they were going to have a long talk. Sean knew who he wanted to be *Mrs.* Cowboy and if that hadn't changed in roughly twenty years, it wasn't likely to now.

Chores over, it was nearly supper time when Sean knocked on the door to Riggs' home. He opened the door and waved him inside.

"I swear I didn't drop by for dinner." Sean threw his palms up. "I have something important to talk about."

Winona joined them, Mary on her hip. "Delores made her fried chicken. Don't try to tell me you didn't know."

"I swear, just lucky. Had no idea."

"Come in, Sean!" Delores called out from the kitchen. "I made enough to take over later, you might as well eat here with the family."

The two little toddlers, Cal and Joey, ran up to him at once and grabbed a hold of each leg.

They babbled in words only their mother could probably understand, but he heard "Shaw-ee" in there somewhere, which was what they called him most of the time.

Riggs picked up Joey and Sean picked up Cal. They carried the boys to the twelve-seat farmer's table in the new formal dining room where Delores had spread out her weekly supper. It had been decided early on that Delores would stay with Riggs and Winona, considering they had twins and only twelve months later, Mary.

After his mother's death, Delores settled into the role of pseudo-mother, cook and housekeeper. But far more family than employee, Delores always made sure Sean had a home-cooked meal, too.

So much had changed in the house since Winona moved in, but Sean admitted all the changes were for the better. They'd added on to the main house where Sean, Colton and Riggs had been raised. Instead of Delores living in a cabin within a short walking distance, they'd made a separate wing of the house for her to live in. Delores and her husband never had any children, and the Henderson boys, Marge's boys, were like her own. Now, Cal, Joey, and Mary were like her grandchildren.

Sometimes a found family really was the best kind. There was a greater appreciation of each other, an under-standing that a loving family wasn't a right but a privilege. With three highchairs, the dining room often resembled a daycare. Every few feet, Sean often found a dropped pacifier on the floor or a plastic teething ring. It was utter chaos most days.

And he loved every minute of it.

He came over every chance he could but lately there hadn't been many. Preoccupied with Mr. Cowboy, he'd only recently had a reprieve.

Delores passed him the mashed potatoes. "How's the contest going?"

"Interesting."

"It certainly has accomplished Beulah's goals," Delores said.

"Guess so. Lots of single women in town, though who knows for how long?"

"And Bonnie." Riggs slid Sean a look that meant his big brother had already read his mind.

Winona and Riggs exchanged a look. They'd just had an entire conversation in the simple glance.

"Yeah, Bonnie." Sean set down his fork. "Is that a problem?"

"No, I just find it interesting Beulah's *niece* is on the show," Riggs said, offering Cal a piece of a roll.

"Well, she *is* an actress," Delores said.

"Without much work lately, I've heard," Winona said.

"Now, I thought you of all people would understand how difficult show business makes things on women of a certain age," Delores scolded.

"Of course, I do. I only want to be sure she came here for the right reasons."

"Yeah, you've said that," Sean said, frustration bubbling up. "Why did *you* come to Stone Ridge, Winona?"

"Sean—" Riggs said in a warning tone.

"No, it's okay, baby." Winona stroked Riggs' arm. "Let's address the elephant in the room. Again. I was thirty-nine and I wanted a baby. I thought I could just get knocked up and walk away, but I fell in love."

Delores smiled, made a cooing sound, and fed Mary a spoonful of baby food. "And maybe Bonnie came here for an acting part and she'll fall in love with Sean all over again."

"Yeah, maybe," Riggs said, but his words were thick with doubt.

Sean heard Delores hopeful and romantic words through Riggs ears:

Yeah, and maybe pigs will fly.

As always, supper was a little like riding a bicycle. Like riding a bicycle, if the bike was on a trapeze, and also on fire. Cal wasn't crazy about his mashed potatoes and decided they might taste better in his hair. When Winona wholeheartedly disagreed, he screamed loud enough to break the sound barrier. Screaming was catching, Sean had already learned. Joey cried immediately following his twin, because they did everything together. And Mary *never* liked being the odd one out. Plus, as a baby, it was her right to scream.

When Sean was here, the adults outnumbered the children. Together, they managed to get through supper, taking turns with the kids. Later, while Delores cleaned up, Winona began the bedtime routine that took hours.

"Let's go into the office," Riggs said, leading the way down the hall. "What's this about?"

"The contract I signed for Mr. Cowboy. How solid is that donation they agreed to?"

Riggs sank into the chair behind his desk. "Solid. It's not a small amount of money."

"Even so, I was an idiot to sign the contract."

"Tried to tell you. But you said, and I quote, 'I can get along with any of these beautiful women.' And if it doesn't work out, no harm done. I still have a good start on the foundation."

"I know what I said." Sean cleared his throat. "I agreed to let them choose the winner, but that was before they brought Bonnie."

"And now?"

"Now, I can't *let* them choose for me."

"Then you'll lose the contribution. That was the deal."

"I'll figure out another way. I want to honor my word, but they didn't play fair with me. They never told me they were bringing on Bonnie."

"You're right." Riggs leaned back in his chair. "And if they'd told you?"

"Yeah, I guess I would have told them to forget it."

"It's a good thing they didn't tell you, then. You can be a little hotheaded at times."

"So, you're saying I should go through with this sham? Honor my word and propose to someone I won't marry?"

"How do you know they won't choose Bonnie?"

"What if they don't?"

"That's the risk you're taking. But you could also wind up with everything. Bonnie, the money for the foundation."

"I've never been much of a gambler."

"I disagree. You're gambling now that Bonnie won't get a hankering to go back to Hollywood after this."

"I'm older now and I think I'm a big enough man to accept I can't be everything to her. If she still wants to act, I'll support her."

"Right. I never told Winona she couldn't have her career. It was her choice to take a long break because of the children." Riggs steepled his fingers together. "Let me ask you this. Have you ever stopped to wonder why you didn't go after her? You've had years to do it. If Winona left me for two *days*, I'd go after her."

"I did go after Bonnie."

They were quiet, remembering their mother's cancer and

how quickly they'd lost her. Painful and difficult times, not knowing how hard their father would take the loss. Not realizing they'd lose him not long after. Bonnie had come home with him, something he'd never forget. It was the one time she'd chosen him over everything else. She'd come home to be with him because he needed her and there had been no question she would be there.

But then she'd left him again. On some level, he'd been waiting for her to come back. Even if on the basis of *Mr. Cowboy*, she'd come home, and that meant something. She'd had no idea what kind of wrath she would encounter from him and he certainly hadn't made it easy in the beginning.

"What no one seems to realize is I ignored the fact I fell in love with a girl who had a big dream. I ignored it as long as I could while I tried to turn her into the kind of wife I wanted. And she tried to be that person. For me."

"Those are some tough truths to face."

"If I *could* love anyone else, I would. Someone more convenient. I tried to forget her, but it didn't work."

"Do you think it's going to be any different this time?"

"I know it will."

"Brother, I hope so, because I do not want to see you lose this opportunity to be happy. To have the family you want."

"That makes two of us."

CHAPTER 25

*L*ike a teenager all over again, Bonnie couldn't stop thinking about Sean. Pretty soon she'd start drawing hearts on napkins and practicing writing her name as "Bonnie Lee Henderson."

Okay, get a grip.

Thankfully, Mama hadn't grilled her the previous evening about Sean, but she'd laid into her bright and early the next morning over coffee, eggs, bacon, and grits.

"If you want Sean back, you're going to have to play a little hard to get, sugar. Don't just let him think he can have you easy as pie."

She took another sip of coffee. "Mama, my eyes are barely open here. And playin' hard to get went out with the phone book."

"I have one under my bed." She quirked a brow. "Something to be said for tradition."

"Don't worry about me. We're just talking, catching up on old times."

"Uh-huh. That's what I thought. And I know exactly what

your old times were. Teenage sex. Lots of rolling around in the hay and knockin' boots, your poor Mama with no idea."

"Mama, I'm thirty-seven, and I've been on my own for years. Are you really going to lecture me on sex?"

Her mother blushed the color of a pink sunset. "Of course not. That's *your* business."

"Thank you."

"Much as I love you, and you know I do, you broke the poor man's heart. I don't want to see you do it all over again."

"*Excuse* me? We broke each other's hearts. Remember, he stopped taking my calls and moved on. Got engaged!"

"And we both know why. He wasn't willing to wait forever."

"It wasn't going to *be* forever."

But of course, with hindsight, it would have at least been several years. She should have been the bigger person and let Sean go. But she hadn't been selfless enough to do that. She'd wanted it all. Had it been up to her, she and Sean would have had a long-distance relationship for years.

At the time, she believed they'd be able to overcome all obstacles, but now she understood that no relationship was unbreakable. She'd juggled several balls in the air, and accidentally dropped the one made out of precious crystal.

"Can I borrow your car today?" Bonnie asked. "I want to go into town and maybe grab lunch."

"Good idea. There are a lot of folks who haven't seen you yet."

Later, Bonnie drove her mother to her latest house-keeping job, then drove downtown simply so she could get better reception. She wanted to check social media and find out how badly she'd been vilified *this* week. Last night, she'd been watching TV when a commercial for *Mr. Cowboy* came on. With no announcement that the show had been canceled, and all the press junkets, she assumed they'd finish. But she saw signs of a show on life support.

"Hey, Bonnie Lee!"

A voice she recognized called out when she walked into the Shady Grind. Jolette Marie, whom she hadn't seen since the night she'd secretly brought her and Sean together.

"I heard y'all were on a break. What happened?"

"Actually, I'm not entirely sure but it looks like we're moving forward." She took a seat at a booth and Jolette Marie joined her, sliding in on the opposite side. "I'm here for the WIFI but I can't talk about the show. Not even to you. I'm sorry."

"Have you checked all the new hashtags? You're trending!"

"*Me?* Not the show? Why?" She pulled out her cell and started swiping.

"After all the hateful comments, there's been a backlash. So many organizations for women have taken up the cause. Agism in Hollywood is a trending hashtag."

"You're kidding." Great, just what she didn't want, more attention called to the fact she'd aged out of most good women's roles.

"It's wrong and there should be something done about it, don't you think?"

"Sure, but it's not that simple."

Bonnie sucked in a breath when she saw the comments on one of the original hateful posts about her. Hundreds of comments returned fire on the original poster, coming to Bonnie's defense, and that of all older women in Hollywood. Someone from an organization for women Bonnie had never heard of started a hashtag and it was indeed trending. #stopagisminHollywood and #IstandwithBonnie.

"I never wanted this to happen." Bonnie set her phone

down and covered her face with her hands. "This is the wrong kind of attention."

Just when she'd begun to get used to the idea of fading into the background, someone was fanning this flame. She just wanted it all to go away and leave her in peace.

Why did she *ever* check social media?

"I thought any publicity was good," Jolette Marie said.

"That's what they say. I'm just tired of it all. All the ups and downs. One day you're a hero, the next day a zero. All I ever loved about this business was performing. But all the rest of it? It's plain awful."

"Like anything else, I guess you take the good with the bad."

"Yes, but in this business the swings are so wide and deep. Unlike anything else I've ever experienced."

"Okay, then. Let's talk about something else. How are you and Sean doing?"

"Better."

Bonnie wasn't going to draw Jolette Marie into their deception.

Maybe it was also too soon to assume everything would work out the way Bonnie wanted. Sean had put plenty of conditions on them in the past. He'd always been a man with definite ideas about his future. Their future.

And with her entire career floundering at the moment, she wasn't in great shape to be anyone's partner. This time around, she wanted to be her best for Sean. Their relationship could never again take a backseat to her dreams. Besides, maybe her dreams had changed.

"What are y'all having?" Their waitress asked, putting down two menus.

"Just some sweet iced tea for now, please."

The waitress left the menus and bustled off.

"I heard it's not the same in Hollywood," Jolette Marie said smugly. "The sweet tea."

"Yes, Sean was right." Bonnie sighed. "He was miserable in L.A. I'm sure he told you all about it."

She nodded. "You can take the cowboy out of Texas, but you can't take the Texas out of the cowboy."

"Or something." Bonnie chuckled.

"He wouldn't have moved there for a minute with anyone but you."

"And I might not have come back for anyone else but him. Both times."

Had everyone forgotten she'd come back with Sean for two *years*, giving up on her dream, while secretly miserable? And she might have stayed that way if the part of a lifetime hadn't come along.

The doors to the Shady Grind swung open again and every woman who'd been on the show and eliminated, less Jessica, waltzed in. All ten of them.

"Boys! We're baaack!" The fitness trainer announced.

The men parted for them like the Red Sea.

Jolette Marie crossed her arms. "Oh yeah. *They* haven't left."

Bonnie sunk a little lower but even so, two seconds later, she was recognized.

A few of them waved happily, obviously having forgotten all about Sean. Some scowled, obviously not quite over him. The fitness trainer, Kristan, strode over to Bonnie's bench and sat. Jolette Marie moved to accommodate her, keeping a frown on her face.

"Bonnie! Give me the scoop. Is it you and Sean for the win, or Tabitha?"

"What about Angela," Bonnie Lee protested. "She's still in the running."

"Yeah, but we heard…" She leaned in closer to whisper. "Lenny drove Tabitha to Sean's cabin yesterday."

Suddenly appreciative of Tabitha's ways of throwing the scent off her, Bonnie shook her head. "I don't know about that, but I wouldn't listen to the rumor mill if I were you."

"Tabitha is not Sean's type," Jolette Marie said.

"Yeah, you've said that, but on the other hand she seems like *every man's* type." She held her hands in the shape of an hourglass. "Don't you agree?"

"I can't talk about the show. It's in the NDA we all signed."

"Sooner or later we're all going to know," Kristan said.

"It will have to be later." Bonnie took a sip of the sweet tea the waitress delivered.

"How can you drink that? It's like sugared water." Kristan pointed to the tea.

"And it's perfect."

"I'll be honest. I always knew you had an edge with him from the moment you showed up. Sean couldn't take his eyes off you," Kristan said.

"He wouldn't dare. Taking his eyes off me meant he'd lose his aim," Bonnie said.

Kristan's eyes widened and she jerked back in surprise. Jolette Marie burst into laughter.

"I'm kidding." Bonnie waited a beat. "He could probably shoot me with his eyes closed."

Jolette Marie nearly slid down the bench laughing so hard. "Please. I'm going to pee if you keep going."

"Why is this *funny*?" Kristan said.

"It's the idea that any man of Stone Ridge would hurt a woman. It's so rare it's laughable."

"Can I be honest?" Kristan glanced at the men surrounding the table with all the women. "I love it here."

"It gets *very* hot in the summer," Jolette Marie said with

her most discouraging tone. "And humid. Plus, the bugs. It's like walking into a sauna filled with mosquitos."

"While that sounds lovely," Kristan said with a mocking tone, "I might just want to find out on my own. If you don't mind."

"Suit yourself." Jolette Marie shrugged.

"Hey, darlin'." Jeremy beckoned to Kristan. "We're waiting for you."

"Oh, sigh. Excuse me." Kristan smiled and joined the rest of the ladies.

"How can you stand it?" Jolette Marie pouted. "They're here to take our cowboys."

"I only need one."

"It's been kind of nice to be one of the few. Always made me feel special."

"Only one man has to make you feel that way."

Jolette Marie scowled. "Well, he took off."

"When you left him at the altar?" Bonnie canted her head.

"Maybe I made a mistake there. I'm still searching. Now Lincoln is out, Jackson out, even Riggs is out. Sean was never an option, of course. All the good ones are taken." She slumped.

"I don't think so. Check out the men holding court with the ladies." Bonnie swept her hand in their direction. "Levi is free and he's hotter than a pistol. I heard *Beau Stephens* is still not married. If Colton ever comes back, he's never been married. And Jeremy is always up for a good time."

"True."

"You know what I think?" Bonnie reached for Jolette Marie's hand. "I think you're still not over your first love."

"Yeah, right." Jolette Marie snorted. "But he never looked back."

"I took off too and look at me now." She held her arms out. "I'm back."

"It's different between you and Sean. You two were meant to be."

"And. yet, we weren't together, for many, many years. Just keep your options open. You never know what could happen. Check this out." She held up her cell with a smirk. "I'm trending."

CHAPTER 26

"Whatever you do, don't get caught in a patch today." Sean instructed Beer. "I don't have time to find you."

Beer yarked as though he understood "wingman" talk.

On board with Bonnie's idea to meet him here, instead of doing the gentleman thing and picking her up, he accepted their time together was now going to be limited. They'd all received word they'd resume production tomorrow.

Sean had been busy with his seduction plans most of the afternoon. Rising at four this morning meant he got all chores done by noon barring any emergencies like a stuck cow. He fed cattle in the north pasture, moved them to the south pasture, rode a fence line, and checked in with Riggs. He had plans to attend a cattle auction next month and wanted Sean to head all operations in the interim.

As a kid, he used to dream about being a cowboy. But he'd lived with his parents in a trailer park where the closest he got was watching old westerns. The dream became reality when he and his brothers were adopted by the Hendersons. They'd first arrived as foster children, but when his parents lost their rights, his chosen mother and father swooped in to adopt all three boys. He was a Henderson through and through, no matter whose DNA rushed through his bloodstream.

Beer barked to be let outside and chase a bird. "Remember what I said."

Yark, yark. He barked and looked at Sean as if he understood.

Maybe Beer wasn't as smart as Sean gave him credit, but he'd always liked to believe the best about people and animals. He talked to the horses, too. When his first rescued wild horse, Tank, had arrived, Levi said he couldn't be broken. Stubborn, it took months to put a saddle on him. But Sean had refused to give up on Tank when he swore he saw the truth in Tank's eyes: he wanted to do better. But it went against his nature. Sean liked to believe that in the end love and devotion had triumphed.

Levi said they'd simply worn him out. He was far more of a pragmatist than Sean had ever been.

He'd adopted Tank but couldn't afford another one.

For that reason alone, Sean got a bit discouraged at times.

He chopped lettuce and tomatoes, sliced avocados and grated cheese. Tonight, Bonnie would get a Tex-Mex meal. On the menu was beef enchiladas with chipotle chili con queso. He wasn't a great cook but had learned a few things by watching his mother and later, Delores, in action. And he could grill the perfect steak.

He heard scratching at the back door and went to let Beer back inside.

Instead, he found Bonnie, looking delicious in her tight jeans and plunging Tee under an unbuttoned flannel shirt. Now, *this* was the Bonnie he remembered.

Rodeo Queen.

Girlfriend.

Love of his life.

"C'mere." He tugged her into his arms. "Why didn't you knock on the front?"

"You have a lot to learn about cloak and dagger, mister." She waggled a finger at him. "We have to be sneaky."

"What about your vehicle?"

"I parked under the tree. If anyone sees it, they'll think my mother came to visit and give you a piece of her mind."

"Still mad at me, is she?"

"If anything, she's frustrated with both of us. But she asked me not to break your heart, as a matter of fact." She tapped his chest with one finger.

"What a wise woman. You should listen to your mother."

"She also thinks I should play hard to get."

"Well, she's wrong, but nobody's perfect." He tugged her into the kitchen.

"What's all this? You're cooking for me?"

"Tex-Mex, like the kind you can't find in Hollywood."

As he recalled, everyone was turning vegan and he'd had a difficult time finding good Mexican food.

"Oh how I miss nachos."

"I'll make you some another time."

"But this looks delicious." She peeked in the oven and found the steak settling. "Red meat? Thank the sweet Christ child."

He removed the steak and brought it to the counter to start slicing. "Not going to lie, Skippy, I'm happy Hollywood didn't turn you vegan."

"Well, it tried. But you can take the girl out of Texas…"

"Good to know."

She came behind him, and wound her arms around his waist, pressing her face against his back. "Sean, I'm giving the money back. It's ridiculous to be paid for falling in love. I'm not acting and it's wrong to take the money."

He dropped the knife and turned, framing her face. "You're *not* giving the money back. This is your livelihood. You might have been working somewhere else if you hadn't come here. Believe me, I'd rather you make a living here than anywhere else."

"Hey, it finally worked out. You used to say how you wished I could find acting work in Stone Ridge. Here I am, working in my hometown."

As a kid, he'd thought it the perfect solution. Stone Ridge was growing now, but he still didn't think they were ready for a theater in town.

"Kerrville has the Playhouse and Cailloux Theater. It's... nice."

She grinned. "And how would *you* know that?"

He'd once told Bonnie he'd rather be dragged naked through a rocky pasture than go to the theater.

He chose his next words carefully. "Robyn took me."

"Oh." She lowered her lashes, avoiding his eyes. "I could never get you to go with me. You never had the time."

He tipped her chin to force her to meet his gaze. "Because I was a stupid guy. We've both grown up a lot. I should have gone with *you* and I'm sorry I didn't."

"I thought you wouldn't go with me because you were this strong alpha cowboy who didn't like or appreciate the theater."

"That's still mostly true."

"But...you'll go with *me* now?"

"Anytime." He brought her hand to his lips and kissed her knuckles. "Let's not forget I went to Hollywood for you. If that's not love I don't know what is."

"That's love."

"I love you, Bonnie. I always have."

"Oh, Sean." She smiled, eyes shiny and wet. "I never

thought I could be this happy again. I forgot what this feels like."

"Me, too." He pressed his forehead to hers, sinking his fingers into her hair.

Bonnie worked her magic on him, sliding her hand under his shirt. Heat pulsed through him and he forgot all about dinner. When it came to Bonnie, he had a difficult time remembering the rest of the world existed. It had always been this way with her, and he'd been shocked to find nothing had changed. He was now a grown man, not a teenager with limited sexual experience.

How did she *still* manage to rock his world?

Hands under her behind, he lifted her, and carried her to the kitchen table to set her down. "This table has never been properly blessed."

"Hmm." She raked her teeth across her lower lip and went for his pants. "Let's do something about that."

Bonnie almost felt guilty being *this* happy. Somewhere in the world, a young (or older) woman was pining away for her lost love. Lonely, and alone with her regrets.

And here she lay, in her lover's bed, rolling in the sheets. Getting her second chance. She hadn't imagined it possible even a month ago. Sean had moved on, and she'd received the message after his engagement to Robyn was announced.

This told her in no uncertain terms, in case she didn't already know: *we're done.*

Now, she was in heaven. After the kitchen table, they'd gone positively vanilla and went for the bed. Hey, they weren't kids anymore. But after the shower stall and kitchen table, Bonnie felt like she'd been starring in her own porn. She'd never been this adventurous with any other man.

"Dinner is served." Sean strode in the bedroom, wearing

nothing but his jeans, unbuttoned at the top. He carried a large skillet and something red and white under his arm.

"I'm starved." She sat up, drooling both at Sean's abs and the delicious smells of steak and queso.

"Good." He threw a checkered tablecloth on the bed and set down the skillet of enchiladas, then took two forks from his back pocket and brandished one. "Eat."

"You don't have to tell me twice." She dug into the delicious tortilla with melted queso and beef. "Yum. I'm so glad you learned to cook."

"Delores taught me." He reached over and took a forkful. "She's busy with Riggs' family and I don't want her cooking for me too."

"Now you'll have to teach me."

"Whatever you want."

He kissed her bare shoulder and slid her a slow smile, reminding her of the past few hours he'd spent giving her orgasm after orgasm.

"What I want is never to leave this room, but we go back tomorrow."

"Soon, this will all be over."

"Over, as in just beginning?"

"Yeah. I would talk about us getting married, but I don't want to rush you. I did that once before."

"Rush me?" She leaned into him. "I don't think you're rushing me. What's it been? Over a decade since you first asked me? I'm ready."

"Yeah?"

"Yeah." She bopped his nose, then offered him a forkful of enchilada.

He laughed when she kissed him, the taste of melted cheese and Sean mixing together in one delicious bite.

"I'll be right back." His warm hand slid down to the small of her back and he popped out of bed, pulling on a t-shirt.

She heard him downstairs, opening the sliders and letting Beer inside. But he was gone so long she began to wonder. Grabbing his flannel button-up, she threw it on quickly. It fell to her knees and she padded down the hallway.

"Sean? Are you coming back?"

No answer. Silence.

"Sean." She stood at the top of the steps and called down. "Where'd you go?"

Beer answered her with a yark and a tail wagging so hard it might fall off.

"Right here." Behind her, Sean stood in the door frame of the spare bedroom at the end of the hall. "I had to find something."

"What did you— oh!" She covered her mouth with her hands, sudden tears filling her eyes.

Sean had dropped to one knee and held a tiny black box in his hands. "This is the ring I had for you before. I could buy you something bigger now but there's something about this ring. I worked hard and saved every penny to get it for you."

And he still owned it.

Overwhelmed, she dropped to her knees. "I want it, and I won't ever need anything else."

"I didn't do this right the first time. I made a lot of assumptions and forgot there were two people in this relationship with hopes and dreams. Your dreams matter to me, Bonnie. *You* matter to me and everything you want. I love you. Will you finally, after all this time, marry me?"

"Yes! Oh, Sean, I love you, I love you, I love you."

She kissed him and let him slip on the ring, a beautiful antique looking gold ring with a small square-shaped diamond in the center surrounded by dozens of smaller ones. The most beautiful ring she'd ever seen. Simple and classic.

Her heart tugged in a sweet swell of emotion. "You've been hanging on to it all these years?"

He nodded. "I wanted to do this privately before I ask you for the show."

"What about the foundation?"

"I'll get the money another way. And there's always the chance they picked you. They always said they'd consider my input, too."

"They'd be stupid not to, right? I think we've created enough conflict for them. Surely they see the story here. Doesn't everyone love a reunion romance?"

"You'll get your flashy, sparkly two-carats from some big-time jeweler in Dallas. They're paying, but I get to pick it out."

She held her hand out, admiring it in the soft ray of dimming sunlight filtering through the windows. "This is the one I'll wear for the rest of my life."

"Okay." He pulled her close. "I'm holding you to it."

"I don't want this day to end. It's been the best of my life."

"Then let's stretch it out a little longer."

CHAPTER 27

*S*tretching out the day lasted only another glorious hour, but eventually Bonnie had to pick up her mother.

Mama appeared haggard as she ambled out to the car, carrying her big blue satchel. Through the years, Bonnie had sent money home so her mother didn't have to work. A bad day on the job for Bonnie meant getting up at four AM in order to be in make-up and hair promptly so she could wait around for hours for her scenes to be filmed.

A bad day for her mother meant her hands hurt from ironing shirts and cleaning toilets.

Once she and Sean were married, Bonnie would have her move in with them like Sean had originally offered. Sometimes the simplest solutions were the best ones.

"Hi, Mama!" She got out and opened the passenger door for her. "Did you have a good day at work?"

"Well, well." She appraised Bonnie, her gaze sliding up and down. "What on earth put the wiggle in *your* walk?"

Engaged!

She was engaged to the love of her life. Something she'd

once taken for granted till the door slammed in her face. It had opened wide again, carrying with it a glorious sweetness she didn't deserve.

"Um, well…" She slipped behind the driver's seat and drove off. "First. I have something to ask you."

"Dinner will be leftovers tonight. Fend for yourself."

"I'll cook for you."

Mama's neck swiveled in surprise. "If you don't want to know what's for dinner, what's the question?"

"*Why* are you still working? I've sent money so you don't *have* to work."

"And it's all sitting at the bank in Kerrville earning interest. I haven't touched it in years."

Bonnie nearly swerved off the road. "What? Why?"

"How else am I going to pay for your wedding to Sean?"

Well, wasn't this working out to be an emotional day? Her mother, for years hanging on to the hope of her and Sean reconciling. Even after Bonnie had given up all hope.

"*We're* both old enough to pay for the wedding. You don't have to do that."

"But, I want to. At least let me help."

"Jesus, Mama. You're going to make me cry all over again."

"He already asked, didn't he?"

Bonnie nodded, not trusting herself to speak.

"Well, Beulah was right. I do hate it when my own sister is always right. It really chaps my hide."

"What does Aunt Beulah have to do with it?"

"She felt guilty all these years. Because of her, you took that first modeling job." She cleared her throat. "Lingerie. She encouraged you. We both think that was the beginning of the end for you and Sean."

"Y'all had nothing to do with it. Sean and I managed to screw things up on our own."

"The least Beulah could do is bring you back, put you right in Sean's line of vision, and see if you two might find your way to each other again."

"She has that much influence?"

"I don't know about influence so much as show biz smarts. That Beulah, she convinced them it would make good TV."

And she hadn't been wrong.

"Lots of changes for me today. I don't know how I'll ever thank her enough for getting me this job."

"All the women in our family are working women." She patted Bonnie's arm. "Listen, I don't mind my job. You have no idea how much I'm needed. The Churchills would be lost without me."

"At least think about the day you retire. I want you to take the money you have in the bank for me and open up a retirement account instead."

She waved her hand dismissively. "Way ahead of you. I took about five percent of what you sent me and started an IRA."

"Oh, Mama. That's great."

"Mrs. Churchill listens to a program every afternoon. It comes right through her computer and we both listen while I'm ironing. Something called 'Girl, you Should be a Millionaire. Lots of good advice on there. *You* might even learn something."

Bonnie smiled. "I think I already have."

THE NEXT DAY, Lenny waited for Bonnie in the Hummer, ready to drive her back to the Truehart mansion.

He reached for her hand and kissed it. "Hello, Miss Bonnie Lee. Your chariot awaits."

By the time they arrived, several vans were already

parked meaning Lori and the crew beat her here. Inside, the crew was setting up cameras and Lori ran around the house with her clipboard, yelling.

Angela greeted Bonnie with a hug. "She's on the warpath. We've lost too much production time. Which is their fault."

"And *we're* going to pay for it."

Tabitha walked up to Bonnie. "Where have *you* been?"

"Staying with my mother, like I said."

"Hm." Tabitha narrowed her eyes and worked her jaw like she didn't quite believe Bonnie.

She *might* be a mind-reader, or perhaps there really was a new wiggle in Bonnie's walk.

"Finally! We're all here," Lori bellowed. "Thank you for joining us, Bonnie. Better late than never. Because we've lost valuable production time, we're going to speed things up. I spoke to Sean and he's already made his decision."

"Tonight, you'll all come downstairs for your exit interviews. I'll slap together a killer montage to pace the show. I've got plenty of unused footage. Then, tomorrow, Sean will choose his bride. Badabing, badabeh, we're done, it's a wrap. My crew will clear out of here."

"Is she talking faster than normal or is that my imagination?" Angela said.

"Oh, my gawd, I might be engaged by tomorrow!" Tabitha jumped up and down. "Wait till they hear back home. My brothers swore no one would *ever* marry me!"

Oh, poor Tabitha.

Bonnie was no longer threatened, just sorry. She'd never met anyone quite so deluded. Or hopeful.

Might be a fine line some days.

"Hey, Lori!" Elton beckoned. "Come look at this."

He seemed to be studying something coming out of one of his monitors. Lori and Elton were animated for several minutes, gesturing back and forth to each other, then finally embracing.

She'd never even seen them touch. *What in the world?*

Lori bustled over again. "Fabulous news! Bonnie's old series is number one on a streaming network this week. Who knows how long it will last, but it will be a giant ratings boost to our own show when it comes out. We'll try to rush to release, obviously. Got to strike while the iron is hot and all that. Take advantage of the old show's resurgence in popularity."

"What show?" Tabitha asked.

"Kavanaugh's Way?" Angela said. "She mentioned it to you before. Don't *tell* me you didn't recognize her."

She shook her head. "Before my time, I guess. Never watched it."

Bonnie sank into the couch. It was bad enough Sean and Robyn had watched the show together but now the entire country would watch a much younger, kickass Bonnie Wheeler. Much as she'd loved her first big break and working with some stellar talent, she'd still been honing her craft. It wasn't her best work by a long shot. She believed her best performance to date was the independent film from the Cannes Film Festival, but no one would be watching that anytime soon. Deep sigh.

"Something wrong?" Angela took a seat beside her.

"Not at all."

She pictured Sean on bended knee and went straight back to her happy place.

Angela cocked her head. "You strike me as being squeamish about all this attention which you have to admit is strange for an actress."

"Yeah, she's generally being weird today." Tabitha joined them, circling her hands in the air all around Bonnie. "*Something* is different."

Bonnie hid her left hand, even though she had purposely removed the ring this morning and put it right back in its box, now in her luggage.

"I'm fine. Ready for this to be over."

"So, you really are an actress," Tabitha said.

"Of course she is!" Angela said. "I've seen her work."

"Well, okay then. I had counted on you being an actress, that's all."

"Why?" Bonnie said.

"D-uh, because you're *acting* about wanting to marry Sean."

"Oh."

"Or *is* she?" Angela smiled wickedly.

"Well, good luck. He and I have a special connection. I know y'all have a history but well…let's just say I think I finally have his attention."

It took everything in Bonnie not to wipe the smug smile off Tabitha's face. Bonnie knew *exactly* how Tabitha had tried to get Sean's attention because he'd later confessed and swore he hadn't even looked when she stripped her blouse off.

Yeah, right.

"Well…too bad for me." Bonnie folded her hands in her lap. "I guess I should give up right now."

"Are you *kidding* me?" Angela wagged her finger from side to side. "Uh-uh."

"I can't tell." Tabitha crossed her arms. "Is she acting?"

"Alright, ladies!" Lori screeched and clapped her hands. "Go upstairs and get your glam on. Angela, we'll do your exit interview first, then the rest."

"I don't care for being rushed like this," Angela said, going up the steps.

"What are you wearing?" Tabitha asked.

"My pride," Angela said. "I know I'm on the chopping block. It's all good."

"I don't know about that," Tabitha said. "It could be Bonnie, after all."

"Yeah, right," Angela muttered under her breath, giving Bonnie a conspiratorial smile.

There would always be a special place in her heart for this show, for these ladies, who'd for lack of a better word, been her co-stars. After this, Bonnie was turning in her membership card to the Screen Actors Guild. Maybe she'd look into community theater work where her experience would be rewarded.

She could be a character actor and take on the type of parts she'd never considered before. The kind where you no longer cared to be the prettiest woman in the room. The type that meant admitting you were getting older and didn't give a hoot. Older also meant experienced. She'd had her moment and the rest of the world, if not Hollywood, saw a woman who had a lot of good years ahead of her.

Bonnie slipped on the dress wardrobe had laid out for her. It was red. A redhead wearing a red dress wasn't always regarded as the best choice. It was, some said, an "in your face" choice. A "screw you and the horse you rode in on" choice. But tonight, she didn't care. She'd record her exit interview doing some of her best work. She'd call on every one of her skills to pull it off. Because Sean had already chosen her.

After the last mascara wand pass and lipstick application, Bonnie walked into the hall where downstairs, she could hear Angela speaking in the calm and professional manner of a financial podcast leader:

"I've had a wonderful time and met so many kind people. Yes, Sean is wonderful. I hope he picks me..."

Bonnie walked further down the hall to Tabitha's room.

Peeking inside, she saw her primping in the mirror. She wore a dress so tight she might have trouble walking. The poor girl's insecurities ran so deep she couldn't even be herself.

With brothers like hers, she'd obviously been told somewhere along the line that all she had to offer were her looks. Maybe even that a man would only want to fool round with her. And this had been reinforced over and over again when her appearance became all that mattered to her.

Because this made her who she was.

Remind you of anyone else?

Thank God she was finally over all that, but how long had it taken? Decades, or from the first time someone told her mother that she ought to put Bonnie in a beauty contest. Even Daddy used to call her his very own little Miss Texas.

Sean claimed to love her for more than her looks, but she hadn't believed him because even she hadn't seen her own value beyond them. Her beauty would get her out of Stone Ridge and get back the life she and Mama had before Daddy died. All the pomp and pageantry of the rodeo, Hollywood style.

"Hey," Bonnie said in the doorway of Tabitha's open door.

She turned and almost spilled out of her dress. "How do I look?"

"Beautiful. Any man would be lucky to have you. You do realize this."

"Oh, sure." She turned back to the mirror, fluffed her perfect hair, licked her bottom lip. "But I hope the man is Sean. This is going to be on film, for all posterity for everyone to see. Including Sean. And either he's going to be reminded how grateful he is to have me as his fiancée, or he will rue the day he let me go."

"Tabitha, if he doesn't pick you, you're going to be alright."

"I can't even think like that. I want to show everyone back home that I can be special. Chosen."

A ball of emotion formed in Bonnie's throat. It was like watching someone boarding the Titanic unable to save them because it might alter the timeline or some such thing.

"You know, a long time ago Sean told me that he didn't love me simply because of my looks."

She snorted and adjusted her cleavage. "Yeah, that's what they all say."

At that moment, Bonnie realized what she both loved and hated about Tabitha. She was *Bonnie* a decade ago. Like looking in a fun house mirror with everything twisted and bent out of shape. Everything Tabitha said and did triggered Bonnie. No wonder she'd been on her last nerve the entire time. It wasn't just Tabitha's relentless pursuit of Sean.

It was Bonnie. She *hated* looking in this particular mirror. No distortion. Plain and simple. *This is your life, Bonnie Lee.* Look back with regret at the stupid mistakes you made based on a false belief.

Or move forward from this point forward.

"Tabitha." Bonnie cleared her throat. "Thing is, it doesn't matter what anyone else says or thinks. It only matters what you believe. You're obviously smart, not just beautiful. And I'm sure you're kind under the right circumstances."

"Then *why* don't I have a husband?"

"You're only twenty-five. Maybe you haven't met him yet."

"But I did. It's Sean, I just know it. He's so nice and cares so much about all of us. I can see how much he hates hurting anyone's feelings. And there was that thing he did with your slimy ex all because he insulted you. He's a real man and all I meet are boys."

"Interesting. You didn't *once* mention how very handsome he is."

Tabitha blinked. "Well, that's obvious. You have eyes and you know how good looking he is."

"That's not the point. What if Sean had all these wonderful qualities but maybe he wasn't *quite* so handsome? Maybe he had a little bit of a gut, or crooked teeth? Wouldn't you still like him?"

"Hm." Tabitha seemed to consider it. "Maybe, but I still want the hot body."

She waltzed by Bonnie, on her way to the exit interview which would be broadcast when the show released. When all the decisions had already been made and all her hopes and dreams were crushed.

CHAPTER 28

*a*fter her exit interview, Bonnie joined Angela and Tabitha in the living room.

"Don't we all look *gorgeous*." Angela kicked up her leg. "With no man to enjoy the fruits of our labor."

"Hey," Elton said from behind the camera he was adjusting. "What about me?"

"Oh, honey, you don't count." Angela waved her hand dismissively, but her smile went a little wider and a whole lot flirtier.

"All I'm saying is I enjoy all the...gorgeous." He sent Angela a slow smile.

"He's cute." Bonnie elbowed Angela.

"He came back earlier than the rest of the crew and gave me some tips for my podcast. I wanted to interview him, but he wouldn't do it. Said it went against union rules."

Bonnie elbowed Angela. "Hey, I have news. My mother listens to your podcast."

Angela brightened. "That's amazing. I have listeners from all over the country, but I've never met any of them in person."

"I think I can arrange an introduction."

Tabitha was pacing the floor, holding a flute of champagne.

"I'm worried about her," Bonnie whispered.

"Me, too. She's going to be extremely happy tonight and come crashing down tomorrow."

Bonnie blinked. "Why do you—"

"Honestly, it's been obvious since day one that Sean still has a thing for you. If I've strategized and calculated right, he's going to ask *you* to marry him."

He already has.

But Bonnie wasn't sure she should reveal that Sean wasn't choosing anyone himself. Unless he worked a way out of this, he'd have to go along with whoever the producers chose, and it could well be Tabitha.

"Shh," Bonnie said. "I feel bad for Tabitha. She's put so much of herself into this."

"Give her some credit. She'll bounce back, but not before millions of tears and drama." She sighed. "That's how she rolls."

Tabitha stopped suddenly in the middle of the room and when Bonnie followed the direction she was looking, Lori had placed two western hats on the table.

"Oh my gawd. I can't...I can't look." Tabitha shielded her eyes.

"And we're rolling, people!" Lori bellowed.

Bonnie and Angela stood to move on either side of Tabitha as Sean entered the room.

Tonight, he was dressed in dark jeans and a starchy white button up shirt. He wore his black Stetson and matching boots. She'd always loved this simple cowboy look on him and it took everything in her not to run and jump into his arms.

He tipped his hat and gave her a little wink. "Hey, ladies.

I've been doing a lot of thinking and I know my future wife is in this room."

Next to Bonnie, Tabitha sighed.

Sean picked up a hat and twirled it in his hands. "Bonnie, will you accept this hat?"

She walked to him, smiled and winked. "Thank you."

This time he slipped it gently on her head, lightly caressing the curve of her face when he did. The gesture was so slight Bonnie thought it was nearly imperceptible to the camera angle.

Sean picked up the last hat and lowered his head as though he would be making a difficult decision.

"And...Tabitha, will you accept this hat?" He seemed close to a grimace as he offered the hat.

Tabitha smiled triumphantly, then did a little spin and victory dance before she walked to meet Sean. "Yes, yes, I will!"

"I'm sorry, Angela," Sean said a moment later, straightening.

Bonnie was the first to embrace Angela. "I'm going to miss you and all your strategizing."

"I accomplished what I wanted to." She leaned in to whisper. "Now, I hope you do the same."

"I'm sorry to see you go." Tabitha opened her arms wide for Angela.

"No, you're not." But she went into the hug and laughed. "I hope Sean finds who he's looking for."

"I'm sure he will," Tabitha sniffed. "And I'll invite you to the wedding."

Not too subtly, Angela rolled her eyes, patting Tabitha's back. "You do that, honey. And remember, no matter what happens here tomorrow, you're a strong and powerful woman with a very good start at your retirement."

Obviously, Bonnie wasn't the only one worried about Tabitha.

"Thank you," Tabitha sniffed, displaying genuine emotion.

"And you're also smart and very capable," Bonnie added.

"May I walk you out?" Sean held his hand out to Angela.

"Yes, please." With one last finger wave, Angela walked toward Sean.

The crew followed with her luggage.

"I'm sure going to miss her," Tabitha said, taking another flute of champagne and plopping down on the couch. "She has a lot of good financial advice."

"She's a good friend."

"A good friend and a not so formidable opponent. It was easier to like her because she never stood a chance with Sean."

"I don't know about that. She made the final three, didn't she?"

"She doesn't even like him and I know he sensed that." She pointed between her and Bonnie. "You and I have always been in a dead heat for his attention."

"Are you saying I'm a formidable opponent?" Bonnie shimmied her shoulders to lighten the mood.

"*I'm* the formidable opponent." Tabitha tapped her chest.

And even though Bonnie knew she'd already won, even if she already had Sean's heart, she had compassion for Tabitha.

She wanted to be *seen*.

Bonnie nodded. "You *are* a formidable opponent."

"Bonnie!" The cook held the cordless phone usually kept in the kitchen. "Telephone."

She took the receiver and walked out of the room for privacy from Tabitha's questioning look.

"Hello?"

"Bonnie! I have fabulous news!" Marvin, her agent, said. "Get this. Netflix wants to bring back new seasons of

Kavanaugh's Way and you'll be the star this time. The head of the Irish mafia. One promised season with options. Surely, you've seen how the old show is trending. Thanks to all this social media attention to agism in Hollywood you're finally getting a role you deserve. You've arrived. Forget *Oopsie Underwear*. How about a reboot of *Kavanaugh's Way*? Can you believe it? In all my years of doing this crazy schtick, I've seen plenty of comebacks. It's happening to *you* now and no one deserves this more. More details to come, but they want to film in Canada in a few months."

Bonnie fisted the handset while her other hand started twitching.

"Marvin, I'm about to film the last episode."

"I know, that's why I wanted to give you the good news. Word is the producers have asked Sean to choose Tabitha. It's part of her contract, apparently…But hey, congratulations on getting this far."

"But…"

Sean always did everything he'd promised. A man of his word, honorable beyond reproach. A man of Stone Ridge. He would also do nothing to jeopardize the Henderson ranch. This was the livelihood of not only him but his family. Riggs. Colton. The legacy of his parents. He wouldn't risk it. Nor would she ask him to.

Not only had the jiggles returned, the stomach cramps had followed. A stone lodged itself in her throat. The floor dropped from below her entire world. She didn't want success *this* way. This felt wrong on every level.

And she couldn't lose Sean. Not again.

"I…I have to go." Bonnie set the phone down and walked back into the living room with Tabitha.

"Important call?" Tabitha smirked.

The confidence now made sense. This was no deluded

woman. Tabitha was the woman who'd entered a contest knowing she'd be chosen. It had been in her contract.

"You know, don't you?" Bonnie accused.

"Know what?"

To anyone else, the sly look would go unnoticed. But as an actor, Bonnie had made a study out of microfacial expressions. She now saw smugness and confidence exuding from a highly intelligent woman she'd completely underestimated.

"You are really good, you know that?"

"I have no idea what you're talking about."

"Sean has to choose you, doesn't he?"

She shrugged. "I don't know if I'd say that."

"Tabitha, surely you can see this isn't real. It's a fantasy."

"It's an opportunity. Look, I know he doesn't love me yet but he could grow to love me."

"You don't love him, either."

"Only because I barely know him." She smoothed the skirt of her dress. "But we're going to get to know each other, outside of these very public dates where I've had to share him with you. Then, I'm sure I'll fall head over heels like you did."

Frustration bubbled up in Bonnie and she fought to keep her composure.

"I can't believe you. And to think I felt bad for you!"

"For me?" She tapped her chest. "Feel bad for yourself, Bonnie. Stop trying to relive your youth. It's time to move on and find someone new. Not some old boyfriend you already had a chance with. It didn't work before. Why would it now?"

"You tell yourself that, but he was not just some old boyfriend. He was my first love and he asked me to marry him a long time ago. I took him for granted and assumed he'd wait for me. He didn't. But if he chooses you, it will be because he's been given no real choice. Think about that!"

And before she turned into Meghan Kavanaugh and ordered a mob hit on Tabitha, Bonnie left the room. Taking shallow breaths, her entire body jiggling, Bonnie went upstairs to be alone. Closing the door to her bedroom with a shaky hand, all the emotions hit her at once. Caught between a sob and a laugh, she reminded herself to breathe. Already, anxiety was cloaking her like a coat.

Even though she realized Sean loved her, even if he'd already given her a ring, she didn't know whether she could watch as he proposed to someone else. Her two lives now juxtaposed, and it seemed her real life was now a theater production. A three act play in which in the final act the hero would choose someone other than the woman he loved. The knowledge this wasn't the way he truly felt just didn't seem enough. She was experiencing the old and tired sense of not being good enough for the role of a lifetime.

This time the choice carried a lot more weight than the chance to be a significant player in a major production. This was her life and she wanted to see Sean make the same tough choice she'd been faced with so many years ago. Choosing him meant giving everything else up. She'd never managed to do that for him.

He'd have to give up his dream if he chose her. He'd do it knowing how difficult it had been for her, and how in the end, he'd ripped the choice away.

Life was funny sometimes. Once, the chance to reprise her most popular role would have been a dream come true. She'd do better this time, with more acting chops. And she'd show people like Vici, and Eric, and all the others that maybe age counted for something in Hollywood. Maybe women actors shouldn't be cast off when they lost their shine. Just maybe they had more to offer than scene decoration.

But as her luck would have it, this new opportunity became yet another difficult choice.

.   .   .

THE NEXT DAY, Sean stared at the dazzling collection of wedding rings from the Dallas jeweler as the camera crew filmed.

Why had he ever agreed to this? He'd essentially handed someone else a choice that no one else should ever make. All because he'd give up on real love, on finding someone who could take the place of what he'd once had with Bonnie.

Yesterday, he'd taken Lori aside and asked whether a decision had been made as to whom he'd choose in the final ceremony.

"I know I agreed that y'all would choose someone for me, but things have changed. You were the ones who brought Bonnie to the show, not me."

"What does that have to do with anything? You *want* to choose Bonnie?"

"I think it would make great TV, don't you? Some of that reality TV butter you love. Reunions are popular, right?"

"Honestly, Sean, after the first night I thought you were going to kill each other. I'm glad you worked it out, dude, but I don't have any real control over who gets chosen. Bonnie came here to be the conflict, and she was never supposed to be an option. And you agreed to let them choose for a donation to the wild horse rescue."

"I know what I agreed to do."

"Are you going to back out now? After all this?"

"I never said that. But I'd like you to put in a good word for Bonnie, if you could."

"I'll see what I can do," she'd said.

Even after walking Angela out to the car and having a nice talk with her, he still couldn't get over the fact that he'd hurt her and all these women. Angela, possibly the least. But Tabitha…even Angela had warned him.

"Watch out for her." Angela hugged him goodbye and after the cameras stopped rolling so Elton could hop in the car with Angela. "Tabitha won't take it well."

Sean's thoughts were yanked back to the present by the jeweler's voice.

"This one is an emerald cut and looks timeless in a variety of settings." He held up the diamond for inspection and it shimmered in the natural light. "Beautiful. Naturally, all our diamonds are ethically sourced. Conflict-free. We track diamonds from mine to market so you can rest assured."

The emerald cut resembled the one he'd already given Bonnie. Quietly, he wondered if the first diamond ring he'd ever purchased was ethically sourced. He'd never thought to ask. Just in case, should he get something different than what she already had, or get the same kind of ring but larger? He should have asked her, damn it. Too late now. She'd said she wouldn't wear any other ring but the one he'd already given her, so was there any point?

And to think when he'd first signed up for this, he couldn't imagine falling for anyone in such a short time. He'd agreed to propose because he figured they could have a long engagement. If the relationship didn't work out, well, been there, done that. He had certainly never imagined being this certain about proposing. But yet here he sat, choosing a ring, knowing he had every intention of getting married, though possibly not to the woman he'd propose.

What a damn mess.

Either keep his word and possibly humiliate Bonnie in front of cast, crew, and later the rest of the country or give up on his dream of starting the wild horse foundation.

Something between Bonnie and him always went spectacularly wrong. Living in different cities. Illness and death. Dreams that took her away. Now his dream could take her away from him, because God knew he wouldn't take it well were the roles reversed.

He would say something when he made this choice. He'd say to Bonnie that he'd chosen her over his dream. She of all people would understand the significance of this.

But Bonnie could still change her mind about living here and try to talk him into leaving again. She'd changed, and so had he, but maybe their fundamental conflicts would return. He was taking a risk and knew this. If not for the way he loved her, he wouldn't be willing to take the chance. But there was really no one else for him. He *had* to try again. Had to risk his heart.

He wiped his brow and viewed the diamond ring display. "What's your advice?"

"It depends on the woman. What is your lovely bride to be like? You know her heart, I'm certain."

"Well, she's beautiful, but not just on the outside. She's kind and smart. You should see her with children. Little boys gravitate toward her because they sense her generous and open heart. She loves you large and doesn't hold back. She's the kind of woman that will forgive a guy and give him a second chance."

Ooops. He glanced up at the camera guy who rolled his hand for Sean to keep going. He thought perhaps he may have given too big of a hint as to who he'd be choosing but he'd already learned Marti, Jr. could do her magic on the cutting floor.

"Spoken like a man in love." He smiled and closed a box, reached for another one and opened it. "I suggest the heart shaped diamond. A unique style with a variation of the brilliant cut. See how the light reflects its spectacular beauty. This is one is two carats for a lady with a big heart."

He set the ring down on the soft blue cloth between them. Sean picked it up, turned and examined it as if he had a clue what he was doing. The moment the man said 'heart shaped' Sean knew it would be the one. For the woman who owned his heart. He could still hope that the producers would see the sense in allowing him to choose Bonnie.

"Yep, this is the one. Can we have it engraved?"

LATER, as Sean was getting dressed for the last episode, Riggs dropped by.

"You ready for this?"

Sean adjusted his ridiculous tie. "One more time with this choke collar around my neck."

"So…Bonnie Lee, yeah?"

"Don't try to talk me out of it. It's already done."

Riggs quirked a brow.

"I gave her the first ring I ever bought. Privately. Now, I hope to give her a huge rock in front of an audience."

"You already asked? That was quick."

"If you call twelve years quick, then, yeah."

Rigg snorted. "Ya got me there. I still remember Dad sitting you down, explaining you couldn't marry her when you were both only eighteen."

"That was just a pipe dream. Dad called it as usual. Horny toad teenager."

"Look. Winona is a realist, Jolette Marie's a romantic, and I got to be a first-hand witness to the carnage Bonnie left behind. I saw you walk around this ranch like someone had hit you over the head with a baseball bat. But don't listen to what anyone else tells you. Do what you want to do. Do what's in your heart. If I'd followed anyone's else advice, including your own, I might not have married Winona. Certainly wouldn't have fallen in love with her."

"I've already admitted I was wrong about her."

"And all I'm saying is maybe I'm wrong about Bonnie.

Maybe she'll put you first this time." Riggs clapped Sean's shoulder. "You *deserve* to be first with her."

"Yeah. Have you noticed no one ever stopped to think whether I should have put her first? It goes both ways. Her dreams were important even if they took her away from me."

"Pretty wise of you, little brother." He cleared his throat. "Just don't forget that you're giving up on a dream, too, if you choose someone other than who the producers want."

"There's always the chance they'll choose Bonnie. A fifty/fifty chance."

"Good for you. Look on the bright side. You might be able to put a big dent in the foundation coffers."

Riggs stayed until it was time for Sean to leave for the Truehart mansion. When he arrived, a small crowd waited out front. A few of the locals, including Lenny.

Lenny waved. "They said we could have a looksee as long as we stay back behind this rope."

Sean spotted Angela in the group, and several of the women he'd let go early on. They all waved happily, making him feel less of a chump.

"Good luck, Sean! You really can't lose in *this* contest." Jeremy saluted him. "And if it's not Tabitha you choose, please introduce me."

"Not before you introduce her to me!" Beau Stephens yelled.

Good to know Tabitha had admirers. Yeah, she'd be fine.

Standing near Beau, Jolette Marie waved. Even Winona was here, holding Mary, giving him a thumbs up. Riggs had probably talked to her. He went over for a little fist bump with Mary.

"Wish me luck, baby girl." He planted a quick kiss on her sweet bald head.

He followed Lori to where he'd stand outside in the garden and let Tabitha go, then propose to Bonnie. The sweat beaded on his forehead at this public display. By nature, he was a private man and this whole thing was way out of his wheelhouse. But if it had brought him Bonnie, it was worth every last uncomfortable feeling.

Lori met him at the end of the lane, a sour expression on her face.

"Who screwed up now?" he said.

"You have to choose Tabitha."

CHAPTER 29

*S*ean's heart must have stopped beating and the blood stopped running through his veins because he instantly went ice cold.

"No, I won't."

"I'm sorry, but it's been decided. I went to bat for Bonnie, I tried, and they weighed your input heavily. But they have a very special vision in mind." Lori waved her hands dismissively. "Oh, you don't have to actually marry Tabitha, of course!"

"Because *that* would be crazy?"

"No one can tell you who to marry. Obviously, it's a free country. But this is a show, our show, and you *have* to pick Tabitha. You agreed to do this. Then, later, you and Bonnie can do whatever you like."

Do whatever they like, after he dropped to one knee and proposed with the heart shaped ring he'd picked out for Bonnie. To another woman. Oh hell no.

And he understood what happened afterward. Plenty of photos together of the happy couple as they held hands, embraced. And finally got to kiss. Shitfire! He was supposed to *cheat* on Bonnie in front of a viewing public. Because it was all "pretend?" There was no such thing as a pretend kiss. Bonnie would not tolerate it, and he couldn't blame her. Neither would he.

"Tell me you're kidding. This is a big end of the series joke on me. Funny. Hahaha. I don't get it but nice try."

"It's not a joke, Sean. *I'm* not funny."

"You're a little funny when you're not trying to be."

"We'll send Bonnie out first. You let her go, nice as you can, and then Tabitha will come out. Propose to her with that rock and badabing—"

"Do *not* say badabey," Sean said through a clenched jaw. "You of all people have to realize what a horrible match we are."

"Who cares?" Lori crossed her arms. "Why *not* choose her when you don't have to marry her anyway?"

Because choices said something, damn it. And this one would break Bonnie's heart. He'd have to spend more time with Tabitha, fool everyone, including the town's residents. What had once seemed harmless felt catastrophic.

"Look at it this way. *Why* would they choose her in the first place?"

"How the hell do I know? The producers like her. She's beautiful and smart, or haven't you *noticed?*"

"And she is not in love with me."

"How do you know?"

"Because she doesn't even *know* me."

"Well given time…you never know…"

"This isn't a game we're playing. It's my life. Remember, I'm not an actor!"

She pointed. "That's why this is called *reality* TV! And you made the decision to do this."

How he wished he'd turned down the idea when Beulah approached him for the fifth time. Should have said no a fifth time and let Jeremy or anyone else do the honors. But then he'd had a so-called "brilliant" idea.

What's in this for me?

"It won't sound real if I propose to Tabitha. You already know I'm a bad actor."

"I'll coach you from the sides like I did with Jessica and we'll do as many takes as needed. Don't worry, I've got you."

Sean straightened, taking the same stance he did with an angry bull or wild, unbroken horse.

Come at me.

"I agreed to this deal before I knew y'all would drag in an old girlfriend to throw me off my game."

"It was supposed to, but you weren't supposed to want *her!*"

"And if she wasn't here, maybe I'd still be fine with y'all choosing someone for me. That was the deal we made. I rightfully guessed I couldn't get to know someone in two weeks. But everything changed when you brought her here so y'all can take the blame for all this mess." He took in a deep breath. "If you take the foundation contribution away, I'll have to live with that."

"But we don't want to do take it away! Hey, I love the wild horses much as anyone else. I want good TV!" Lori shook a fist. "Choosing Bonnie is just so damn predicable. I don't understand you people. As God as my witness, I will never do reality TV again!"

"Nice work, Scarlett."

"I'm bringing Bonnie out first and you do whatever you have to do." She huffed.

"Great. *Do* it!"

The first woman they led out was supposed to be the one getting the heave-ho, so they'd send Bonnie. Then everyone here would see and know who he'd supposedly "chosen."

"Rolling!" said Elton.

While he waited for Bonnie to be led out, a memory sliced through him of the younger man who'd felt abandoned by her. Abandoned by his parents, when they chose their addiction over him and his brothers.

Abandoned by the woman he loved when she chose to pursue her passion.

He and Bonnie had a history of choices behind them. Choosing each other. *Not* choosing each other.

With the benefit of a clear lens and greater wisdom and maturity, he now saw that years ago, it was he who had failed to choose *her*.

"Bonnie, you're up!" Lori called. "I'm so sorry, kid. It's the end of the line for you. The producers went another way."

Wow. Shades of Hollywood right here in Stone Ridge.

The producers went another way, Bonnie.

Someone shorter.

Someone taller.

Someone blonder.

Someone younger.

Someone thinner.

Someone curvier.

Someone better known.

Someone lesser known.

She'd spent years trying to fit her own character into personas so she could work. In the process, she'd nearly lost herself. For a while, she'd forgotten who she was at her core. A small-town girl with big dreams. The daughter of a rodeo champ and a good woman. A hard worker who didn't expect to have anything handed to her.

With a spike of dread clogging her windpipe, Bonnie understood Sean had been forced into a corner. When his own dream was on the line, he'd had to make a choice. Worse, she couldn't blame him. While this didn't mean he'd *marry* Tabitha, it did mean a lot of other devastating things. He'd have to kiss her for the cameras, be forced to pose for joyous photos of the happy couple. Play into the lie for a couple of weeks until he could find a way to break it off. In theory, this pretend engagement might work but reality was a completely different story.

Reality meant she'd watch the only man she'd ever loved with another woman.

Meanwhile, in private, Tabitha would do her thing, which she had already demonstrated once by removing her top to display the "merchandise."

Tabitha smirked. "Nice meeting you, Bonnie! When you go back to Hollywood, send me and Sean a postcard."

"Screw you, Tabitha," Elton muttered from behind the camera following Bonnie. "You're a sore winner."

You'll be okay. At least she had work ahead of her. She'd simply bury herself deep into performing and try to forget her loss. The role of reprising Meghan Kavanaugh, a decade later, would have once been a dream come true. Now it came shaded with the knowledge it was truly her second choice. She didn't want to leave here, her hometown, the place with salt of the earth people who had welcomed her back with open arms.

Moving toward the garden, Bonnie heard the audible gasp of the crowed gathered behind the rope to watch the last episode. Jolette Marie's sign had dropped along with her jaw. Eve and Daisy both wiped tears from their eyes and hugged. Aunt Beulah's lips were pursed tightly in a vicious scowl. And Lenny? He crossed his heart and mouthed, "love you."

Tears sprung but she tamped them down. She never thought she'd come this far in a stupid dating contest but now the stakes were higher than she'd have ever imagined. It wasn't supposed to matter, but it did. It was a choice, like so many others he'd made in the past.

Like giving up on her and letting her go. For years. She'd followed dreams which led her away from him but never made the choice to give him up. Until he'd forced her hand.

Moving slowly, as if she could stop time itself, Bonnie clasped her hands together and reached Sean.

His eyes had moved to their darker hue, and a worry line creased between his brows. He had to know how much this would hurt. She'd walk away before she had to watch him kiss Tabitha. No. Not happening.

"Hi," she said, trying not to meet his eyes for long.

He took her hand in his. "Bonnie, you and I have a painful history, and when you first showed up, I honestly wanted you gone."

"Yes, I know. And I wanted to *be* gone." She tried to lighten the mood.

"Please forgive me."

"It's okay," she said, biting her lower lip and lowering her eyes so she wouldn't have to look in his eyes. "I understand."

She would forgive him, of course, even if they couldn't be together. As always, Sean wanted to do the right thing.

And this time, she wasn't the only one who needed him.

"No, it's *not* okay." He shook his head. "I gave up on you once before. I'm not doing it again."

She didn't know if she could trust her ears. "I'm...not sure I understand."

Sean would do what the producers asked of him. What he'd agreed to do. She wanted him to have his dream, too. Glancing around wildly, her gaze landed on Elton and the crew. In the past she'd done this whenever she'd dropped a line of script. Begged for the P.A., for someone, anyone, to feed her the line. Now confusion clouded her. She turned in a semi-circle, looking for help. Something had gone wildly off script. Could it be...reality? Imagine that, *reality* going off script. She choked back a sound between a laugh and a sob.

Sean had let go her hands.

When she turned to him, he'd dropped to one knee.

CHAPTER 30

A loud gasp came from one of the onlookers. A cry. Some laughter and words which sounded like, "I knew it, I *knew* it!"

"Shh!" Lori hissed to the crowd, but Elton sniffed and rubbed his eyes.

"Sean." Bonnie whispered and reached for his hand. "What are you doing? What about—"

"I'll find another way. It may take a while but that's alright. There's something else I've waited for a lot longer. Right now, I'm doing what *I* want." He held out a ring box and opened it for her. "This is my choice."

A beautiful, very large, heart-shaped ring glinted in the light. "Oh. My Lord. You're..."

"Proposing."

This caused a commotion on the set. Lori stalked away, still wearing her headphones, so until she yanked them off, she nearly took audio down. Tabitha walked outside, staying out of camera view, with arms crossed, her scowl deep. Two seconds later, she went back inside, attempting to slam the slider doors. But Elton smiled and made the hand motion to keep going. An assistant dropped a light and it clattered behind them. Another crew member fell in a rose bush and cursed.

Bonnie heard Lenny's voice: "Sean is fixin' to get married to Bonnie Lee. If that don't beat all."

"About time!" Aunt Beulah said.

"Bless his heart," said Mama.

Sean would not be deterred. "I choose you and I will always choose you."

"Sean." She reached to palm his chin. "I love you so much."

Bringing her hand to his lips, he brushed a kiss on her palm.

"Bonnie, I've loved you for over half my life. We're both older now, and wiser, I hope. But one thing hasn't changed. We belong together just like we did years ago. I let my pride get in the way before, but it won't happen again. You're everything I've ever wanted. Would you marry me?"

Bonnie clutched his hands, cried, and said yes over and over again. Yes, for the second time, or third time, gosh, who was counting anymore? This was the *last* time she'd say "yes" to his proposal. This *yes* would stick. Forever.

Behind the barricade, more sounds of approval. Hoots and hollers. Whistles. Good to know their little town approved of Bonnie and Sean 2.0. Good to know, but not *necessary.*

She was certain and that's all that mattered.

They finally kissed for the cameras, and if it seemed to others this might not be their first time, as if maybe they'd *practiced* recently, she hoped no one would take deeper notice. A bottle of champagne was uncorked and poured, and congratulations came from the crew.

Angela broke through the roped barricade and hugged Bonnie.

"Honestly, you two make *such* a cute couple."

272

Some of the earlier contestants had come along and hugged Sean first, then Bonnie.

"This was such fun," said Kristan.

"I've met someone special," said another woman. "I'm going to stick around for a while."

"Where's Tabitha?" said Jeremy, a wolfish smile on his lips.

Probably sulking.

"I'm sure she'll be out in a while to say hello to everyone," Bonnie said.

The wardrove crew joined in, hair and make-up attacking Bonnie with brushes and more lipstick. They'd obviously been focusing on Tabitha.

While they waited for Bonnie, they filmed Sean answering questions. She couldn't hear the questions, or his answers, and figured she'd have to listen with everyone else when the show finally aired.

Everything moved swiftly and they were ushered through posed photos in different settings. Photos of them in a clinch, the glimmering pool in the background. One of Sean playfully appearing to push Bonnie in the pool. Another of her tugging at his tie, as if she might do the same.

After a while they were led inside, where two chairs had been set up in the dining room for the interview they'd finally do together.

Lori, who had been drinking champagne as well and chatting with the rest of the crew, appeared to have finally unclenched.

She'd changed into a black shift dress and red high heels, hair and make-up making her look extremely glamorous. Bonnie did a double-take.

"So, you two have a history together. This is sort of a shocking revelation. I mean, the first night didn't go so well, did it?"

"No, guess not," Sean chuckled. "She broke my heart. What do you expect?"

Bonnie squeezed his hand. "We were high school sweethearts."

"Ah, young love. How sweet. And where do you two think you'll be settling after the wedding?" Lori asked, the hint of a wicked gleam in her eye.

"Stone Ridge, of course." Sean squeezed her hand.

"This is home," Bonnie said.

"Interesting. I was just checking our social media with updates when I saw that Bonnie also has some news."

Sean glanced at her with curiosity, the hint of a smile on his lips.

Bonnie's foot jiggled to the point her shoe nearly came off.

"I…well, since you mentioned it. Just before the final ceremony, I received word that Netflix is bringing back a reboot of *Kavanaugh's Way*. They've asked me to come back as the head of the crime fighting family in a starring role this time."

Sean stiffened next to her and he let go of her hand.

"Congratulations," Lori said.

Bonnie threaded her arm through Sean's. "Thank you, but I'm not taking the role. It's a nice offer, however, and good to know Hollywood doesn't believe all women nearing forty should be relegated to modeling adult diapers."

Lori blinked. "I'm sorry. You're not *taking* the role?"

"No. I'm not."

"I'm just saying, I don't know if *I'd* turn down the opportunity to work with Sahara Rhodes," Lori said. "She's amazing."

"*Who?*" Sean said.

Lori snorted. "Only one of the greatest female influencers in our business. Anytime you see a bestselling hit on the biggest streaming network there is, she's at the helm of it with her own production company. Her mission is for both women *and* minorities to be properly represented. She scours fiction books and makes series out of them. Some of them win Emmys. Everything she touches is gold."

"She's amazing, true, and it would be an honor to work with her," Bonnie said, wishing she'd have had time to talk to Sean privately before someone else gave him the news.

"But...?"

"That part of my life is over. I look forward to getting married, settling down, having a family."

Sean smiled and lowered his head.

"What do you think, Sean?" Lori pressed.

"I think my fiancée and I are going to talk about this. Possibly in private."

"Sounds like a good idea," Lori said.

Now Bonnie stiffened. She did *not* want to talk about the reboot. She'd made her decision. Even the thought of recreating the role of Meghan Kavanaugh had caused her shakes and cramps to return. Life would be easier if she could just stay in her hometown and shut out the rest of the world. So far, this had worked well. She didn't see why it couldn't continue.

A few more lighthearted comments on the roping event, the schoolhouse event, and giving a mention to Bonnie and Sean's date at the Shady Grind, and the interview at last concluded.

Then, the "wrap up" party began. All the women contestants made their way inside the mansion, even Jessica. Music boomed through the speakers, and caterers arrived to serve appetizers and more alcohol. The kitchen was filled to overflowing with women chatting and catching up.

Jessica hugged Bonnie warmly, then Sean. "Thank you for

being so supportive when I was falling apart. You're like the big sister I never had."

"How did things go when you got back home?" Bonnie squeezed Jessica's shoulder.

"Well, we're talking. There's so much to work to do and I'm not sure if we'll ever get there."

"Keep trying," Sean said. "Some of us are dense."

Later, Angela and Elton seemed to be flirting as he mixed drinks in a tumbler. Jolette Marie was hanging with Daisy and Wade, also here. Eve and Jackson were canoodling in a corner, him stroking her big pregnant belly. Mama and Aunt Beulah were deep in conversation with Lori, of all people.

Tabitha approached. "See you, Sean. It took courage to do what you did. I'll give you that."

"Not really. Courage is getting in the corral with a pissed off bull."

Bonnie offered Tabitha her hand. "No hard feelings."

Surprisingly, Tabitha accepted the offer with a smile. "The competitor in me hates to lose. But the realist in me knows I never stood a chance."

Once more, Bonnie wished she'd given Tabitha a little more credit.

This day had seemed interminable, and as night fell, clean up began. People began to leave, offering their goodbyes and congratulations.

"Will I see you at home, sugar?" Mama turned to Bonnie after hugging Sean.

"Do you mind if I get an early start on the marriage, Miss Maybelle? I really have waited a long time."

Mama sniffed and tilted her chin. "I guess you have. She has a ring on her finger so that's alright by me."

"Miss Beulah," Sean said, giving her a hug. "I'm sorry I'm late in thanking you, but thanks for bringing Bonnie on the show. If not for you, who knows when she would have made her way home again."

Aunt Beulah gave him a wide smile. "You're welcome. I do what I can, son. I do what I can."

The crew came in to strike the set, cords and cameras were rolled up, and cars and trucks were packed. Mr. Truehart would get his mansion back. Bonnie thought she might actually miss this place a little, and the comradery she'd had with the girls when they were in this together.

But for now, she was going home with her cowboy.

CHAPTER 31

*B*onnie didn't think Sean was angry, but in the spirit of healthy relationships everywhere, she brought up the subject hanging between them as he drove home.

"I didn't tell you about the show because I'd just learned about the offer. But you can ask me anything you want."

"Why aren't you taking the role?"

She blinked. "Do you want me to?"

"Tell me what *you* want."

"I don't want to leave you." She brought his free hand to her lips and kissed it. "That *all* I want."

"Hm." He didn't sound convinced, and several minutes later, he pulled up to the driveway and shut off his head-lights. "It sounds like a great opportunity."

Bonnie was still salivating over working with someone like Sahara, a little tidbit her agent had neglected to mention. Yet she'd doubled checked on social media and Lori was correct. Sahara had already voiced her excitement over a new project involving the female head of an Irish mafia.

Working with a woman who might make a difference in

the way older women were viewed in Hollywood could be career changing. Bringing back the show with Bonnie as the head of the mafia family would accomplish this goal and much more.

"It's being filmed in *British Columbia*. For six *weeks*."

"Okay," Sean said and didn't sound at all bothered. "At least it isn't Hollywood."

How could he be okay with her leaving him for six weeks? He'd given up the donation to the wild horses' foundation. This was the least she could give up. One meaty role, but with no guarantees it would grow into another great series run. Nothing in show business was ever guaranteed.

"We just got engaged. Six weeks can feel like a long time."

"So, we'll live in Canada for six weeks. We can even split our time between Texas and wherever you're going to be working."

Okay, she had to have heard wrong. Her cowboy, in *Canada*?

And yet, it had a nice ring to it. *My Canadian Cowboy*. Someone should make that movie.

"I meant it, Sean. I'm giving up acting to be a full-time wife and partner and maybe, if I get lucky, a mother. If I feel like indulging my acting chops, I'll find something in regional theater."

"No," Sean said. "This isn't going to work for me."

His voice sounded abrupt and cold.

"*No?*"

This couldn't be happening. Not after all the hell they'd been through to get back together.

"Isn't...isn't going to work for you?"

"Skippy, I don't *want* you to give up acting. That's part of what makes you who you are, and the woman I love." He unbuckled his seat belt and turned in his seat to face her.

"But—"

"If I'm upset at all, it's because you have so little faith in me. Admit it. You were *afraid* to tell me. For us to work in a healthy way, we have to be open about our dreams and desires." He winked. "Both in and out of the bedroom."

This man was constantly surprising her. "You're right, and I'm sorry. I didn't want you to think you'd come second again."

"I *chose* you, Bonnie, in front of however many viewers will eventually watch. And believe me, I realized exactly what I was getting myself into. I'm not a kid anymore, but a grown ass man. I realize there are times when I might not be able to come first with you, like when we have children. Believe me, I've seen this firsthand with Riggs and Winona. Sometimes the kid needs you more. We'll work it out. I'm not going to be one of those ridiculous men who are jealous of their own baby."

She chuckled and pressed her forehead to his. "I'll think about it. But we'll make the decision together."

"That's all I'm asking. Let me into these decisions as your partner. I want you to be happy for a very long time. Whatever it takes."

"Speaking of whatever it takes, I'm going to get you the donation they were supposed to make. You had to give that up for me."

"Totally worth it." Then Sean came around the passenger side of the truck and held out his hand.

Her gown, the least attractive choice wardrobe had since they'd expected her to go home, made a sliding noise as she moved. The dress, too short for her, forced her to move one leg out of the car at a time so it wouldn't ride up to her hips.

"Another wardrobe malfunction?" Sean waggled his eyebrows, expression hopeful.

"We can have all the malfunctions you want once we get inside."

"Promises, promises." Sean lifted her into his arms and carried her to the door.

"Are you going to do something old-fashioned like carry me through the threshold?"

"Is that old-fashioned?"

"Maybe old school, but I'm in if you are."

"Here we go." He unlocked the door, juggling her in his arms, swung open the door and strode inside.

"Wow. You didn't drop me once."

"Special skill of mine."

Beer met them at the door, yarking, and doing his guard dog imitation.

"Beer, make yourself scarce."

The dog sniffed the air, then turned, and went back to his perch on the couch.

"Best wing man ever. Knows when to disappear and I never have to ask twice."

Sean carried her up the staircase, and Bonnie toed off her strappy heels as he walked. In the bedroom, he set her down on the edge of the bed as if she was something precious and breakable.

He pulled off his jacket, then squatted next to her, and framed her face between his big hands. "Damn but I love you, woman."

She wrapped her arms around his neck and pulled him close. "Show me."

"This time, I'm going to take my time."

"Whatever you say."

Everything slowed to a crawl as his hard masculine mouth took hers in a hot and fierce kiss. The kisses were both hot and lazy as he made his way down her body. He kissed her shoulder, sliding the strap of her bra down with his teeth.

Her hands quickly moved under his shirt, luxuriating in

warm skin and taught muscles. His weight pressed against her, and she moaned at the slight scrape of razor stubble brushing against her exposed nipples. Before long they were bared to each other, and he thrust into her making them both gasp. Bonnie clung to him, wanting this never to end. As promised, he moved slow, leaving her with a desperate sense of urgency. They came together in an explosion of heat and love.

Much later, Bonnie woke in Sean's arms, sated and content. Head on his chest, she listened to the steady thud of his heart. Years ago, she'd never imagined this kind of happiness for herself. The type of joy which depended less on outside forces she couldn't control and more on her own heart.

"Are you awake?" Sean spoke softly, his fingers lightly touching the crow of her hair.

"Yes." She mumbled.

"I have something for you." Disentangling, he reached for something in the drawer of his nightstand and handed her an envelope.

"What's this? I already have the ring, two of them in fact. And a proposal. You built our dream house. Honestly, baby, you're spoiling me."

"No, I haven't spoiled you enough. This is me playing catch up."

He watched her from under hooded eyes as she sat up and opened the envelope. Inside were two tickets to a regional theater production of West Side Story.

"We're going to the theater!" She happily waved them in the air.

"I thought it was about time." He tugged her back into his arms.

"Oh, Sean. You're too good to me."

"Hey, I'm just getting started. You were the one who for

years put up with a stubborn cowboy who had specific ideas about our life together. Where we should live, how we should live, when we should get married. I didn't give you any room to grow."

"Even then, you were the best man I've ever known."

"C'mere."

He kissed her then, another long and deep kiss that reached all the way to her heart. She'd finally followed said heart, which told her years ago that Sean was her soulmate. For years she denied the quiet sounds of her soul, chasing the dream of stardom instead.

Until she followed her heart all the way home.

Now she could clearly see she'd always had everything she ever needed, right at home.

EIGHT WEEKS LATER, production of the Kavanaugh's Way reboot began filming in Vancouver, British Columbia.

Bonnie Wheeler was listed among the stellar all-start cast, and with her was someone else who'd gained his own celebrity status. She shared the off-camera spotlight with Sean, which she didn't mind a bit. He was popular with the cast and crew, especially women. A bit of a flirt, he enjoyed the attention. Mr. Cowboy had eased him into it, after all. He was often asked about his experiences on the show and swore he never wanted in front of a camera again. But she wasn't the only one who noticed an ease and confidence with which he now spoke to complete strangers.

Her cowboy was much more of a rancher now, at home with movie executives and movie stars in addition to cattle and horses. She acknowledged maybe it *hadn't* been his media training for Mr. Cowboy, but simply that "her" Sean had grown up. She was getting to know the grown man all over again and every small nuance gave her one more reason to love him.

The crew, director and co-stars of Kavanaugh's Way had all been sworn to secrecy over Mr. Cowboy, but photos were eventually leaked. Bonnie and Sean were spotted at the airport together and the Internet went wild with rumors. And as it turned out, the producers of Mr. Cowboy had underestimated audience delight in a later in life reconnection of teenage sweethearts. In a complete flip, Bonnie became the front runner and fan favorite.

Meanwhile, she was deep into the creative process of recreating the now bloodthirsty and vindictive Meghan Kavanaugh. The years in between, and loss of her family members, had made her vengeful and ruthless. She went after her enemies without an ounce of remorse. And she appeared to love no one but herself. Viewers were going to love to hate Meghan. An absolute dream of a meaty character to play, and it helped she was the antithesis of Bonnie Lee Wheeler soon-to-be-Henderson.

It was a common joke on the set that Bonnie and Meghan were as different as tea and coffee. One could be made stronger when steeped in hot water. The other was particularly bitter the longer it roasted.

Even if Bonnie's workdays ordering mob hits and betraying people were long and punishing, she had every night with Sean. Wrapped up tight in each other's arms, and under a multitude of blankets, they were simply two lifelong Texans trying to stay warm in Canada.

They were having a late dinner when he pulled out his phone and displayed his social media account with well over a million followers.

"Are you as famous as I am?" He slid her a slow smile.

Sean was using his newfound celebrity to bring attention to the plight of wild horses, and it was working. He spoke and wrote with such authority on the subject that within weeks he'd been approached to be the research consultant for a planned documentary on the plight of the wild horses.

"Not nearly as famous. It helps to be a handsome cowboy who wants to save the world." She crawled into his lap and fed him a bite of the cheesecake they'd ordered from room service.

"Not the world. Just a hundred thousand horses."

"Is that all?" She licked a hint of cheesecake from his lower lip. "You're too good. I can't compete with you. I'm the lady who ordered a hit today on my oldest friend. Face it, I'm bad."

"How *bad*?" He quirked a brow.

"Pretty evil. Save me, Mr. Cowboy."

He picked her up and carried her to the bed. "I think I can help you, little lady."

"Oh, yeah. I know you can."

EPILOGUE

Six months later

"What did we miss?" Riggs and Winona blustered into the Shady Grind, late as usual. They'd informed Sean they were trying a new thing where they got out of the house once a week for "date night." But as frazzled parents of three, they were often late.

"Just the montage," Sean answered.

Montage. To think a year ago, he wouldn't have used the word in casual conversation. This morning, he'd moved cattle from the north pasture while Bonnie was still sleeping. He might have cursed a time or two when a cow refused to get in line.

He might still occasionally lose his temper but now he was using words like "montage." His emails were from documentary producers and an occasional movie star or two wanting to be involved. He'd come up in the world, he guessed, and Mr. Cowboy had done that for him. Since it started, ratings were through the roof, according to Lori. Tonight was the final episode and everyone who hadn't already been there wanted to watch Sean propose to Bonnie.

"Where's Bonnie?" Winona asked.

"Signing autographs." He pointed to where she stood at the bar chatting. "Pretty soon I might have to go over there and intervene. Seems like the meaner her character on Kavanaugh's Way became, the nicer Bonnie did. She has a hard time saying no. So, I have to say it for her."

Tonight, as in every night since the show released its first episode, the Shady Grind was hosting a Ladies' Night. Drinks were half off and the joint thick with women. Many of the contest entrants, including Tabitha, here with Dr. Grant tonight. She was considering a position with the new women's clinic he'd started, but from the sultry looks she threw Dr. Grant, she was considering a whole lot more than a job.

Jessica and Angela were the only ones missing. Jessica, because she was apparently planning her wedding again with the same guy from before. And Angela was back in New York City, where she'd hooked up with Elton. They were working together on her popular podcast and apparently also getting to know each other on a whole new level. All of them were keeping in touch via email and social media.

Until tonight, he and Bonnie had stayed home to watch Mr. Cowboy. It hit a little close to home for both of them and they were frankly tired of the spotlight after the six weeks spent in Canada.

Plus, they were both a little unnerved by what cuts and edits Lori might use and how it would make them look. For his part, Sean didn't like watching himself. It was damn embarrassing, but yes, he was curious. They'd both done interviews apart from each other, and early on made a pledge they wouldn't talk about it but simply watch together when the time came.

By now, he'd watched many of the interviews with the individual women. In particular Tabitha's interviews reassured him he'd seen right through her and he felt relief that "Mr. Cowboy nation" agreed Tabitha should have never gone as far as she did.

In one interview, after the event at Wade's rodeo school Tabitha had said:

"Oh yeah, oh yeah! Did you see how he caught me in his arms? I'm sorry, girls, he's mine. Y'all don't stand a chance."

Bonnie had laughed when Sean winced, then teased him about taking Tabitha aside the first night. He explained he'd done that simply to make Bonnie jealous.

This was his story, and he was sticking to it.

Everyone on Mr. Cowboy had signed NDAs, so he would never be able to share that he'd agreed for the producers to choose for him. Good thing because he'd look like a chump and he knew it now.

No one would ever share how the producers heavily favorited Tabitha as the winner. In a Zoom conversation a week ago, Lori had warned that she'd cut the show to make it look as if Sean might have slightly favored Tabitha. It was all about leaving those cookie crumbs and trails so viewers would stay tuned in to the next episode. By now, they had the viewing public on edge, wondering if Sean would be stupid enough to choose Tabitha. They were rooting heavily for Sean to choose Bonnie, insinuating that if he didn't he had "a screw loose."

"Their journey back to each other...will love work better the second time around?" The narrator intoned as the last episode began. *"Or will Sean choose someone else? Get ready for the dramatic conclusion!"*

Bonnie finally extricated herself and slid back into the

bench seat next to Sean. She said hello to Riggs and Winona, then squeezed his hand.

"Are you ready?"

"I know what happens." He smiled and put his arm around her.

For the next hour, Sean watched himself on the screen. But mostly, he kept his eye on Bonnie. He watched as she tearfully hugged Angela goodbye, then later listened as she talked to Tabitha, assuring her that she had far more to offer than her looks. Later, he barely contained his temper when he watched Tabitha tell Bonnie that she should move on and let go of past relationships.

Finally, he saw Bonnie as she approached the patio, knowing she was the first. Which meant she'd be eliminated. Her eyes, her entire face, showed a devastating sense of loss that gripped him by the heart ventricles.

"You really thought he was going to let you go?" Winona said softly.

"Well…" Bonnie said.

"Crazy," Riggs shook his head and muttered.

Ignoring everyone else, Sean brought their clasped hands to his lips and brushed a kiss across her knuckles. "Do you not realize I've been in love with you since I was sixteen years old?"

"Forgive me for sometimes forgetting I'm the luckiest woman alive."

The show concluded to wild applause, Lori doing such an excellent job of misleading viewers of the final outcome that some of the patrons did double-takes, wondering if maybe Sean selected Tabitha, then changed his mind.

But in the end, everyone here got the happy ending they'd wanted.

Including him.

. . .

LATER, at home, Sean was getting ready for bed when he decided to check his email for the first time today.

"Did you ever hear back from Colton?" Bonnie asked.

"I'm checking."

He'd emailed Colton weeks ago, as he tended to do every now and again to see if his brother was still among the living. Usually, terse replies came back with words like "still in this hell," and "might get some R&R next month." Nothing ever came of it, of course. Colton hadn't been home in years.

Sean's last email had been equally pithy and to the point:

Getting married to Bonnie Lee. Would like you to be there.

No answer had been forthcoming for weeks, and now finally, a reply as concerning as it was short:

I'll be there. There's been some trouble, but I think I'm finally coming to the end of it.

Bonnie read the reply when he showed it to her. "What does that mean?"

"I don't know, baby. I don't know."

"He'll come. I know he wouldn't miss our wedding." She took his hand and led him to bed. "Let's not think about it now."

I HOPE you've enjoyed Sean and Bonnie's second chance, later in life romance.

Next up in this series, pre-order Soldier Cowboy and read what happens when Colton finally comes home to Stone Ridge.

To download a Heatherly Bell starter library, keep up with the latest shenanigans and never miss a new release or sale, sign up for my newsletter!

ABOUT THE AUTHOR

Heatherly Bell is the author of over fifty published titles of contemporary romance under two different pen names.

She lives for coffee, craves cupcakes, and occasionally wears real pants. She lives in Northern California with her family.

You may reach her at
heatherly@heatherlybell.com